Michael Con[illegible]
and educated [illegible]'s School. He
started a career as a chartered accountant
and went on to become a management
consultant. Then he went into the
catering business, managing an inn in
South Devon for three years and
a hotel in the West Indies for another
three. He currently works for the British
Columbia Forestry Service as well as
writing. Married with three children,
he lives on Vancouver Island.

Mirror Image

MICHAEL G. CONEY

SPHERE BOOKS LIMITED
30/32 Gray's Inn Road, London WC1X 8JL

First published in Great Britain
by Victor Gollancz Ltd 1973

Published by Sphere Books 1975

TRADE
MARK

Set in Linotype Times

Printed in Great Britain by
Hazell Watson & Viney Ltd
Aylesbury, Bucks

ONE

Three rough timber huts rose on stilts from the warm brown tidal waters of the delta. For the past week twelve men and six women had lived in these huts. Eighteen humans until this morning when, suddenly, there were seventeen. The waters swirled past the piling as Stordahl clung to the crude ladder, still uneasy with shock, while the body of Cable drifted with the tide face-down. If Cable could be said to have a face any more. . . .

The huts stood in a triangle with the entrances facing inward; these openings were now crowded with colonists watching the flurry of bloody activity as the body drifted on, presently hesitating against the twisting roots of one of the mangrove-like trees which, apart from the tall reeds, were the delta's only visible form of plant life. The water was now seething around Cable and his clothes were gone; there were brief glimpses of white flesh before this turned crimson as the shoal of small silver fish ripped and fed with needle teeth.

'Stay where you are, all of you!' shouted Stordahl – unnecessarily, because nobody was about to step into that water. Several people, including the Supervisor himself, had seen what happened to Cable, yet no one ventured to assist. That would have been pointless from the first instant when a fish, rising glittering from the dull water, had torn out Cable's throat.

'It jumped,' someone was muttering. 'It jumped clear out of the water and went for his neck as though it knew how to finish him quick. I. . . .' The man swallowed nervously, staring at the suddenly menacing waters. 'I could have sworn it had . . . wings. . . .' Behind him, a woman wept softly.

Later Stordahl called a meeting. 'This is our first setback,' he said, watching their faces carefully. He stood at the entrance to Hut One with ten men behind him; fifteen yards of murky water separated him from Huts Two and Three. Men and women thronged the entrances but nobody cared to cross the intervening distance. The tide was falling; about six inches of water remained and the body of Cable was now grounded thirty yards away, the fleshless rib cage exposed. A vague shape moved in the branches above the body, oozing formlessly through the dark foliage like a giant amoeba.

'And naturally,' continued Stordahl, 'we are deeply shocked. Suddenly, the planet seems hostile. After a few months of having it easy, we've had a reminder that our environment is alien. Back in the colony, under the domes, we developed a sense of security – but we knew that sooner or later we would have to venture out and explore our surroundings.'

So the expedition to the delta had been mounted; difficulties in growing Earth-type crops at the colony on the plain had been partly responsible for the decision. Armed with sacks of super-rice seedlings they had travelled the short distance to the coast – the plant had been developed for use in saline, tidal waters, and promised to supplement the largely imported food supplies. Small experimental paddy-fields had been constructed and planting, until now, had proceeded daily. The seedlings appeared to be taking well.

A woman spoke sharply across from Hut Three. 'If you think I'm going to work knee-deep in water with those fish around you're damned well mistaken, Mr. Stordahl.' There was a murmur of agreement from the other colonists.

'We'll work when the tide is below the level of the paddy-field banks,' Stordahl informed her coldly.

'How will we be sure that the fish aren't already in the enclosures?' someone asked nervously.

A large lizard watched them unblinking from among the upturned bowl-shaped leaves of a nearby mangrove. 'Like this,' said Stordahl, climbing to the ground. The tide was down to the last two inches; nevertheless slime and ochre water rose to the knees of his thigh-boots. Anxious faces regarded him, scanning the surrounding film of water closely.

Stordahl moved away from the triangle of huts, drew his gun and sent a pulse crackling among the branches of the mangrove. The lizard fell, smoking, and hit the water with an audible hiss. Stordahl took it by the tail – it was about two and a half feet long – and dragged it across to one of the small enclosures which held some two feet of water left by the receding tide. He threw the lizard in. It floated to the surface, rolling slowly. Nothing happened.

'Satisfied?' Stordahl climbed to the bank of clay and upright piles and jumped into the water. He waded about casually, examining the super-rice seedlings which already projected above the surface. Despite his apparent confidence he found that he was fingering his throat nervously, visualizing the terrifyingly abrupt death of Cable. The diabolical killer fish had been about the size and shape of a Terrestrial piranha, although in the brief glimpse he had caught he had seen a peculiar, almost transparent membrane running the length of the flank. . . . It was the first time they had seen such a fish, and they had been here for a week. Stordahl hoped the fish were not capable of learning by experience where the food supply was. . . .

It was much later in the day that the team suffered the second and final disaster. Work had proceeded from midmorning onward without incident and as the early rain gave way to bright watery sunshine the morale of the team rose. The women were planting the seedlings, bent double with arms plunged below the surface, while the men were engaged in construction of a further enclosure, driving short piles hewn from the mangroves to reinforce the banks of muddy clay. Stordahl himself had climbed back to Hut One to radio his daily report back to the colony and to ascertain the latest news. Following the death of Cable, he had decided that the present team should be relieved the next day – a week in these surroundings was enough for anyone, but progress to date had satisfied him that the project was worthwhile. Now he could go back to his normal duties as Colony Supervisor, sending back somebody else in charge of the new team.

He had just made contact with Bill Myers when he heard the screams from outside. He dropped the mike and ran to the hut entrance.

The tide was slipping in slowly across the gleaming mud, a creeping iridescence flecked with scum. In the paddyfields the colonists thrashed and flailed, shouting. A number were struggling towards the huts; others twisted on the ground or lay still, while among them glittered silver shapes.

Stordahl half climbed, half fell down the ladder, drawing his pistol as he sank into the mud. 'Hurry!' he shouted.

The glistening forms flitted in from the sea, a huge shoal of the killer fish, underterred by the shallow water. They were skimming the surface with the thin membrane of their wings outspread and fluttering, diving into the deeper pools, re-emerging and gaining height, gliding across the intervening stretch of uncovered mud, diving into the water of the enclosures. The colonists were struggling from the paddy-fields, beating them off; Stordahl saw another man go down with a metallic gleam at his throat and the crimson blood pumping. The narrow beam of his laser probed the air, bringing down two fish in quick succession as he hurried to assist the wounded back to the huts. People passed him going the other way, paddling through the clinging mud with faces blank with fear, making for the safety of the huts' height. They fought at the foot of the ladders, screaming, while the killer fish veered around them like hungry gulls. Stordahl switched his pistol to broad beam for short-range work, frying a small flight of fish as they headed towards him.

There were no wounded whom Stordahl could assist. He realized this as he stood half-way between the huts and the enclosures, his feet sinking deeper into mud. People were either hurrying for the huts, or dead. Those behind him were alive, but there was no movement from those lying around the enclosures, merely the impression of shifting silver mounds as the fish wrenched and tore and fed in their dozens. Stordahl turned back and made for the nearest hut, climbing the ladder one-handed and burning any fish which swooped too close.

Seven more lives had been lost. That night, the colonists were besieged by fluttering fish which found the height of the huts no obstacle; indeed they seemed to be attracted by the light and, despite guards at the windows and entrances, were constantly finding the way in, where they dashed themselves against the lamps and fell to the floor, thrashing and snapping at anything within reach. . . . They were accustomed to spending minutes at a time out of the water, and took a long time to die.

The following morning, as soon as the tide was low enough, the remainder of the colonists left the huts and made for the vehicles on the high ground about a mile away. The journey back to the colony was a silent one; the setback had become a rout. At a later meeting it was agreed to postpone all attempts to cultivate super-rice in the delta until some defence against the piranavas, as they came to be known, was devised. The eroding tide began to smooth away the traces of the colony's first unsuccessful experiment.

* * *

Colonists en masse tend to be phlegmatic and by the end of the week the disaster at the delta had become history. There were so many other matters to think of. The dead were mourned as is fitting but the grief was short-lived, and life on the new planet resumed its normal busy course.

Until one day Stordahl, with an unaccustomed hour or two to spare, set off in the direction of a small hillock. . . .

The low knoll was capped with a grove of cuptrees and he paused some two hundred yards from the nearest; turned, and surveyed the embryo colony, white blisters on the wet plain, with some pride. He would have to think of a name for the site before someone else did. As Supervisor, it was his prerogative, failing instructions from the top. It was an oversight by Hetherington, the colony's financial backer, not to have named the first town; the armless tycoon back on Earth had already named the planet Marilyn, after his blonde and reputedly oversexed wife. Alex Stordahl, Supervisor, standing on the slopes of a low hill on the planet Marilyn, smiled to himself. He had met the original Marilyn, once.

Fifteen large silver domes were clustered on the broad plain; they glittered in the unusual Marilyn morning sunlight, as did the ground foliage and the groves of cuptrees. Last night, like every night and most days, it had rained heavily. Around the domes moved the half-tracks and people miniature with distance. There seemed to be a lot of colonists about this morning, due as much to the unusual weather as to the overcrowded living quarters. Almost five hundred people lived in those domes. To the right, or east, of the camp was a black area of vitrified soil, legacy of the shuttle service performed by Hetherington Ferry IV some months ago while the FTL starship *Hetherington Endeavour* orbited, disgorging.

This landing pad bore testimony to the colony's virility;

building work was in progress using local materials. Five families were constructing timber cabins from felled cuptrees, taking advantage of the only firm dry ground for miles around. Stordahl had warned them that such a site might in time be liable to subsidence and eventually become a lake, but they had proceeded nevertheless. Anything, they said, was better than living in those damned domes, with no privacy. At least, the women had said that. Their husbands, being male and therefore susceptible to reason, had said nothing, but built the cabins on platforms in the manner of houseboats.

Alex Stordahl looked north; forty miles beyond the camp the plain rose to a long crescent-shaped mountain range. Stark and jagged in the clear morning sun, these mountains curved from a point due north of the camp to somewhere south of west. Aerial surveys had revealed a vast desert beyond the mountains, and spectroscopic analysis had shown this to consist of huge surface deposits of ferrous oxide. There was also considerable radioactivity. This readily obtainable source of wealth had been of great interest to the financier and was the principal reason for the founding of the colony on the planet Marilyn.

Hetherington's last message had inquired when the hell Stordahl proposed to send an exploratory team into the desert. Stordahl had replied to the effect that he would do so when he was good and ready. This would, in fact, be within the next week, but Stordahl was an independent personality who disliked giving his boss the impression that he jumped to obey commands. . . .

Apart from the disaster at the delta, in the six months of the colony's existence they had lost two other members, their zoologist and his wife. These two had taken a half-track and ploughed off into the distance one day two months ago; they had not returned.

Stordahl had blamed himself for that; he should have realized that Arnott Walsh was getting impatient. The fauna of Marilyn had, apart from the occasional elephant worm, shunned the camp area and Walsh had been champing at the bit, having to be satisfied with telescopic views of lizard-things slinking around the distant cuptree groves, in addition to the few specimens Stordahl had brought back from the ill-fated delta expedition.

Walsh's wife had been no happier; they were both highly

regarded in their profession and had been accustomed to World Government sponsored expeditions complete with fully-equipped enclosed vehicles and teams of technical assistants. Hetherington's shoestring operation complete with cramped accommodation, no laboratory, and open half-tracks had not, apparently, appealed to them. If they had known it was going to be like this, they had said, they would never have come.

In fact Hetherington would never have included them in the colony if he had not found out that the World Government was prepared to make a grant towards the colony if research work such as zoology were carried out in addition to the usual exploitation of resources. So the Walshes were signed up, Hetherington calculating that the grant would be well in excess of the cost of their passage and upkeep.

But Alex Stordahl, who had supervised colonies before, had insisted on a six months' settling down period before any work of a research nature commenced apart from essential investigations into food sources such as the delta project. Even six months, he felt, was barely enough to get the housing and supplies sorted out, test the local water (heavy in minerals but drinkable) and sink the wells, set up the essential laboratories, plant crops, explore briefly the vicinity and make provision for unexpected attack. Five hundred assorted people, including a few children, take a great deal of organizing.

So far it had gone well, apart from the disappearance of the Walshes and the failure of the super-rice, and Stordahl felt, on this optimistic morning, that they were ready to go at last. Teams in half-tracks supported by the colony's one helicopter would now start commercial exploration. Within a few days they would be analysing samples from the desert and a few months later, all being well, the smelting plant would arrive from Earth with its attendant team who would themselves become additional members of the community.

For this was a community. Stordahl had insisted from the start; it was not just a factory with accommodation. The intention was to colonize Marilyn, to provide a new world for people to live in; not merely to set up a trading post, a small industrial offshoot of the Hetherington empire.

People were going to live here. If Stordahl liked it enough, he might stay here himself when his contract was up.

His gaze dropped from the mountain to the camp, and he wondered how many times he had thought the same thing. This was his eighth planet, and he had always moved on. *I'm forty years old,* he thought; and with the thought came its inevitable companion: *I wonder if I ought to get married again.*

The girl was twenty yards away; her hair was long and black and it hid her face as she bent low, examining the ground, parting the saucerplants to get at the soil. He called to her.

'Joan!'

She looked up, smiling towards him. Her face was flushed. She was very pretty. *Damn Hetherington,* he thought.

'What?'

'Nothing,' he said, smiling back.

Damn Hetherington and his animal assumptions. 'I've interviewed the applicants personally,' the man had said. 'There are an equal number of men and women, plus a few children just to make people think they're building for the future, you know. Equal males and females – that way everyone can get his oats. I think you'll like your girl.'

Stordahl had stared at the armless obscenity behind the mahogany desk, holding on to his fury and his job. *My God,* he thought, *does he expect us all to walk up the gangplank two by two?* And for the next week before blast-off he had been wondering what his assigned bedmate would be like, suspecting that she would be the twin sister of the blonde and breasty Marilyn, who had wandered into the room during his talk with Hetherington, given him a suggestive look, then sat on the table and fondled the tycoon's thinning hair.

Hetherington couldn't have known, could he, that Stordahl's wife and child had died a year ago when the westbound monocar from Capital City had been blown from the rail by the latest cult of have-nots?

And Joan, who he had avoided meeting until the last possible moment aboard *Hetherington Endeavour,* had turned out to be so very nice. So anxious to please, so desperately afraid that he wouldn't like her (because, after all, there were some two hundred and fifty other women aboard), so young and sweet and pretty and unHetherington-like that he wondered what the hell was the matter with him, because he couldn't fancy her.

Even now, they had never been to bed together; because Stordahl knew that, at the moment of impact, the ghost of Hetherington would appear leering in his mind's eye, saying: 'I knew you'd like her. . . .'

'Come on up here,' he called.

The wind was as reliable as the rain on Marilyn. During most of the day it blew from the south-east – from the sea to the desert as the reflective land heated and the air rose. In the late afternoon it reversed direction, bringing with it fine particles of dust which caused spectacular auroral displays in the rays of the sinking sun. At present the wind blew towards the hills; as Joan arrived at his side her face was framed in flying hair like a dark-petalled flower, a black tulip.

'Well . . . what do you think of Marilyn?'

'Attractive, possibly unpredictable. Definitely a man's girl,' she replied, smiling.

'I mean the planet.'

'So do I,' she said innocently. 'All virgin planets are men's girls. A man can see the possibilities, whereas a woman tends to view with suspicion.'

Stordahl laughed. 'Not to change the subject, what did you think of Hetherington's wife? Obviously you met her.'

'I only hope she never takes it into her head to visit the place,' said Joan seriously. 'Our boss could have trouble with her in an easy-going environment like this.'

'Easy-going?' repeated Stordahl in mock horror. 'Are you suggesting I run a slack ship?'

'There has been certain intermingling of the sexes in segregated dormitory domes,' she explained carefully. 'You know, like two in a sleeping bag.'

'I didn't realize accommodation was quite so cramped.'

'Why do you think the families are moving out and building? They don't mind for themselves, but they think it's bad for the kids to see a bag bursting at the seams, groaning and heaving in the middle of the night like two snakes trying to shed the same skin.'

'It's all part of growing up, for the colony as well as the kids. I don't believe in strict rules about this sort of thing. Neither, apparently, does Hetherington. Equal numbers of men and women; it's just too much of a coincidence to mean anything other than sex.'

'You're laughing at me again, Alex. All the same, I suppose you're right. You can't force people to pair off, but you can give them the chance.' She looked, suddenly, a little sad. 'And when they do, permanently, I mean, they'll have the incentive to move out, like the families. That way they do all necessary building work willingly, in their spare time. You're a devious sort of man.'

'It's better this way than compelling people to give up their evenings to construct cabins; with teams and rosters and waiting lists and all the grumbling and friction that would entail.'

'Are . . . are you thinking of moving out?' asked Joan hesitantly. 'Community living is all very well, but the Supervisor ought to have his own house.'

'If I do, Joan, I'll give you the first option on sharing it with me,' he said, and wished he hadn't.

'Thank you. . . . You were very fond of your wife, Alex? I'd heard she was . . . dead.'

'We got along. . . .' *At least I chose her myself*, he thought savagely, wondering how to change the subject without appearing too rude. Obscurely, he didn't want to be rude to Joan.

'There was a daughter?'

'She was five,' he said shortly, this time leaving no doubt that he did not want the subject pursued.

'I'm sorry, Alex. Sometimes it's better to talk about these things. . . . Shall we walk on a bit? Let's have a look around the cuptrees and see if there are any of those big lizards around. We've both brought guns.'

He hesitated. He had left the camp on the spur of the moment, delighted by the morning sunshine, with no intention of turning his stroll into a full-scale exploration. Joan had tagged along and he had let her come, partly for company and partly because of his own rule that no unaccompanied person should travel more than a quarter mile from the camp perimeter.

Curiosity got the better of him and he started on up the hill, Joan at his side with drawn hand gun. After all, he told himself, he was about to perform the duties of the missing Arnott Walsh and investigate the local fauna.

They halted twenty yards from the nearest tree and

stared into the forest of thick trunks beyond. Nothing moved apart from a tiny gliding lizard which leaped from a twig and plunged deep among the cuptrees, paper-thin membranes stretched taut between short limbs. In flight, the creature resembled the killer fish of the delta. . . . Even the wind had dropped and the multi-branched trees stood still as though watchful with bated breath while the grove got a close sight of Man.

'We're not going in there,' stated Alex Stordahl definitely. 'Later perhaps, with ten men properly armed. This time we'll just walk around the edge, keeping in sight of the colony.' Back among the domes, men with binoculars would be watching them, and telescopic cameras would be whirring. They walked again, eastward.

The ground was pitted with the holes of elephant worms, open sores over two feet in diameter interrupting the green carpet of the saucerplants. Here and there little clusters of taller plants grew with tulip-shaped heads on slender stalks. Bending down, Stordahl snapped off a plant and stuffed it in the pocket of his windbreaker.

'I may as well take something back for Briggs,' he remarked. Briggs was the colony botanist and agriculturalist, now also doubling as zoologist in the absence of Walsh. 'You notice this plant is the same species as the saucerplants and cuptrees?' He wondered if all plant life on Marilyn would exhibit this strange reversal of the Terrestrial system whereby nourishment is obtained by capillary action from the roots up. In which case Briggs would have the pleasure of sorting out his own genera before arriving at the subdivision of species.

Joan wasn't listening. She caught his arm suddenly. 'Quiet,' she whispered. 'I thought I saw something. Coming out of that hole.' She indicated a burrow some twenty yards away, near the trees.

'Probably an elephant worm,' he whispered back.

'No. It was a different shape. If it had any shape at all. . . . It just poked its head out, a sort of amorphous lump, then it went back again.'

Now the forest, accustomed to their presence, was beginning to stir again with small rustlings and shrill, tiny sounds. Against the sky, the curious leaves of the cuptrees waved in the resumed breeze, and a dark bank of cloud was sweeping in from the south-west. The two humans stood silent, watching.

This time Stordahl saw the creature emerge. It oozed out from the burrow shapeless, a grey tube of protoplasm like a flaccid maggot until it lay clear of the hole, when it seemed to expand, questing this way and that with stumpy pseudopods. It grew tall, rising from the ground, still featureless apart from the lumpy protuberances which changed position constantly. Soon it was all of six feet high tapering to a rounded apex, reminding Stordahl of nothing so much as his crude childhood attempts at building snowmen. Shockingly, the similarity intensified.

'My God,' he whispered. 'It's growing eyes.'

Two eyes stared at them with blind fixation, the head became more clearly defined, and the gash of a mouth appeared.

Stordahl gripped his gun.

There was a heavy crashing within the forest and they swung around. A giant lizard-like creature stood among the thinning perimeter trees. Its mouth hung open, drooling as the eyes stared unblinking. It was over twenty feet long from its carnivorous fanged jaws to its pointed tail and it stood over six feet tall at the shoulder. A feature rather less reptilian was its obvious masculinity. Almost with relief Stordahl levelled his gun at it. This was the sort of creature he understood.

But the giant lizard's attention was fixed on the strange object in the open. With patent hunger it regarded the mound of protoplasm and its tongue flickered as it moved forward with surprising quietness.

The dead eyes swivelled and the mound had seen the lizard. Again the shape began to change as the flesh expanded, swelling rapidly like the defence mechanism of the puffer fish, but extending horizontally, extruding limbs, projecting a tail.

Joan whispered something, incredulously.

The shape had achieved at least four times its original volume and its outline was sharpening, becoming more definite. The long tail shifted, the cruel jaw drooped. . . .

And there were two great lizards at the edge of the forest.

The original reptile threw back its head, uttered a coughing roar, and moved forward purposefully; while the pseudo-lizard lowered its head, shuffled and presented its flank.

The creatures met and wheeled in a giant gavotte.

Then, ponderously, they copulated.

TWO

The violent Marilyn rain roared deafeningly on the roof of the dome as they entered the tiny laboratory of Briggs, biologist. He stood with his back to them, apparently deep in thought. Alex Stordahl gave him the benefit of the doubt. He probably *was* deep in thought, although it would have been characteristic of the moody biologist to have ignored their presence deliberately.

'Ah, Briggs,' said Stordahl allowing the man no further time for dumb insubordination. The role of Colony Supervisor could be difficult in that most members of the community knew more, in their own fields, than did the Supervisor; and some were quick to take advantage of this.

'Stordahl. Miss Er—' Briggs had a bad memory for names, or maybe a shrewd system for making people feel insignificant. 'I was observing your little escapade. I find it interesting. Very interesting. . . . Um.'

'Any ideas?' asked Stordahl casually, sitting down and motioning Joan to do likewise, thereby leaving the biologist still standing, as there were only two chairs available. Briggs, a small man, sat awkwardly on the laboratory desk, his legs swinging.

'Possibly, possibly. . . . Ah, what were your impressions, as the man on the spot?'

'I can only summarize the obvious, Briggs. The thing emerged from a hole which might have been an elephant worm burrow – which makes it likely, though not conclusive, that its natural habitat is underground. When it became aware of Joan and me, it changed shape. Its colour, which had been uniform grey, changed also and became lighter. Its upper extremity took on the approximation of a head, and something which looked very much like eyes and a mouth appeared.'

'You were wearing a white jacket. The rather shapeless windbreaker affair you have on now.'

'That's right. You think there was some degree of imitation.'

Briggs chuckled with little mirth. 'Of course. But the

imitation was more successful in the case of the giant reptile.'

'It was amazing,' broke in Joan. 'In a matter of seconds the thing *was* a lizard. It was utterly convincing. It even fooled the real lizard. . . .' She broke off abruptly, blushing.

Stordhal said hurriedly: 'I've got a theory. I thought of it on the way back. Shoot me down if you like.'

'Go ahead.'

Stordahl, realizing he was laying himself open to sarcasm, one of Briggs's less popular weapons, went on more slowly: 'We've seen various types of life forms since we've been on Marilyn. Mostly of the lizard type, different shapes and sizes but still identifiable as belonging to the same species. Then this shape came up out of a burrow. It's different. The first observed land creature to be significantly at variance from the rest.'

'Well?' Briggs was looking indulgent.

'Well,' Stordahl plunged on, 'suppose it's *not* different. Suppose it's the same species again. Suppose there is only one basic land-based life form, which changes shape at will.'

'Very neat,' said Briggs approvingly.

'Possible?'

'Possible,' conceded the biologist, 'but not really likely. You see, the change in shape was triggered off. It was a reflex, brought on by a stimulus. It saw you, it changed shape. Then it saw the lizard, and it changed shape again. If your theory were correct I could swallow the second change, but not the first.'

'Why not?' asked Stordahl irritably. He glanced at his watch. 'Look, I've got to address the colony soon. Let's discuss it later, when we've seen the film. Coming right before the meeting, this thing is a damned nuisance. The whole camp will be talking about it. The wider issues could get neglected.'

'Bear with me for a moment. Ask yourself, why would the creature change its form into that of a man? Remember, sex resulted from the second transformation.'

'All right. What do you think?' asked Stordahl resignedly.

'I think the change of shape is a defence mechanism. As a general rule animals are not cannibalistic, so what better defence is there than to assume the shape of the species you are threatened by? Imagine this amorphous creature to be naturally non-aggressive, then you have a marvellous system for survival in a hostile environment!' Behind the pebble lenses, Briggs's eyes were gleaming with enthusiasm. 'Now, *that's* why it began to turn into a man.'

'But the sexual act? Isn't that taking it a bit far? It would have been meaningless, surely, to the creature?'

'Strangely enough there are parallels on Earth. Take the case of an ape colony. Among the great apes you'll naturally get large, dominant males in a tribe. At the same time there will be younger males not yet strong or big enough to constitute a real threat to their elders, but who will nevertheless cause those elders some uneasy moments. The dominant males see a future threat, and will often attack the younger males. To combat this, the young males frequently employ a defence tactic which I reckon is similar to that used by these shapeless things. The young ape, on being threatened, will turn his back on the larger male and present his, ah, hindquarters in a female attitude of submissive invitation. You often get the larger male then mounting the smaller and simulating the sex act. Pointless, of course, but instinctive and, from the point of view of the young male, a necessary defence. Like the pointless but necessary act you witnessed this morning.'

'Could be,' admitted Stordahl reluctantly. 'After all, you're the expert. In the absence of Walsh,' he couldn't help adding.

'I've no doubt Professor Walsh would agree with my opinions,' replied Briggs stiffly.

'I'm sure. Well, we'd better get going, Joan. I don't suppose we'll really know much more until we capture one of those things.' He got to his feet. 'Oh, by the way, I've got something for you, Briggs.' He brought the plant from his pocket and handed it over.

The biologist glanced at it briefly. 'Same thing again,' he observed. 'See?' he pointed to the tulip-shaped cup. 'Just like the cuptrees and saucerplants. This plant catches the rain in its cup, the moisture then seeps down through the fibres of the stem and drains out through the roots. An unusual system, but perfectly logical.' He glanced out of the window. 'In view of the everlasting rain. . . . When Entwhistle's fit again he'll be able to go into the matter more thoroughly.'

Stordahl and Joan left the biologist to his deliberations. The girl was silent as they walked down the narrow, limp-walled corridor between the various laboratories of the totally inadequate research dome. They turned into the short tunnel leading to the next dome, the men's dormitory where the meeting was to be held.

'Anything the matter?' asked Stordahl.

Joan hesitated then, as they were about to leave the tunnel, she burst out: 'Why do you have to be so childish, Alex?'

'What do you mean?'

'Trying to needle Briggs like that. Everything you said, you were trying to annoy him. Why? What's the point?'

'He always tries to needle me,' replied Stordahl, surprised. 'It's a sort of game.'

'I don't like it. It seems to me that we've got enough to contend with on Marilyn as it is, without making things more difficult. We ought to pull together, not squabble like kids. You hardly listened to what he was saying just now, because all the time you were trying to think of ways you could outwit him. I thought his ideas made sense, myself.'

Stordahl was suddenly contrite. 'You're right,' he said. 'And Briggs did talk sense. There's just something about the man which annoys me. He's so damned smug and egotistical. I suppose it's just his way; he's a good man at his job, I'll grant him that.'

'That's better, love.' Joan took his hand.

He regarded her in surprise, was about to say something but changed his mind. Her hand felt comfortable in his, but he was glad Hetherington wasn't around. . . .

'One thing Briggs hasn't thought of yet,' he said. 'That thing took the shape of a human being, or began to. Now just suppose the lizard hadn't arrived at that moment. What shape would the thing have taken, eventually?

'What – or who – would it have looked like?'

As they stepped into the men's dormitory dome where the meeting was to be held, the sudden noise was almost overwhelming. Most of the colony members were already congregated and the hubbub of five hundred voices competed deafeningly with the drumming of the rain on the walls and roof. Stordahl released Joan's hand, embarrassed as the faces of those nearest turned towards them. He looked around anxiously; the dormitory was far too small for this sort of crowd.

He had the irrational – or perhaps sensible – thought that one well-placed mortar shell from a hostile alien could wipe out the colony.

Fortunately there was no evidence that Marilyn possessed life forms of sufficient intelligence to have discovered fire, let alone constructed a mortar, although the amorphous creature of the morning could possibly present a new factor.

As he walked to the temporary platform against the wall of the dome he overheard snatches of conversation; everybody seemed to be discussing the new creature and some interesting theories were being aired. He got the impression that the entire colony had spent the morning with field glasses pressed to their eyes, observing. There was a disturbing undercurrent of mild alarm.

He allowed another five minutes for the late-comers to straggle in and pack themselves in place, then thumped the table for order.

'Friends,' he shouted as the talking died. 'The purpose of this meeting is to summarize our achievements to date and, I will tell you in advance, to inform you that the period of settling-in is now officially over. But first I wish to put your minds at rest concerning the strange creature which was sighted this morning.

'Briefly, I have had preliminary discussions with Professor Briggs' – he nodded at the small figure sidling in at the entrance – ' and it appears to us that the creature will present no danger. Of course, it's too early to say with complete certainty, but Professor Briggs considers that the creature's ability to change shape at will is in the nature of a defence mechanism, thereby suggesting that the thing is not particularly aggressive. After all, there was no sign of aggression in the manner in which it dealt with the giant lizard.' He paused for a laugh, and got it.

'Naturally we shall secure one of these creatures at the earliest opportunity for the purpose of observation; meanwhile the customary precautions will be taken. I hardly need to remind you that you will carry arms at all times, and must not leave the camp area alone, or at night. Other restrictions are now being relaxed, however, and you may now do whatever private sightseeing or exploring you wish, in your own time, within five miles of the camp. A roster will be drawn up for pleasure use of the vehicles. If you intend to go far I advise you to use these vehicles. Not only for convenience, but because we have observed that the noise of the half-tracks will scare off even the largest of the Marilyn reptiles. You will of course report any observations of interest. Remember, we're all learning about this planet; any information, no matter how insignificant, helps build up the picture.'

Stordahl paused, knowing the next moments would inevitably cause difficulty.

'The first stage of our operation is now over,' he said slowly, 'and we must look to the future. As from now, this is no longer a camp; it is a township which I would like to take this opportunity of naming Alice, after the Australian city of that name. Alice is now established and we are all set to go.'

There was a murmur of approval and Stordahl drew a deep breath. 'Tomorrow, a team of fifty-four men and women will leave Alice with equipment and supplies for a journey of some sixty miles north-west to the desert area beyond the mountains. They will set up a base which will, in effect, become our second city. It will be manned continuously; the roster will be posted on the notice board later today. Everybody, without exception, will serve approximately one week in ten at this desert camp. A few must become permanent residents there.'

The stunned silence quickly changed to an aghast buzz of conversation. A man shouted: 'Are there no exceptions? What about me? I'm needed here!' Stordahl recognized him as Lever, the surveyor, who was engaged in a scheme for land drainage to provide a firm footing for the permanent cabins.

'There are no exceptions!' he called out above the din. 'I want you all to understand one thing.' The noise subsided and he continued more quietly. 'You are not free agents on this planet. You are employees of the Hetherington Organization. The organization has paid your passage here, your accommodation, your food. In return the organization expects a profit. You have ample leisure time for your private projects such as house building and community work, but your working day belongs to the organization. You are all on a five-year contract. At the end of that time you may leave Marilyn and the organization, or you may stay on and sign on for another term.

'Or, if you are willing to take the chance, you can stay on Marilyn but outside the organization and take up farming, or set up shop in competition to the company store, or whatever. The steelworks will be in operation by then, the population will have risen and there should be plenty of scope. But not for another four and a half Standard years.' He eyed them grimly, awaiting further reactions.

'Mr. Stordahl!' A man called from the back of the hall. It was James Walters, who was erecting a cabin on the fused soil to the east of the colony. 'I've got a wife and kids. I'm building a house. Do you expect me to ship them all out to the desert every ten weeks?'

'I'm afraid that's just what you'll have to do, James,' replied Stordahl. 'You knew the set-up before you signed on. We can arrange for the kids to be looked after here at Alice, but you and your wife will have to do your spell in the desert with the rest of us.'

Briggs spoke up next. 'What the hell can I do in the desert?' he asked belligerently. 'This is democracy gone mad. I'm far more use here than I ever could be in the desert. What can a biologist do in a place where nothing grows?'

'We'll try to find you a scorpion or two,' replied Stordahl unkindly, and it got a laugh, as Briggs was unpopular. Stordahl glanced guiltily at Joan, but she was studiously regarding her feet.

'You're quite right, Stordahl,' came an unexpected cry. Charlton the mineralogist pushed forward and turned to face the crowd. 'He's right, all of you. We knew this had to come. We knew, when it came, that we wouldn't like it, and we'd complain. So that's what we're doing. But we've got to face facts, and the facts are that the purpose of this so-called colony is to produce the goods for shipment. The first six months are over, and we've worked hard, and everything's gone well. We're established. We feel settled in. We feel we can live here on Marilyn. The air's breathable, we haven't gone down with the plague, we haven't been eaten by tentacled aliens. But now, as Stordahl says, we're ready to go. We've got to produce the goods. And we've got to do it together; this is no place for individualists and farmers and dreamers; not yet. Give it a few years, get the plant in operation and the place on a commercial basis, and then we'll see. But not yet. In ten years we'll all have our farms and shops and businesses, and it'll be the new arrivals who are working for the organization. The place will grow that fast. I know. I've seen it before!' He turned and grinned at Stordahl as the crowd's mood changed subtly to cautious optimism.

You've seen it before, thought Stordahl grimly. *You've been on as many worlds as I have, but you've worked for the organization all your life and, Charlton, you've never owned a farm or shop yet; and you're not likely to, because you're a Hetherington man through and through. I expect you've made that speech a few times too, supporting other Supervisors like me, who are ashamed that they are glad you said what you did. And when it comes to prospecting in the desert, who is more important than a mineralogist? You've got to do your turn at the desert camp, and you know it, Charlton. And you're going to make damned sure you drag everyone else there, too. . . .*

Stordahl himself had signed on with Hetherington when the world Emigration Commission finally ran out of government support and money, and private enterprise took over the job of shipping out fugitives from the overcrowded Earth. The challenge of the new worlds was in his blood and when the Commission finally, regretfully released him he had jumped at the chance Hetherington had offered; he knew it would be the only chance he'd get. The Commission would never function again; the public outcry against the expense of maintaining struggling colonies which took years to become self-supporting was too great.

Today, more than ever, he was realizing the difference between the self-governing Earth colony, and the commercial colony. On a strange, alien planet it was a simple basic difference.

On an Earth-sponsored colony, a man used to say to himself: 'I am building for the future of myself and my family.'

On a commercial colony, he said: 'In a few years' time I will be building for the future of myself and my family.'

Just a few years' difference, that's all.

The meeting was breaking up now, in a better mood

than had seemed possible, thanks to Charlton. People were drifting out and, no doubt, beginning to congregate around the notice board to await the posting of the roster. Stordahl felt a little weak from reaction and decided, cowardly, to get someone else to put the roster up. Joan, for instance. She could deny responsibility and tell the inevitable bleaters who wanted their dates changed for inevitably convincing reasons to refer the matter to the Supervisor in writing.

'Went quite well.' Charlton was regarding him. 'You'll become an organization man in time, Stordahl. Treat them firm and promise them everything; that's the system. I've seen all this before.'

Stordahl muttered something and moved away with Joan.

'I don't like that man,' she said hotly. 'I don't like any man who refers to me as "them". I'm me and you're you and Lever, say, is Lever. We're individuals and we're not fools and we don't like to be patronized.'

'Take it easy, Joan.' Stordahl was surprised by her vehemence. 'In a way he was right, although he may have expressed himself badly just now. I don't like the man either. But there will be plenty of time to be individual, when our contracts are over.'

'In four and a half Standard years' time.'

'That's right.'

'I don't think you get my point, Alex. You and the other top men like Charlton are well paid, but ninety per cent of the members of this colony get next to nothing. Just their food and a dome over their heads. All for the chance of making a new life on a new world.'

'Be reasonable, Joan. It takes five years of work to pay off the cost of transporting a man here. That's what determines the length of the contract. After that, you can renew at full pay.'

'And what happens if the Hetherington Organization finds the operation is uneconomic in five years' time, and closes it down?' asked Joan quietly.

THREE

Early the following morning Alex Stordahl set out on a tour of inspection of the base, well waterproofed against the streaming Marilyn rain. As he paddled across the muddy ground between domes he was mildly surprised to find himself in good spirits despite the weather, and attributed this to the air of anticipation which hung over the place. There had been much discussion during the previous afternoon and evening; wherever he went, little knots of people were talking over the situation and speculating as to the problems of the future.

By late afternoon, when the wind had changed and the rain ceased, the whole thing seemed to have been talked out and an atmosphere of cautious optimism was prevalent. Even those detailed for the expedition to the desert appeared to be looking forward to a change of scenery. At night people sat in the mild air outside the domes and held impromptu parties, silvered by the bright light of Marilyn's huge moon.

Stordahl pushed his way through the entrance to the dome which housed the vehicles and equipment for the expedition. This was the largest building of the Alice complex; when the vehicles were gone it was intended to convert it into a community dome, with a bar, restaurant, and theatre. In anticipation of this a dramatic society had already been formed whose members spent much of their leisure time rehearsing for the opening night of a musical comedy scheduled for the following week.

At present, however, the dome was the scene of a more utilitarian activity. Men and women swarmed everywhere, taking the covers from the huge, balloon-tyred vehicles, checking their reactors and generally making ready for the voyage. The equipment and supplies were already aboard the trailers; these long vehicles had been shipped from Earth fully laden with carefully checked inventories. It was thought that this would save time, prevent mistakes being made, and lessen the opportunities for sabotage. It would not be necessary to open up the trailers until the desert site was reached.

Stordahl saw Bill Myers, his assistant, supervising a group of men running through the starting procedure on a nearby vehicle. He walked over, ploughing through discarded polythene wrappings.

'How's it going, Bill?'

The sandy-haired man looked down from his seat in the high cab of the tractor. 'Oh, morning, Alex. . . . Fine, fine. There's not a lot to do now. We've got most of the covers off; I'm just checking over the motors.' He glanced around the dome; there were six of the balloon-tyred tractors and twelve trailers, similarly shod to deal with the extremes of Marilyn ground conditions. 'We should be ready to roll in a couple of hours.'

Stordahl grinned up. 'I should think these are more comfortable than the half-tracks.' The tractors had fully-enclosed cabs, air-conditioned with well-upholstered seating.

'You're right. I'm looking forward to driving a proper vehicle again.'

Myers was in charge of the desert expedition. He, like Stordahl, had worked for the Emigration Commission before its demise. They knew each other's methods, having been involved together in the initial stages of colonization of two planets in the Vega sector. Stordahl had been pleased when Hetherington had informed him Myers was to be his second-in-command. He had every confidence in leaving Myers to lead the desert expedition. He, Stordahl, intended to relieve Myers the next week, unless anything unexpected cropped up at Alice.

'I'm going to come with you part of the way,' Stordahl said. 'Briggs and I will take a few men and try to catch one of the amorphs for examination. We'll take a half-track and leave your column after about twenty miles, then make a wide arc back here.'

'The amorphs. . . .' Myers looked thoughtful. 'Have you seen the film yet?'

'No. Briggs and I are going to take a look at it this morning. I expect he's already run it through. It's early to tell, but I've a feeling this could be important. No life form like this has ever been encountered before.'

'This imitation thing. How accurate could it be? I mean, could this creature duplicate a man exactly?' Myers chuckled, but the sound held undercurrents of alarm. 'If they got into the base, we wouldn't know whether we were in bed with a girl or an alien.'

'I don't suppose the resemblance would go so far as to include speech.'

Myers laughed outright. 'In that case the women had better watch out. They may find themselves replaced.'

Stordahl left Myers to his work and, outside, climbed on to a half-track and started it up. He headed in the direction of the building site.

At this hour the partially completed cabins were deserted, the owners at various jobs around the colony. As the skidding motion of the half-track steadied with the fused soil to a firmer though noisier ride, Stordahl caught sight of Lever, the surveyor, measuring up a site. He drove over and stopped.

Lever indicated the area he had marked off. 'This is the sixth site,' he said, 'and there's no room for any more on the fused ground. Do we have to wait for ships to take off before we can get building sites? It's not as if you can call these sites perfect. People coming out from Earth want a garden around their house – a bit of greenery to look at. Nothing will grow on this. And I can't see anything other than rice growing on the virgin soil. It's too wet.'

Stordahl glanced at the paddy-fields to the north of the building site. The super-rice was coming along reasonably well, although the site was not so suitable as the delta. Here, the saucerplants kept crowding out the seedlings. Experiments with other crops had so far failed although research was going on. The colony was still dependent for food on the shipments of concentrates from the organization.

Lever went on: 'What happened to your requisition for PVC drainage pipes? Is the stuff coming on the next ship? There's a good sloping stretch of land between here and the base. It only needs drainage putting in to make it perfect for crops, housing, or whatever you like.'

'The ship's not due for three Standard months,' replied Stordahl. 'And it's going to be loaded with equipment for the steelworks. There may not be room for a load of pipes.' He hadn't the heart to tell Lever that his requisition had already been refused by the organization, on the grounds of cost. Find a local solution, they had said. Use your ingenuity with the materials at hand.

'Three months?' echoed Lever, reddening. 'That's nine months between ships! Do they intend us to live in domes and eat pills and rice for five years? What sort of thing have we got ourselves into?'

'Hold it, Lever. It's not as bad as that. Once the plant is in operation there'll be regular ships coming to take away the production. They'll be able to bring whatever we need.'

'You didn't tell us there wouldn't be another ship for three months,' muttered the surveyor. 'When you told us we were starting for the desert today, we all assumed there'd be a ship along right away.'

Worried, Stordahl mounted the half-track and left. One of the more difficult facets of his job was to prevent the colony, light-years from Earth, from getting the impression it had been abandoned. A rumour is all that is needed to break the morale of a colony – a rumour that they had been written off the books and forgotten.

It had happened to him once before, and had cost twenty-three lives in quelling a completely pointless mutiny. . . .

The film was inconclusive. As the screen brightened and the tape pattered around the spool, Stordahl stood up.

'It's OK,' he said. 'It shows us what happened, but it doesn't tell us anything new.'

'True,' admitted Briggs. 'But it confirms one very important point which you might have missed in your, ah, astonishment at the time.'

'Oh?'

'Yes. The question of sex. I may have misled you with my comparison with the apes and their homosexual defence mechanism. . . . This film shows, quite clearly, that the true, aggressive lizard was male. Sex is a little more obvious here than among Terrestrial reptiles. And the amorph, as people seem to be calling it, became female.'

'I'd gathered that much already.'

'But don't you see the significance?' persisted Briggs. 'This knocks out the imitation theory. The amorph did not simply assume the shape of the creature which threatened it. There were essential differences. It became a female of the species. It was able to achieve a subtle distinction from the form of the male.'

Stordahl stared at the biologist. 'You're right,' he said slowly. 'It's not a blind, instinctive imitation. But it does rather lend weight to my original idea that there's only one species of animal on Marilyn, and that animal has no permanent shape but can change at will into another form. And even breed as such, if the mood takes it.'

'I wish you'd forget that nonsense, Stordahl,' said Briggs irritably. 'There's no reason, evolutionwise or otherwise, for such a creature.'

'Does there have to be a reason for anything? What is the reason for Man?'

'Oh, for God's sake,' snapped Briggs. 'Don't go all philosophical on me. There's always some sort of reason, granted the initial existence of life.'

'Sorry.' Stordahl was contrite; he had gone too far again. 'It's time we were getting ready for our trip,' he said, changing the subject.

They left the room and walked in silence down the corridor.

The undulating plain was uniformly green although the flat saucerplants had given way to taller vegetation similar to the tulip plant they had discovered near the cuptree grove. Twenty miles away the tall mountains rose jagged against the sky; emerald forests could be discerned among the foothills. The huge wheels of the tractors swished through the vegetation; the larger, nuclear-powered vehicles were almost soundless compared with the little half-tracks snarling alongside. In the main, the animals kept their distance. A herd of large upright reptiles stood watching about a mile away, their craggy heads swivelling slowly as the caravan moved across the plain. Earlier, they had startled one of these beasts; it must have been sleeping, comatose though upright on thick-thighed hind legs. It had awoken suddenly, given them a startled glance from cold eyes, then moved off rapidly in a two-legged run, surprisingly graceful despite its size. Otherwise they had seen very little in the way of life for the past few miles apart from the tiny lizards which scuttled terrified from beneath the lumbering vehicles.

Stordahl and Briggs were mounted on the bumpy seats of a half-track, followed by two similar vehicles carrying the rest of the hunting party; they moved up and down the flanks of the convoy like outriders.

'Time we were leaving them,' remarked Stordahl. He accelerated alongside the leading tractor and waved to the driver, who gestered back, peering down at them from the height of his cab. Stordahl veered southward, followed by the rest of his party.

'Bearing in mind that the amorphs seem to live in burrows,' said Briggs, 'I suggest that we take a wide curve towards the base, taking in that hill' – he pointed ahead – 'and that one, and the one to the east of it. The burrows are far more frequent around the lower slopes of the knolls, and it seems that the amorphs use the same burrows as the elephant worms.'

'Could be,' agreed Stordahl. 'I was going to take that route, anyway. We'll pass the first knoll again, that way.'

Shortly after leaving base they had skirted a low hill hooded with cuptrees and, through field glasses, had got a good sight of a number of amorphs moving about the fringe of the grove. The creatures changed shape constantly, but so far as they could make out this was for purpose of locomotion rather than defence. Snake-like amorphs climbed trees, and they even saw one form itself into a sphere and descend the slope rolling rapidly. Then an arm of the grove had hidden the group from view as the convoy moved on. Convinced that there was no shortage of amorphs Stordahl had stuck to his original plan of remaining with the convoy until they were half-way to the mountains.

Within half an hour they were at the foot of the first knoll. Like all the others they had seen, the hillock rose gently from the plain and appeared to be almost circular, with the inevitable clump of cuptrees at the summit. Beyond it, about six miles, rose a curious plume of what looked like smoke. They stopped the vehicles and dismounted.

'Right.' Stordahl regarded his team. 'I take it you're all armed. It's likely there are a few of those giant lizards among the trees; so if you see one, shout and run like hell for the half-tracks. Don't use your guns except as a last resort. It looks as though the reptiles are lacking in brain capacity, so you could have a hell of a job stopping one with a shell. By the look of the one I saw yesterday, it would have attacked even with its head blown off.'

As an added precaution, Stordahl unshipped from the half-tracks a high-powered laser rifle; a bulky weapon, but effective at any range.

'We'll be OK,' Briggs said confidently. 'You just keep us covered with that thing while we do the hunting. I don't think this will take long.' He took the bundled net from the vehicle and shook it free.

The hunting party moved quickly up the hill towards the first of the trees. Stordahl followed more slowly, rifle at the ready. He estimated that the grove measured approximately half a mile in diameter – plenty of cover for the larger reptiles.

They crept among the trees in single file, Briggs leading and Stordahl bringing up the rear. The grove was silent as though examining them watchfully, and the rain had ceased. It was mid-afternoon; before long the breeze would be blowing from the desert. An occasional small lizard darted among their feet, and in the upturned branches of the cuptrees they saw further creatures of the gliding variety, peering down at them with bright eyes. The whole place smelled dank, and from time to time they were obliged to climb over rotting trunks festooned with creeping plants. Briggs halted the party to examine a plant and, with difficulty, hacked through the tough creeper and secured a specimen to take back for Ward Entwhistle, the colony botanist whose initial work Briggs had been undertaking while the other man recovered from bronchitis in the sick bay.

Suddenly the column halted again. Briggs turned around, finger to his lips, then pointed upward.

Slung among the branches of a cuptree was a snake-like creature, slender, at first glance almost indistinguishable from the creeping plants. Then it moved, and the uppermost extremity turned; it was watching them. Stordahl joined Briggs.

'What do you think?' he whispered.

'It could be,' Briggs replied. 'It's thinner than the other we saw climbing trees. More ropy. It could be an amorph taking on the appearance of a creeper. Let's watch for a while and see what happens.'

So the group stood silent. Gradually the forest, encouraged by their immobility, came to life about them. Tiny forms started to glide from tree to tree, others bounded along the branches monkey-like with prehensile tails. Shrill squeals and tiny squeaks reached their ears.

And the creature in the tree began to change shape. Slowly at first the sinuous body slithered through the branches, contracting, drawing in on itself, the green hue shifting subtly through yellow to orange, then a neutral brown. The tail, now short and stumpy, divided; further limbs sprouted from the new, thickened body. The head became distinct, flowing like a drifting mist through a variety of forms until, undeniably, they were being watched by a human face. . . .

A human face with human features, but with a curious inhuman anonymity of expression. . . .

The legs had formed, the creature clung to the tree with hands; on each hand were four fingers and an opposed thumb. It blinked at them, a human blink in no way reptilian; and a strange indistinct corona surrounded its head. It was wearing clothes; a brown smock.

'It's coming down,' whispered Briggs. 'God, the thing's coming down to us!'

But suddenly the creature froze in its descent, its grip on the trunk tightened and Stordahl could have sworn that the pink flesh of the hands turned white at the pressure. The head turned away from them, the mouth opened, showing fangs; a forked tongue flickered. The jaw lengthened and the countenance was changing again, becoming reptilian. . . .

'Look out!'

Stordahl brought his rifle to the shoulder and thumbed the trigger in the same movement, sweeping the forest in the direction the creature was looking, raising a crackling cloud of steam from the damp vegetation through which loomed the vast bulk of a giant lizard. The group of men scattered, diving for concealment and loosing off a fusillade of shots at the new arrival.

Roaring with pain the monster paused, its tiny eyes fixed on Stordahl until, desperately, the man swept the narrow beam of the laser across the terrible head and the eyes exploded in steam and blood. The creature thundered agony and, veering, crashed away through the trees to suffer noisily in the distance.

The men were picking themselves up and regrouping around the cuptree.

'Close,' observed one. 'Too damned close for me.' He glanced nervously back the way they had come.

The amorph regarded them from the tree. It hadn't moved. Its appearance was once more human.

'The thing warned us,' Stordahl said shakily. 'It saw that brute of a lizard coming and it changed shape to let us know.'

'Nonsense,' retorted Briggs, himself again. 'It assumed the form of the most imminent danger as a defence mechanism.'

The amorph was once more descending the tree. It stepped to the ground and stood before them, an anonymous human, apparently unafraid.

'Who are you?' someone asked idiotically.

They covered it with their guns. Its mouth opened; it now had human teeth, a human tongue. Its lips twisted experimentally.

'Who?' it said. 'Who are you?'

FOUR

There was an immediate babble of conversation. Guns were lowered and men crowded around the amorph, questioning it, forgetting in their surprise that a few minutes ago the thing had resembled nothing on Earth.

'Back off, men!' Stordahl shouted. 'Keep it covered!'

'It's only an imitation. A facsimile,' added Briggs. 'It repeated what it heard.'

The group calmed down. They stood in a semi-circle, again regarding the amorph with due wariness.

'Let me try,' said Briggs. He addressed the creature. 'You are a native of this planet?' he asked slowly.

The amorph paused, then answered distinctly: 'No.'

Briggs started. They stared at the amorph.

'It replied,' said Stordahl incredulously. 'It answered you in English. So much for the imitation theory.' Through his amazement, he was aware of a feeling of satisfaction.

'What world do you come from?' asked Briggs, recovering.

'From Earth,' replied the amorph definitely. The odd corona about its head had coalesced into thick, long brown hair; but its face still held the indefinable air of anonymity. Its expression was constantly altering, smiling, grimacing.

'I don't get it,' said Briggs. 'We call this planet Marilyn,' he stated carefully. 'The world we come from, we call Earth. Now, where do you come from?'

'Earth,' repeated the amorph. It frowned suddenly. 'Earth is the third from the sun, and there are eight other planets of which Jupiter is the largest. Earth has one satellite which we call the Moon.'

'I guess we're talking about the same place,' said somebody, and laughed, high-pitched, hysterical.

'What is your name?' asked Briggs.

The amorph stared around, gazing at each of the men in turn with an expression of bewilderment. 'Name?' it repeated faintly. 'Name? I don't know. . . . I have so many names, so many shapes. . . . Sometimes I am a worm, sometimes a lizard, or a snake. . . . But a name, now? I don't know. . . .'

Briggs glared at the amorph aggressively. 'How the hell did you get here?'

The creature's expression cleared. 'On a ship,' it stated.

'And the name of the ship?'

'The *Hetherington Endeavour.*'

'Oh? I didn't see you on board,' observed Briggs sarcastically.

'Then how did I get here?'

'You tell me,' snapped Briggs, annoyed at a chuckle from one of the men. 'Come on, Stordahl. Let's get this thing back to the base. I can't get any sense out of it. This is a job for Santana. I can't deal with this sort of double-talk.'

'Good idea.' Stordahl took the creature by the arm, one of them took the other arm, and it came along, unresisting. It smiled at Stordahl suddenly and the smile touched a chord in his memory, and for a moment he chased an elusive resemblance. . . .

They reached the half-track and Stordahl abruptly felt reluctant about locking the creature in the large cage which was bolted to the rear of his vehicle. The others must have had the same thought and they paused uncertainly, regarding the amorph.

'My God,' muttered one of them. 'It's a woman.'

She stood before them smiling and she was nobody anyone knew, yet she was familiar to all of them. There was a belt around her waist which they hadn't noticed before; what they had thought to be a sexless smock was a short dress.

'You know . . .' the man hesitated, then continued sheepishly, 'she reminds me, just a bit, of my wife.'

And yet there was something faintly masculine about the good looks of the creature; her face was a shade too strong for perfect femininity. 'I suppose she is a woman . . .' someone murmured. 'I mean, she looks like a woman.'

Curious, Stordahl thought. *This is an alien animal. Whatever it says, it must be an alien animal, and now there's a question as to its sex. And nobody is suggesting the obvious way to find out. And if they did suggest that way, I wouldn't allow it. This thing has a dignity. . . .*

And then he thought: *I'm kidding myself. I don't want to strip the clothes off this thing because . . . I don't want to. It's not right to do that to . . . to whom?* Again the half-memory. . . .

'Are you a man or a woman?' he asked the amorph.

The bewildered look again, and no reply.

This was ridiculous. What did it matter, right at this moment? 'Put it in the cage,' snapped Stordahl.

Stordahl drove, carefully avoiding the bumps while Briggs sat with his seat reversed, murmuring to the amorph through the bars of the cage. It seemed that Briggs had regained interest now that there were no witnesses to his unsuccessful attempts at communication.

Stordahl twisted around in his seat. 'How are you making out?' he asked.

'Interesting. This is most interesting. The creature shows no fear whatsoever of the method of transport, or of myself.' He leaned away again, his face close to the bars. Stordahl looked around again after a quick glance ahead to make sure there were no potholes forthcoming, and saw the amorph was sitting at the forward end of the cage, near Briggs. It seemed to be changing shape again, facially at least.

'What's happening there?' Stordahl asked, after carefully navigating through a group of elephant worm burrows. 'The thing looks different.'

'I think it's becoming male,' replied Briggs abstractedly, in between firing complex questions at the amorph. Suddenly he swivelled around to face forward again. 'Look here, Stordahl. This is a very strange thing. I've been trying it out, testing its knowledge on my own subject. It seems to have a complete, instinctive grasp of Terrestrial biology. If that were not impossible, I would say it knew the subject backward, already.'

'It did say it came from Earth.'

'My God, Stordahl. Do you believe that? How could a thing like this have come on the same ship as ourselves? To say nothing of all the other amorphs we've seen around the place.'

'Unlikely.' The creature so disturbed and baffled Stordahl that he admitted privately he would rather leave it to the experts. He had never encountered such a life form on any of the other planets he had visited; neither, so far as he knew, had anyone else. The thing was uncanny, sitting there in the cage, changing shape apparently at will and discussing biology with Briggs. The thought of it behind him gave him a prickling sensation at the back of his neck. He consoled himself with the thought that the creature did not seem to be dangerous. So far as they knew. And they knew nothing.

'I wonder if we ought to leave it. Let it go, I mean.'

'What!' Briggs stared at him in outrage. 'Turn him loose? You must be joking. What sort of a Supervisor do you call yourself? It's our duty to investigate this thing, for the sake of the colony, as well as for science. You must be mad, Stordahl!'

'You referred to it as him. A while ago it was she. The thing's weird, we don't know a thing about it, and now we're taking it back to the colony. We've no idea what to expect. We don't know what it can do, and I'm not sure I want to find out. The amorphs have never bothered us in the past. They've never come near the base and I'm not sure that it's a good idea they should. We ought to study them in the field, in their natural environment.'

'If you think I can't keep any experiment under control —' began Briggs stiffly.

'I'm sure you can, under normal circumstances. But this isn't normal. It concerns the emotions as well as the intellect. Haven't you noticed?'

'Noticed what?'

Stordahl took a deep breath, aware that he was going to be laughed at again; but the thing had to be said. 'That creature has an empathetic link with us.'

'What on Earth do you mean?'

'When it was a woman I . . . liked it. I thought it was pleasant. It emitted an aura of companionship and . . . well, friendliness. Now, suddenly, I can't stand the sight of it. I looked around just now, and the thing seemed evil. It's not imagination. The brute definitely plays on my emotions. I begin to wonder just what sort of an effect it could have on me, if it chose.'

Briggs chuckled, an unpleasantly triumphant sound. 'Funny you should say that. When it was a woman, I wasn't too happy. The thing seemed vapid and unformed. But now . . . he and I have had the most interesting talk and we seem to see eye to eye on everything. I like him. He's great!'

Something in the biologist's voice triggered off an alarm signal in Stordahl's mind. He swung around and got a quick sight of the object in the cage. He braked sharply; the half-track skidded to a halt on the wet ground. The other vehicles stopped alongside, wondering what was happening.

Stordahl jumped to the ground, backed away from the vehicle, staring, the hair prickling at the back of his neck.

Briggs stood beside the cage, smiling, his hand resting on the bars with a proprietory air.

Inside the cage, also smiling, correspondingly dressed to the last shirt button, was a perfect facsimile of Briggs.

At last the vehicles got under way again, a compromise having been reached between Stordahl and Briggs. The amorph was to be allowed within the outer perimeter of the base but was to be housed in a metal shed of a type normally intended for use as an emergency shelter in the event of attack. There were a number of these sheds at the base which were at present being used as storehouses. Stordahl reasoned that although the creature might change its shape in order to escape from a cage, it would have difficulty in getting out of a sealed, locked unit built to withstand nuclear attack.

'Who said the defence mechanism didn't invoke an exact replica?' asked Briggs triumphantly.

'I did,' replied Stordahl shortly. 'And I was right, in the case of our first sighting. And in the case of this . . . thing. Remember, it was a woman, earlier.'

'That's where you're wrong again, Stordahl. We only thought it was a woman. In fact it was a composite of all of us. It happened to look female, but that was pure chance. Confronted by a group of human beings, the amorph, in order to defend itself in the only way it knows, assumed a shape which it borrowed from observation of each of us. That's why its expression kept changing, and the lines of its face shifting. It was uncertain. It did its best to please.'

'It was a woman,' persisted Stordahl. 'And the one we have on film was a female reptile.'

'The woman was your imagination. The female reptile

I can explain. Look at it this way. The only way you knew the true lizard was male was because you could see the external genitalia they have on this planet. Your supposed female imitation would, given a few more seconds, have become male. The reproduction wasn't complete, that's all. Take the external genitals from a male Marilyn lizard and what have you got, in appearance? A female Marilyn lizard.' Briggs leaned back in his seat smugly, then took a quick look behind as though to reassure himself that his facsimile was still faithful.

'Look, Briggs.' Stordahl adopted a reasonable tone. 'I'm willing to accept that you may be right, in view of the evidence in that cage. But don't let's get carried away by this thing. There are a lot of implications which you may have missed in your delight at being duplicated.'

'For instance?'

'The conversations. The language. The knowledge of Earth, of biology. You said the thing knew as much as yourself.'

'That follows. It's become a replica. God, think of the possibilities; the two of us working together.'

'Yes. But *how* does it know the language? This isn't just an external resemblance, like a chameleon changing colour.'

'I realize that,' said Briggs shortly. 'Of course the amorph is telepathic. It's obvious. The resemblance is complete. It knows everything I know. And quite a few things I've forgotten, no doubt. I wonder. . . .' He turned around, scrutinizing the amorph thoughtfully. 'I wonder if it possesses free will, in its present form?'

'I hope not,' said Stordahl. 'Because if it does, and it's able to know everything we know, then it places us at a hell of a disadvantage. Because we have no access to the amorph's knowledge. We can't read *its* mind.' He turned, stared at the creature. 'What is your name?' he asked.

'Alfred Briggs.'

'What are you thinking about?'

The duplicate Briggs smiled back; a bland, enigmatic smile.

'I'm thinking I don't like you very much,' it said. 'I don't know why, but I'm thinking you're a difficult man to get on with.'

* * * *

'Take the wheel for a while, Briggs,' commanded Stordahl grimly. 'I'm going to have a talk with this thing.' The colony domes were in sight now; the afternoon was nudging evening and the western sky was a rainbow kaleidoscope of shifting colours as the sun's slanting rays were refracted by the desert dust. They stopped the vehicle briefly while they exchanged seats; Stordahl swivelled his to face rearward. The amorph watched him with interest. It was wearing, unbelievably, pebble lenses – or a very good organic replica.

Stordahl was silent for a while; thinking out the situation and giving the amorph a chance to assimilate his thoughts. Telepathy, although much speculated about, had never yet been encountered in a form which allowed even one-way communication between different species – which made the present problem difficult to assess. In any case, could he and the amorph, at this moment, be regarded as belonging to different species? What is the distinction between species? In the present situation no distinction was applicable. The amorph was *every* species. It was a basic life. In its ability to adapt almost instantly in mind and form, it was the quintessence of evolution.

My God, he thought in sudden alarm, *it's the perfect creature. If it has free will....*

'Are you reading my mind?' he asked.

Something was bothering the amorph. It had commenced to grimace again; a tic plucked at its mouth, a repeated fleeting grin, mirthless. 'I don't understand,' it replied.

'You have a knowledge of biology. Briggs says so. In fact you just told me you *are* Briggs. Now . . .' Stordahl concentrated hard. 'I'm visualizing a Terrestrial plant. I want you to tell me the name of it, and what it looks like.' A tulip, a black tulip on a slender stem, waving in a warm spring breeze; bending low before it was Margaret, a small trowel in her hand. . . . 'Alex,' she said, 'your mind is too orderly. You've planted these things straight, so they've come up like a row of soldiers. Next spring, just dot them at random like the clicks of a Geiger counter. It looks much better that way. . . .' He jerked his mind back to the present, concentrated on the flower, warm purple-black. . . .

'I've no idea what plant you're thinking about.'

The planes of the face were irregular; the resemblance to Briggs was fading by the minute. . . .

It's turning into me, thought Stordahl. *God, this is weird. . . .* 'Who are you? What is your name?' he asked again.

'My name?' Through the flowering features of the face an unmistakable concern showed. 'My name . . . my name must be . . . was . . . Alfred Briggs.'

'You're not sure?'

'How can I be sure? I have . . . no control over my name. My name is what I am. . . . What am I?'

What are you? wondered Stordahl. Because the amorph was becoming smaller, contracting within itself as the spectacles melted into the eyes and the clothes became absorbed by the body. . . .

I'm five-foot-eleven and Briggs is five-six. . . .

And still the amorph shrank.

It held on to the bars of the cage with one small hand as the half-track swayed and bumped across the slippery, uneven ground and the base Alice loomed nearer.

It was going to wear . . . it was almost wearing blue, squared white, gingham, short, childish, and the hair verged on the golden side of light brown.

But it was still too tall, too tall, and the inhuman composite between Briggs and the person it was tending towards was . . . terrifying; because when you see a person you dislike transformed, slowly, into one whom you loved but didn't expect to see again, and the transformation begins to stop while incomplete, then the agony in the mind and the emotions is too great and you can only run, get away, try to forget by thinking and talking frantically about something else. . . .

Stordahl swung his seat around, forward; his face felt clammy in the breeze. 'We're almost there,' he said, high-pitched so that Briggs glanced at him sharply. 'We're almost there. I wonder how the convoy's doing. I hope they reach the desert by nightfall. I must call them up when we get back. . . .'

Briggs twisted and looked at the cage. 'What have you done to the amorph?'

'It . . . began to change again and I couldn't get any sense out of it.'

It began to change, oh God. Oh, God. . . .

FIVE

He ordered Briggs to stop the half-track some two hundred yards from the nearest dome and climbed down, informing the biologist that he would send an emergency shelter along immediately. As he continued on the second vehicle, he saw Briggs seat himself before the amorph again, and begin talking to it. Already the creature was growing taller.

Joan greeted him at the radio dome; her expression was anxious. A knot of people were gathered at the entrance to the dome, talking quietly, their expressions grave in the evening twilight.

'They're having trouble in the desert,' she told him.

'Oh, hell. But they got there all right?' He accompanied her into the radio room, a tiny bubble of plastic allowing them barely space to squeeze in behind the operator. Headphones clamped to his ears, the man did not look around.

'They arrived half an hour ago,' Joan told Stordahl.

The operator was speaking. 'Yes . . . yes . . . I see . . . I'll tell him.'

Stordahl tapped him on the shoulder. The man started and looked around, then said: 'He's here now. I'll hand you over.' Addressing Stordahl he said: 'It's Mr. Myers.'

'Hello? That you, Bill?' Stordahl bent over the operator's shoulder shouting at the mike. 'What's the trouble?' He slipped the headphones on. 'Let me sit here will you?' The operator scrambled out of the seat and Stordahl replaced him.

'Alex? Any luck with the hunting?' Myers sounded cheerful enough.

'We'll talk about that later. What about you? I hear you're having difficulty.'

Reception was good; the voice came back clearly. 'Just a small point we wouldn't have guessed from the original survey. The desert surface is in constant motion shifting with the wind all the time. It's fine dust, mostly ferrous oxide, incredibly rich. Hetherington will flip. All you have to do is scoop the stuff up. But there's a snag.' Myers paused expectantly; the faint sound of shouted orders came through.

'What's the snag, Bill?'

'For one thing we can't get the vehicles any distance into the desert. Even the balloon tyres bog down. We've abandoned one tractor and trailer already. Have to pick it up in the morning. Probably have to winch it out; the stuff's like quicksand. So that means at present we've got no way of testing below the surface; we can't tell how deep it is, or what's underneath. We may have to use the copter and sonar. Believe me, Alex, it's more like an ocean than a desert. A boat would stand a better chance than a vehicle.'

Ferrous oxide, in vast surface deposits. They had expected this, but it was another thing to have expectations confirmed by a physical test on the spot.

For centuries the industry of Earth had been based on iron as a staple commodity. Easy to obtain, easy to work, with countless uses either pure or as a multitude of alloys, the metal had always been taken for granted. Until the conquest of space. Then, for the first time, it became apparent that the prosaic metal was not so common as had been thought. Alien races had been encountered, intelligent races whose development had been retarded merely due to scarcity of an easily worked hard metal. Aluminium, for instance, was frequently present on a planet in huge quantities; but how would a race unused to metalworking recognize it for what it could be? How could they conceive from a deposit of bauxite that from it could be obtained a light durable metal, when their natural growth of knowledge of metalworking stopped dead at bronze? Aluminium was the commonest metal in the known galaxy, yet the method of obtaining it from raw oxide had not been perfected on Earth until the twentieth century.

There was still no lack of iron on Earth, but the cost of shipping it to the farther outposts, even by FTL transports was prohibitive. In the sector which included the planet Marilyn there was little iron. Hetherington had known what he was doing, when he sent the *Endeavour* on its journey. Soon he would be able to handle the entire steel industry throughout a group of colonized worlds – extraction, refining, transport, and distribution. . . .

But now there was a human problem; Myers had encountered difficulties. 'It's grim here, Alex. The men are tired and we're trying to inflate the domes and the oxide is getting into everything. It's like dust, pulverized dust. God knows what sort of mess the equipment will be in, after a few days of this.'

'You'd better sleep in the trucks,' Stordahl suggested.

'I was thinking of that myself. In the morning the wind should be blowing inland, through the mountain pass and across the desert. That won't be so bad. But you ought to see it here, Alex. It's a fantastic sight. The wind has drifted the dust right up the foothills, so that the whole terrain slopes away from us here, like a huge scarlet bowl. And all the time the wind keeps slopping the dust up to the rim of the bowl, where we are. It comes in waves; the desert's cooling fast and you can almost see the cold air pressing down on it. . . .'

Myers was abruptly silent; sounds of distant shouting came through the headphones.

'Are you OK?' shouted Stordahl anxiously.

'. . . amazing.' Myers' voice came back. 'There must have been a pocket of warm air out there, trapped under the dust. It exploded in a fountain, about half a mile away, a tremendous spout of bright red as though a huge artery had been severed. It's blown back at us; everything's covered. . . . It's clearing a bit. I can see again. Oh, my God. We're going to have to dig that tractor out in the morning. No winch will shift that. It's buried half-way up the sides. . . .'

'Has everyone got their masks on?' asked Stordahl sharply.

'You kidding? You couldn't live two minutes here without breathing gear. Look, I'd better sign off now. There's a hell of a lot to do. I don't fancy working under lights in this. I'll call you back at . . . say o-seven hundred. OK?'

'Right. I'll be waiting.' Stordahl removed the headphones and stood, frowning worriedly. If Bill Myers said it was bad out there, then it must be very bad indeed. . . .

Joan was waiting for him as he left the radio dome. 'What did he say?' she asked.

'Conditions are bad but it should be better in the morning. It seems that work will have to cease there in mid-afternoon before things gets uncomfortable. That rather cuts down the day. . . . And once the wind shifts, I think they'll have to stay in the domes. Anyway, we'll leave Bill to sort that one out. How are things going back here?'

Joan hesitated; the burly figure of Lever stood nearby, obviously waiting. 'Mr. Lever wants a word with you,' she said. 'He seems to be the spokesman for a few of the colonists. He says it's urgent.'

Lever was striding towards them. 'You're damned right it's urgent, Stordahl,' he said forcefully. 'And it's not a few colonists I represent; it's practically every man and woman in this place. We want you to answer a few questions.' He stood with hands on hips, staring aggressively.

Stordahl was normally a patient man, such a characteristic is a prerequisite for a Colony Supervisor; but the events of the day had combined to wear his nerves thin and Lever's attitude provoked a flash of white fury.

'Just who the hell do you think you are?' he yelled, stepping close to the other man. 'You can get right back to your friends and tell them to get stuffed! Now get out of my sight, Lever, before I throw you in the cells!' He swung around and stormed off, leaving Lever staring after him open-mouthed.

Joan was beside him, practically running to keep up. Stordahl glared down at her. 'First that fool Briggs,' he snarled, 'and that weirdie we picked up. Then Myers can't cope. Now Lever sets himself up as a union man. God, what a day. . . .'

A man approached them, seemed about to speak, then, seeing Stordahl's face, veered away. 'Hey, you!' shouted the Supervisor. 'Williams, or whatever your damned name is. Get some men and take an emergency shelter over beyond the domes, where Briggs is. Make sure he locks up that damned amorph. I'll hold you personally responsible if it gets out!'

'Yes, sir,' said the man timidly, and ran. Stordahl gazed after him with satisfaction. He'd scared the bastard. The lights came on abruptly, flooding the colony area and silvering the domes; Stordahl squinted up at them furiously, feeling exposed. 'Let's get inside,' he muttered. He shoved his way through the nearest entrance and found himself in the equipment tent, now empty of vehicles but littered with a rippling sea of discarded wrappings. 'Oh, God,' he muttered. 'Do I have to tell them to do everything? They've had all day to clear the place up.' The reaction was setting in now, and he felt weak, and in need of a drink, and a friend, and sympathy. 'What's the matter with everyone, Joan?' he asked plaintively.

'I think maybe you've had enough for one day,' she said carefully. 'Let's go along to your office and have a drink.'

Later, four Scotches later, he was regarding Joan mournfully over the rim of his glass. 'I should have gone with the desert party,' he said. 'I ought to have been there. It's unknown territory, and I sent Bill Myers instead of going myself. I had an idea it was going to be rough, and I didn't want to go.'

'Of course you didn't want to go,' Joan agreed softly. 'And neither did anyone else. As you said, we've got used to it here, and there's a lot to do. But your place right now is here with the rest of us. Bill's had difficulties in the desert, sure, but he can manage. That's what he's for. It was always intended that he should take charge of the party. He's the man with experience at that sort of thing. Your job is supervision generally, organizing and dealing with people. That's what you're good at.'

'You mean like just now?' Stordahl asked bitterly.

'Everybody blows their top from time to time. It's natural. This may sound hackneyed, but you'll feel better in the morning. Lever's problem can wait till then. Have another drink and forget about it.'

'Thanks, Joan. . . . Look, it's not just Lever, or Bill Myers. . . . The fact is, I'm bothered about the amorph. The thing's uncanny. It scares me. Do you know what it did . . .?'

She rose to her feet with a mock oh-my-God expression and sat on the arm of his chair, placing her fingers over his lips. 'Not now,' she said gently. 'In the morning. Let's talk about something else.'

Obediently he tried to relax. 'What shall we talk about?' he asked.

The glow of Scotch had spread through Joan and she had a topic all ready, but regretfully decided that this was not the time.

Morning came and with it the drifting rain and, surprisingly, things did begin to go a little better. Stordahl's first call was the radio dome; Bill Myers came through right on time. The party had spent an uncomfortable night in the transport but no damage had been done. They were up at dawn and the domes had been successfully inflated. The wind had abated and was at present no more than a light breeze, funnelling down the pass and away across the desert. In the new mood of optimism prevailing the buried tractor did not appear so insuperable a problem; a pontoon of duckboards had been extended to provide easy access and a team of men were in the process of digging the wheels clear. Myers felt that they would recover the vehicle by noon; meanwhile, the rest of the party was transferring the equipment and provisions into the domes, the trailers having proved to be by no means dust-proof. Stordahl left the radio dome with the feeling that things at the site were well under control.

Outside the dome Joan was waiting for him and, inevitably, Lever. The meeting could not be postponed any longer, it seemed. The colonists were getting restless. With surprising tact, Lever made no reference to Stordahl's outburst of the previous night. Joan must have spoken to the man, thought Stordahl.

The equipment dome, now renamed the Community Hall, had been cleared of the debris left by the exploration party and was packed with colonists seated on the ground. Lever led the way to the far end where a table and chairs had been set up; in traditional style, the table bore nothing but a carafe of water circled by upturned tumblers. Stordahl grinned to himself at this; obviously Lever intended to organize his meeting properly. The man had had second thoughts after his precipitous approach of the previous night.

Stordahl sat down; Lever stood and tapped for order with a spoon. Apparently there was no gavel in the inventory.

'Friends,' shouted Lever. 'The purpose of this meeting is, as you know, to discuss the unexpected – not to say ominous – piece of news which leaked out yesterday. That is to say, the news that we cannot expect a ship for another three months.' He turned to Stordahl. 'This is unfortunate. From the point of view of everyone here, Mr. Stordahl, it is essential that morale be maintained in an environment which is, to say the least, isolated. There are other points which I should like to raise in the course of the meeting, but I think we ought to start with this main issue. Bearing in mind that you previously led us to believe that the organization would be paying us a call, bringing mail, and so on, every six months, what have you to say about this surprising – may I say sinister? – revelation?' He sat down abruptly, somehow triumphantly, with the air of one who had placed his opponent's bishop in serious jeopardy.

Stordahl stood. They were all watching him, and he could understand their feelings. In essence, the situation had not changed significantly since the previous meeting when Charlton had come to his aid. But now Charlton, together with several other die-hard organization men, was at the desert site. . . . He would have to go it alone.

'It's disappointing,' he told them. 'But it's not in any way significant. We've only just started here, after all. A week ago I received a personal radio message from Mr. J. Wallace Hetherington requesting a progress report. This I furnished as, in fact, I have been doing each week. He expressed complete confidence in the way things were going and, due to my information that we had no immediate requirements, decided to cancel the scheduled ship and divert it to Sunda where an unfortunate explosion had destroyed a large quantity of supplies. That's all there is to it.' He sat down, not really believing Lever would let things go at that.

The surveyor rose to his feet slowly, a pained expression on his face. 'Oh, dear,' he said smoothly. 'What an unfortunate coincidence. So they had a big bang on Sunda and needed our food. Their need is greater than ours, so the ship was diverted. And they've got our mail, too. And the supplies of mutated seed that Mr. Entwhistle radioed for, as our vegetables all seem to have rotted. What with eating our food, and growing our crops, and reading our mail, they're going to be a busy lot of little bastards on Sunda.'

'Don't be a damned fool, Lever,' Stordahl said quietly. 'This isn't helping us, you know.'

'Don't be a damned fool, he tells me!' Lever roared. 'This isn't helping us, he says. Just tell me this, Stordahl. How long do you expect us to live on chemicals? This is a community of human beings, not a laboratory experiment. When are they going to ship in the livestock? The cattle, the sheep, the pigs?' He abruptly dropped his voice to a silky murmur, keeping his eyes on the crowd. 'There's a rumour going around, Mr. Supervisor, and it's worrying us a lot, so some of us can't sleep nights and we're wondering if it's all worthwhile, considering what we're paid. The rumour is that the only people who stand to gain from this operation is the Hetherington Organization. The rumour is that there was never any intention of encouraging colonization. The rumour is that we're stuck on this planet as factory workers at minimum pay, and that's the way it always will be. In short, the rumour is that we're slaves. Slaves, Mr. Supervisor. A dirty word. Is it true?'

'Of course not,' said Stordahl wearily. 'We've been through all this before. You have my personal word that food, livestock, and seed – and the mail – will be here on the next ship in three months' time.'

'And what is your word worth, Mr. Stordahl?'

'Goddamn it!' shouted Stordahl. 'I'll resign if it doesn't come! Does that satisfy you?'

'And go back to Earth?'

'Yes! Do you think I'd work for a bunch of exploiters?'

Lever chuckled softly; the trap was sprung. 'And just how do you think you'd get back to Earth, Mr. Stordahl?'

Stordahl gazed at the audience helplessly. This was playing with words. True, the people here had to take a lot on trust, but although Hetherington might in some ways be ruthless, he would never ruin the reputation of his organization by giving colonists less than a fair deal. How could he make these people understand that? They were carried away, whisked like leaves on the stream of Lever's oratory, flowing headlong to the whirlpool of mutiny. And what possible good would mutiny serve? With each person voluntarily breaking his contract, Hetherington would have every reason for abandoning the colony to its fate. But Hetherington didn't want that, otherwise he would never have set up the operation in the first place. What was it all about? What the hell was Lever after?

'What do you want, Lever?' he asked quietly. 'Do you imagine this place could be self-supporting, immediately? Is that what you're saying? That we'd be better off without the organization?'

For the first time Lever looked uncertain. Stordahl could almost see his mind working. This, it seemed, was the crunch. The audience was hushed, watching the surveyor as he stood before them, irresolute. Stordahl had the incredible notion that the colony would do whatever Lever decided. How could he, the Supervisor, have got so out of touch with the feelings of the place as a whole? Why was a mass of people so much more stupid than its component members?

Irrelevantly, what would a composite amorph do?

Joan, too, sensed the danger; she stood at the end of the table and tapped loudly for attention. All eyes swung to her, even Lever's – and there was something akin to gratitude in the surveyor's glance.

'If I might help you all to make up your minds,' she began, 'as this seems to be a time for decision, though God alone knows why. There are a lot of advantages to be gained from independence, as we all know. For instance, we would all be able to start building our individual houses right away, without having to put in the first eight hours in each day working for the organization. We might find ourselves short of a few items like plumbing supplies, and nails, and electrical fittings, and other things I can't think of now so perhaps don't matter. But at least we would be able to build, quickly, a hut or something for each of us. Or, failing that, find a cave.

'We have diverse individual skills. Mr. Lever, for instance, is a surveyor. In the simplicity of our independent life such skills would not be needed and I'm sure Mr. Lever, for one, would enjoy becoming a farmer. I would like to be a farmer's wife myself, though perhaps not Mr. Lever's wife. We would find that we had quite a lot of farmers. Granted, there would be no crops to plant because we have no seed, neither would we have animals because the livestock isn't due for three months; but there are the local reptiles. We have insufficient fencing materials for all our prospective farmers, so we would have to hunt the reptiles with guns. And later on, when the ammunition ran out, we could use spears or clubs; there's always a way.

'And in case you think this is beginning to sound a little primitive – I mean, prehistoric man used to live in caves and club his quarry to death, didn't he? – don't forget we have an advantage over him. We have discovered fire. We can cook our reptiles. We're round about Cro-Magnon. Who knows, in a few million years we might conquer space.

Now, there's something to look forward to, you stupid bastards!'

Joan's eyes were glistening with tears; she swung around and pushed her way out of the dome. For a while no one spoke, then Lever leaned across and addressed Stordahl quietly.

'Game to you, Mr. Supervisor. Between you and me, why the hell don't you marry that girl?'

Avio Santana was a man of a little below medium height with dark hair, a swarthy complexion and an expression of permanent sadness. Avio Santana was the colony psychiatrist and this doleful countenance – which was genuine – had played a large part in the success which had attended his career to date. His patients did not wish to be jollied along; the hearty couchside manner was for his less successful colleagues. Santana had made it on his face. Not that he did not possess considerable skill; but it is a fact that your average mental patient would rather be confronted by a psychiatrist as miserable as himself. Santana would sit beside the couch and fix his deep-set eyes on theirs and listen in obvious sympathy and sorrow to their outpourings. It had been said that his career was successful and, measured in terms of hard cash, it was. It is another fact that a psychiatrist's patients never really get better, and thereby supply a constant source of income. The treatment is the approach. . . .

There was consternation in the teeming brains of the wealthier female residents of New London N.W. when Santana announced his intention of quitting his practice and leaving for an unknown planet named Marilyn, in the employment of a vulgar commercial enterprise named the Hetherington Organization, or something. They couldn't understand it. They twittered about it over innumerable cups of tea in innumerable Regency-furnished apartments and they all agreed that, if the man actually left, that is to say abandoned them, they would go mad. Stark, raving mad. Their cups rattled in their trembling saucers as they said it.

They told Santana this, individually as they lay on the couch, gazing into his unfathomable eyes. They begged him to stay; it was his duty; my God, he couldn't leave them like this. But he was adamant, and sadly recommended Dr.

Blenkinsop down the road. And before long, as is the way of such people, they became vindictive. A rumour was carried sibilant from one ear to the next, until New London N.W. hissed with the news from an informed source that Avio Santana was leaving Earth in a hurry, before he was caught up with. He had, it seemed, made advances to a female patient who was under the influence of hypnosis.

The rumour gathered circumstance with strength, and the luckless patient was identified; one Gloria Hewitt, a wealthy, attractive young wife of an industrialist. Some said she got what she asked for, because she was not a popular figure in the area; she had a streak of vulgarity as wide as a motorway. Nevertheless it was a dreadful thing to happen to a girl and the ladies of New London shuddered delightedly at the closeness of their respective escapes. Of course, they assured one another, they had always been on their guard from the first moment they had clapped eyes on that little Latin quack. There was something about his manner, apart from that uncanny facial resemblance to Svengali. . . .

Stordahl entered Santana's little consulting dome without knocking, to find the psychiatrist was busy. 'I'm sorry, Avio,' he apologized, and turned to leave.

'Don't go,' called the other, and something in his voice made Stordahl turn back immediately. He looked at the psychiatrist for the first time and was surprised at the appearance of the man; there was an unhealthy pallor to his skin and he seemed to be trembling.

'What's the trouble?' Stordahl glanced in the direction of the couch, then hastily averted his eyes; a girl was lying there. *Her* problem was no business of his. 'You don't look so good, Avio. The old stomach problem?' Santana smoked incessantly and suffered from heartburn.

Santana was silent for a moment, thoughtful. Then he looked at Stordahl. 'Alex,' he began, 'I like to think we're good friends. . . .'

'You Latin types are too emotional,' remarked Stordahl.

Santana's expression did not change. 'Nevertheless I intend to presume on your friendship and be frank with you. . . . Now, you must have guessed that I left Earth for a reason.'

'Everybody does.'

'I had a thriving practice. I had everything going for me

and I like to think I was doing my patients some good. Certainly the business was constantly expanding through recommendation, so I must have helped them in some way.'

'Why should there be any doubt?' asked Stordahl curiously.

'My patients were wealthy, Alex. Mostly women, middle-aged. To some, it might have looked as though I were specializing in the patient, rather than the illness. And I will admit that many of my patients were, to put it bluntly hypochondriacs. But most of them weren't; they were genuine cases, and surely a rich woman has as much right to be treated for a mental disturbance as anyone else.'

'There's no need to defend yourself, Avio. The point is, it appeared you were doing a good job.'

Santana shrugged. 'Perhaps. Anyway, to cut a long story short, I did a very stupid thing. I fell in love. . . .'

'Oh, God. . . .' Stordahl guessed what was coming.

'A young patient, attractive, wealthy and . . . married. At the time I would have said that I couldn't help it; I was obsessed with her. Her husband got to know, and there was unpleasantness and threats and, looking back, I feel maybe that I could have avoided it. I could have recommended her to someone else as soon as I saw her, because that was the moment when I fell in love. But I didn't. I was weak. And so eventually . . . I came here.'

'I've heard of worse reasons,' observed Stordahl. 'These things happen.'

'Her name was Gloria Hewitt. You may have heard of her; she was an actress. Her name was Gloria Bliss before she married Hewitt.'

'I've heard of her.' And with the name came the face . . . the face, and surely, Stordahl thought, staring, his first real look at the girl on the couch. . . .

'Yes.' Santana turned his gaze to the girl and took her hand. 'This is Gloria Bliss.'

'What the hell's she doing here, Avio?' Stordahl asked roughly.

The expression on the psychiatrist's face was tortured. 'This is her, Alex. This is Gloria, as I knew her.

'But an hour ago, she was an amorph.'

'What!'

'Briggs asked me to do an examination. We brought the

amorph here. At the time it resembled Briggs, and I was going to test his protective imitation theory. Briggs left me with the thing, and it began to change. And I thought it would assume my shape. I was almost looking forward to it; it would have been interesting. . . . The last thing I expected was what eventually happened. And Alex, this girl *is* Gloria, exactly as I remember her. And she remembers the things we did together. Don't you, my dear?'

The girl smiled. She was beautiful. 'Of course I remember, Avio,' she replied. 'How could I forget?'

SIX

The vehicle meandered westward.

Stordahl was following a hunch which had been growing in his mind since the day before yesterday when, shortly before capturing the amorph, they had sighted a thin column of smoke in the distance. At the time it had been disregarded in the main interest of the expedition; tacitly it had been assumed that lightning had struck a tree and set dead wood on fire – and Stordahl had not pursued the matter. He had his own ideas as to the source of the smoke and wished to follow them up in private.

Joan, however, had insisted on coming along.

Mid-morning; the rain drizzled and the sun hid behind the customary banks of grey cloud. They were making good progress and, by setting a course close by the hills, Stordahl was able to avoid the worst of the boggy low-lying ground. As they passed the first knoll they got a good view of a group of amorphs moving about in front of the trees. The creatures changed shape constantly; flattening themselves out like large pancakes, then rising from the centre, conical, until they became slender branching stems in apparent imitation of the cuptrees. They tended to follow one another in their transformations; one would grow tall, then the others would follow until there were more than a dozen slim shapes on the hillside. Then the branches merged, and broadened, and became large bowls held up to the falling rain.

Joan broke her long silence. 'They're drinking,' she observed quietly, as though not wishing to disturb the distant forms. 'They're drinking the rain as it falls.'

'It could be,' replied Stordahl. 'Although I should have thought they got enough moisture through absorption in their more shapeless form. Maybe. . . .' A fanciful thought struck him. 'Maybe they're young ones, practising shapes.'

'Now you're assuming they've got some sort of intelligence,' remarked Joan.

'They may have. How can we tell? As soon as they come under our influence it becomes impossible to study them, because our very presence makes them something different. We've got to find some method of observing them without their knowing. Then we might find out what makes them tick.'

They skirted the hill and left the amorphs behind. Setting a course south of east, Stordahl headed for the next knoll. The saucerplants over which they travelled were changing, becoming even more fleshy. Little spurts of juice spat from under the fat front wheels of the half-track.

'They're like succulents,' Joan observed. 'We ought to take a few of them back for analysis.'

Stordahl braked and they got down, stepping on to the plants which snapped under their weight and exuded a milky liquid. They gathered a number of the plants and put them in the container on the rear platform of the vehicle.

'Don't do that!' snapped Stordahl suddenly.

He was too late; Joan had touched her tongue to a spot of liquid on her finger. She smiled at his concern. 'It's obviously the same species as the plants near the base,' she reassured him. 'They're not poisonous.' She smacked her lips. 'In fact, it tastes quite pleasant.'

He shrugged. 'Oh, well. No doubt we'll be eating the stuff sometime. We haven't had much luck in getting the Terrestrial crops to grow.'

'That's because we haven't been trying hard enough,' Joan said pointedly.

'Whose side are you on, Joan?'

'I think I've made myself clear. I'm for the organization so long as it acts in good faith. If I see signs that the organization isn't looking after us the way it ought – like by delaying tactics – then I begin to lose confidence. In which case I'm for the colony as an entity. But that doesn't mean I'd back talk of mutiny. I reckon my views are about average. My own feeling is that we should step up colony activities such as building and investigate the possibility of making use of local food. Entwhistle spends his time cataloguing plants and compiling lists and reports for his foundation back on Earth, when he ought to be finding out whether we can eat the damned things and grow them as a crop.'

'You may have something there,' admitted Stordahl. 'It would be good for morale if people spent a little more time working for the day when we become independent.'

'It will be a safeguard,' Joan said. 'You asked me; now tell me. Which side are *you* on?'

'I suppose I'm pretty well neutral,' he answered evasively. 'I want to see a colony here, not merely a metal-works. But at the same time I've got to remember I'm paid by the organization to do a job. I can't jeopardize the project for the sake of a future colony.'

'Will you move on, after your contract's over?'

'That depends on what I'm offered. And the offer will depend on how I make out here.'

'And how do you think you're making out?'

'Early to tell. And a big factor of uncertainty has entered into the whole thing.'

'You mean the amorphs?'

'Yes. . . . We didn't expect them. We don't know what their capabilities are. . . . Never mind.' He broke off, gazing ahead. The fine rain was restricting visibility, but in the distance he thought he could see a shape, rectangular and incongruous against the flat plain, just at the point where it curved gently upward to a low hill.

In the lee of the hill, sheltered from the rain-bearing south-westerlies. . . .

The obvious place to build a house.

They were nearer now and the structure was plainly in view. A low, sloping roof with a jutting chimney; a door and a square aperture for a window in the wall facing them. Closer still, they saw that the place was constructed on typical log cabin lines with horizontal timbers caulked with mud, ascending alternatively at the corners.

As they pulled up, a tall weather-beaten man with an impressive growth of beard stepped out of the doorway and stood watching them. There was wariness in his stance, preparedness.

'Hello there, Arnott,' Stordahl called casually as he dismounted.

Smiling uncertainly, Arnott Walsh moved forward to greet them.

They shook hands and Stordahl felt his assumed air of nonchalance becoming unreal as Walsh led them into his cabin. The interior was furnished much as he had expected: rough wooden chairs and a crude table. One wall was entirely taken up by the stone fireplace and a door in another wall, Stordahl supposed, led to the kitchen. He wondered what Walsh used for tools and utensils. The question was soon solved when the door opened and Katie Walsh entered carrying a saucepan of unmistakable organization issue.

Joan ran forward at the sight of Walsh's wife and the two embraced with feminine effusiveness. Then Joan held the elder woman at arm's length and gazed into her face. 'Katie!' she exclaimed. 'You're looking great. This life must suit you.'

Mrs. Walsh smiled. 'I've never felt better. Briggs and Entwhistle would never believe this, but I think it's something to do with the diet.'

It was no secret in the colony that Katie Walsh had been seriously ill. This fact had emerged on her first visit to the doctor one week after touchdown on Marilyn, and immediately the question arose as to whether Walsh had known of her illness before they left Earth. Katie Walsh had cancer of the stomach and Jerry Singer, the colony doctor, entertained doubts as to her chances of survival for longer than a year. She should never have come; moreover, if her illness had been known at the time of departure she would not have been allowed to come. But now she was here, and there was nothing that could be done. . . . Or so Stordahl had understood at the time. And over the weeks Katie had become thinner and more haggard and there were many who thought privately that Singer's estimate of a year was optimistic.

Then the Walshes had disappeared. . . .

'What do you eat here, Arnott?' asked Stordahl, glad of a chance to postpone the awkward moment of asking Walsh what the hell he was doing here, anyway.

'This and that,' answered the zoologist airily. 'It's surprising what you can find, when you've got to. Plants, roots, and the local fauna.' He gestured to a huge ham of smoked meat hanging from a peg at the fireplace. 'It can taste very good. Will you stay to lunch?'

'Thanks. . . . We'd like that.' *This is unreal,* thought Stordahl. *Unreal. . . . What are we doing, sitting here like this, as though this were the most normal visit in the world . . .?*

Katie Walsh disappeared into the kitchen, returned with more organization pans, and knelt before the fire, prodding at the smoking logs. When the flames were to her satisfaction, she hung the pots from hooks set into the stones. Stordahl watched her thoughtfully.

'There's a lot of work gone into this place,' he observed. 'Back at the colony, we haven't yet completed one cabin. How did you do it, Arnott?' And an unformed question in his mind resolved itself. Six chairs? Why were there six chairs in this room?

'Our time is our own,' replied the zoologist. 'Mind you, it was hard work. There's still a hell of a lot to do. We've still got to build a proper john. And there's the stone retaining wall for the well not finished yet, and the drainage system to put in. . . .'

'Don't try to kid me, Arnott. Who helped you? Do others from the colony know about this place? Voluntary work parties?'

Walsh chuckled uneasily. 'Nothing like that. When you're thrown on your own resources, you make use of what's available. I have a local labour force, you might call it. Eh, Katie?'

Mrs. Walsh looked up from stirring the contents of one of the pots. Her face was flushed with the heat; Stordahl thought: *'She's quite pretty. . . .*

'The goolies help us,' she said frankly. 'I expect you've come across them. They live in burrows on this hill. They can look like humans when they want, and work like humans too. They never get tired or bored with the work; in fact I don't think they've got minds of their own. But when they're in human shape they understand what we say, and they do what we ask. It's very convenient. I feel quite guilty about using them sometimes, but Arnott says it's all right.' She gave her husband a look of rather embarrassing devotion.

'We call them amorphs,' said Stordahl hastily.

Walsh laughed. 'Now that sounds a bit more complimentary than goolies, eh, Katie? Amorphs they shall be, from now on. They're useful creatures. I've never come across anything like them before. It's a defence mechanism, as I expect you've found. But not only do they look like the subject; to all intents and purposes they become the subject, complete with characteristics, intelligence, and a borrowed memory. Many times I've told myself I ought to dissect one, to find out whether the resemblance is internal too.'

'Why don't you?'

'I'm a zoologist, Alex, and in the course of my profession I've had occasion to open many animals. But I draw the line at the amorph. How can you kill and dissect something which looks like a human being?'

Katie Walsh made a face. 'Can't we talk about something else?' she asked. 'Lunch is ready.' She was spooning the contents of the pots on to earthenware plates. 'I'm rather glad Arnott has given up his job. Sometimes it could be rather gruesome. Now, tell us how things are going at the colony. I saw a convoy of trucks the other day. You've sent the desert party out?'

Conversation continued on these lines throughout the meal; it was apparent that the Walshes were hungry for news despite their self-imposed exile. The meal itself interested Stordahl; it consisted of meat (he tried not to think of it as lizard) stewed with herbs—there was, surprisingly, a savoury suggestion of garlic. Two vegetables were present, cooked separately. One was a root; Walsh described it as being from a variety of saucerplant. The other, green, was simply the boiled leaves of the fleshy succulent which Joan had rashly tasted earlier. There was an amused triumph in the way she glanced at Stordahl on hearing this.

'But how did you find out these things were edible?' asked Stordahl.

'By eating them, of course,' Walsh replied. 'In the circumstances we had no choice.'

This gave Stordahl his chance. 'What circumstances?' he asked. 'Weren't we feeding you well enough at Alice?'

Walsh glanced at him sharply. 'Alice? Oh, I see. We all have our ghosts, Alex, don't we? You want to know why we left your cozy little set-up; that's it? Don't tell me it hurt your pride. . . . No, I'm being unfair. You know about Katie, you know what Singer said. Well, after that there didn't seem to be much point in staying on. We wanted our future right away. So we left. Katie looks much better, don't you think?'

'She does. I'm very glad to see it. Tell me, did you know about her illness before you left Earth?'

Walsh looked uncomfortable. His wife answered for

him. 'Of course we knew,' she said firmly. 'We didn't know quite how bad it was, but we suspected I'd got it. If I'd had the operation then, I'd have missed the ship. So we came on, and I found things had . . . worsened. So Arnott and I decided to make the most of the time we had together. And strangely enough, since we've been here, I've felt much better. I really think I'm cured. It's a miracle.'

'Why not come back and let Singer check you out?'

'No!' Walsh answered vehemently. Embarrassed by his outburst, he apologized: 'Sorry, but we'd rather go it alone. It's become almost a superstition: if Katie went to the colony, she'd . . . never come back. I can't explain it, but that's the way we feel.'

'Suit yourself.' Stordahl glanced at his watch. 'We must get going. It's been very pleasant. . . .' Again the unreal feeling. 'Keep in touch, won't you, Arnott? We need you in many ways, so I'll drop by from time to time. I don't suppose you'd object to doing a few observations for us in your spare time, particularly as you've got to know the amorphs. I'll stretch a point and pay you in kind; tools, hardware, whatever you might need.'

'Of course.' Walsh extended his hand. 'See you again, then.'

They climbed on to the half-track and drove off.

Five minutes later they were out of sight of the cabin, around the curve of the hill. Stordahl drove slowly, his eyes searching the slopes. A movement caught his eye; they were being watched. From the fringe of the trees, Katie Walsh waved to them.

'They're nice people,' said Joan. 'I'm sorry they're not coming back.'

Stordahl said nothing, scanning the slopes, his lips compressed. Joan glanced at him curiously.

'There,' he said. 'Look there.'

Katie Walsh sat on a fallen tree stump; her back was to them. As she heard the half-track she turned, saw them, and waved. . . .

'What . . .?' Joan stared, her eyes widening.

'Mrs. Walsh gets around,' said Stordahl tightly. 'Didn't you know?'

Farther on, Katie Walsh stooped low, gathering succulents for the pot.

'Oh, God . . .' muttered Joan. 'Oh, God . . . God. . . .'

Abruptly Stordahl swung the half-track around and headed back for the colony.

'But she knew everything. . . .' Joan was almost pleading. 'She knew what happened on Earth, she knew all about the colony, she even . . . called the amorphs goolies, and said how they helped.'

'She only knew what was in Arnott Walsh's mind: she knew what he knew. She was what he *thought* she was. Didn't you notice, she was a little bit prettier than we remembered Katie Walsh? A little bit nicer? Arnott Walsh has found his ideal. He won't be coming back to the colony. Neither will he send Katie in for an examination.'

Joan was almost crying. 'That poor man. Living with one of those. . . . Are you sure it wasn't. . . .'

'Living with five of those, to judge by the chairs. Five perfect women who do just as he wants. He's not so badly off. Singer told me, privately, that Katie only had a couple of months to live at most. She must have died, say, four or five months ago. The Katie we were talking to – he must have been living with her for a few months, continuously. Does anything occur to you?'

'What do you mean?'

'She stayed as Katie. Her form didn't begin to change as a result of our presence.

'The facsimile of Katie Walsh has become permanent. . . .'

SEVEN

Myers's voice was loud and clear. 'Technically, we can beat this thing. The original idea of building a railroad and transporting the oxide in open wagons won't do, obviously. But it would be possible to use closed vehicles. Tank wagons, for instance. It ought to be possible to pump the oxide from the surface, like a liquid. Which leads to something else. It might be more economic to forget the idea of rail transport altogether and pump the stuff directly to the steelworks by pipeline.'

'I see. . . .' Stordahl was interested.

'I don't see why it shouldn't work. It'd be cheaper than a railroad in the long run, and much quicker. We could pipe through a continuous supply from up here.'

'That sounds great.'

'Unfortunately there are other problems. As things are, you'll never get anyone to work up here. The environment is appalling. In any other circumstances the men would be on strike already. It's only the fact that this is a new planet which keeps them going. They expect some hardship at first, but sooner or later they expect management to do something about it.'

Is it that bad?'

'Worse.' Despite this, Myers sounded as cheerful as ever. 'It's unbelievable. All of us, men and women, have got dust in our clothes, in our hair, in our beds, everywhere. Even the food tastes of iron oxide. Short of setting up a large dome for a completely enclosed environment I don't know what we can do. And in any case people always object to sealed domes. They say they feel like caged animals. And even if we did that, they'd have to go outside to work.'

Stordahl pondered for a monent, then gave up. 'Look, Bill. I don't have much experience of this kind of thing. When I worked for the government we had it easy. We colonized planets which were ideal, otherwise we didn't colonize. What do you people do in this sort of situation?'

'Charlton had a suggestion, but it's expensive. If Hetherington wants his steel, he'll have to pay for it. There's a system which has been used before in this sort of situation; I think it would work here. It involves fixing the surface of the desert so that it doesn't shift with the wind. There are two ways of doing it. The cheap way is to use a plant they call Wilton lichen. It extracts moisture from the atmosphere and grows like hell in almost any climate. Spread that over the desert and we'd have no problem.'

'The desert covers half a million square miles, Bill.'

'So you drop the stuff by air within a radius that should keep us clear of the dust; say from here to a point about fifty miles away. It would bind the dust within the year.'

'And the other possibility?'

'The expensive way? Spray a similar area with stuff called polybind. The cost is fantastic, but the job could be done in a couple of weeks.'

'Thanks very much, Bill. Stick it out for the time being, will you? I'll be out to relieve you in a couple of days. Then you can come back to Alice and breathe fresh air again. Meanwhile I'll include your suggestions in my report to Hetherington and let him decide. Neither of these methods has ever had any ecological side-effects, have they?'

'Not so far, which is just as well. The cost of removing either the lichen or the polybind would be astronomical.'

'I can imagine. Same time tomorrow, then?'

' 'Bye, Alex.'

Stordahl handed the headphones back to the operator and hurried out. It promised to be a busy morning. After yesterday's meeting with Arnott Walsh he had instructed Avio Santana to go ahead with investigating the mental nature of the amorph, whatever his personal feelings might be. Walsh was hampered by his scruples from dissecting the things; Santana was supposed to have the skill to get to the bottom of a creature without using a knife.

The gloomy psychiatrist was looking a little more cheerful. Briggs was with him and the amorph sat in a chair; it was now an indeterminate hermaphrodite, presumably an amalgam of the fatal Gloria and Briggs himself.

'Ah, Stordahl,' said Briggs as the Supervisor entered. 'Santana and I have been carrying out a few tests.'

'Anything new?'

'We think so. We have an interesting theory which has fitted the results of all our tests so far. . . . As Santana had the original idea,' said Briggs magnanimously, 'I'd better hand you over to him.'

The psychiatrist shifted his sorrowful gaze from the partial Gloria to Stordahl. 'First, I'll just run through what we know,' he said. 'Which won't take long because frankly we know very little. Item one. The amorph, when approached by another creature, changes shape. Conclusion, a defence mechanism. Item two. The shape assumed tends to be of the same species as the other creature, but not necessarily the same sex. Conclusion, it is not a simple duplication. Further, the shape assumed can be a striking likeness of an actual person whom the amorph has never seen, like Katie Walsh, or . . . Gloria Hewitt. Conclusion, the amorph is able to extract information from the mind of the other creature, man or animal.

'This is further borne out by Brigg's observation that the amorph in his form knew biology, and my own observation that the pseudo Gloria Hewitt knew things about me which were only known to the real Gloria and me.'

'I'll go along with that,' agreed Stordahl. 'The fake Katie Walsh knew all about the colony.'

'I don't like the word "fake",' Santana said. 'The thing is no fake from its own point of view. It is a totally unconscious imitation; in its human form it is convinced in its own mind that it is the person it represents. Which brings us to an interesting point. Take the case of Katie Walsh, the amorph. The woman you saw thought she was Katie. But her physical and mental make-up came from Arnott Walsh's mind.

'She is therefore incomplete. She will know everything Walsh knew about Katie, but cannot know anything secret to the real Katie.'

'That's the way it seemed to me,' observed Stordahl. 'She'll be an idealized version of the real thing. It raises some interesting implications. . . . And another thing. There were several Katies. What would be their attitude to each other?'

Santana drew thoughtfully at his cigarette. 'It may be that the concept is meaningless. Each one thinks she is Katie; each one thinks the others are amorphs. As to their combined and individual attitude, I think it would be whatever Walsh wanted it to be. If he said, "Kill", they might do just that. Provided it was in his own mind to kill, and he was not merely uttering a word. They would obey, provided he truly desired them to.'

'A ruthless man could recruit an army,' murmured Briggs.

'True. And we can draw another conclusion from Alex's observation of Katie Walsh. The longer an amorph spends in the company of the object person, the more permanently the facsimile becomes fixed. After a few months with Walsh the imitation Katie showed no signs of alteration during conversation with Alex and Joan. It stayed as Katie Walsh. It might always remain that way; which raises another point.

'It will never grow old. It will always be Katie, exactly as Walsh remembered her.'

'Until the amorph itself dies.'

'Presumably. I suppose they do die. I wonder how they reproduce, when in human form. There's a hell of a lot we don't know.' Santana paused. 'Anyhow . . . we must now pass on to the realms of speculation. And the most important consideration from the human standpoint is: what will a man see, when he meets an unformed armorp? I think I have the answer to this. It depends on a facet of a man's mind about which nothing to date has been known or possibly even thought of.

'I call it the Te factor.'

The rain was sporadic; quick bursts pattered like bird's feet on the outside of the small dome. Inside, two men and one amorph sat regarding another man attentively. Santana's expression was morose and withdrawn; constantly his eyes flickered to the hermaphrodite amorph and away again. 'The Te factor,' he was repeating. 'From the Latin Te, meaning you, or thou. The factor which has its seat in the emotions and was secret to the mind until now, when it reaches out and shapes the amorph. This factor cannot be described as love, although it is related to love.

'It is an outgoing emotion which until now has been repressed, because to reveal the truth completely and unstintedly to the object person is something we cannot do. There is something within us that prevents this; possibly fear of rejection. We may not even admit it to ourselves. . . . We sometimes do our best; we tell a person we love them, but we don't tell them everything. The real emotion lies bottled up in our minds; *we* feel it, but the object person only knows what they are told. It is not entirely love. The nearest word to describe it is . . . compatibility. It seems that the object person is not merely loved, but that he or she is part of you – a hackneyed saying come true. Unlike love, it has nothing to do with sex.

'So imagine your unformed amorph, threatened. It has the capacity to change form as a defence mechanism. What better defence, then, than to assume the shape of the person most compatible with the aggressor?

'And as an added benefit, it is only possible to imitate the mind in as much as the aggressor knows the mind of his . . . shall we say, Te? The one person whom the aggressor will ignore the faults of and tend to see through rose-tinted spectacles.'

Santana almost smiled at them, almost. A grim rictus of the lips. 'And so we discover ourselves through the amorph.

'Who is my Te? I would never have admitted, even to myself, that it was Gloria Hewitt. I have known girls infinitely more worthy, with whom I have considered myself more thoroughly in love. Yet my true emotions now tell me, through the amorph, that Gloria was the girl for me. . . .

'And you, Briggs. We know who is your Te. You have to confess your own self-centred egotism when you are alone with an amorph. Your Te is yourself. . . .'

Briggs grinned briefly, shifting in his chair. 'Never did get on with women,' he murmured. 'Or men either, for that matter. Always reckoned the only sensible conversation was when I was talking to myself over the lab bench. This proves it.'

Santana continued. 'The social dangers to the colony must not be ignored. In the future there will be many unfair accusations between husband and wife, because the true feelings of either can be tested with an amorph. I say unfair, because nobody can help who his Te is. He might try his hardest to make a marriage work out, and think he is succeeding, only to find some girl whom he thought he had forgotten reappear like a ghost to threaten his married life. Arnott Walsh is one of the lucky ones. He married the perfect partner for him, and when she died she was replaced by his Te, and his life resumed with hardly a break. Lucky man. . . .'

Santana looked directly at Stordahl. 'Your wife died in

unfortunate circumstances, Alex. It is possible you may meet her again. I wonder. . . .'

The test had been in progress for an hour, supervised by Stordahl and Santana. Briggs had been an obvious subject; his companion had been selected after a short series of tests. It had rather distressed Stordahl, the speed with which they had found another person so egotistical as to have a Te who was himself. It seemed a sad comment on the supposed community spirit of the colony. . . .

The two men sat with an amorph in an enclosed glass booth, brightly lit. Briggs and Lever, the surveyor. The amorph was by now a perfect Briggs/Lever composite. Its expression had settled, its form was complete. It was answering complex questions on the subjects of both biology and surveying. Briggs and Lever put the questions; outside the booth Stordahl and Santana sat in darkness, monitoring the conversation with headphones.

An experiment with genius which Stordhal almost hoped would not succeed. . . .

Briggs was speaking; he addressed the amorph. 'Let me see, what the hell was the name of that professor at college? Face like a sheep. Astonishing how memory fails one. . . .'

'Lister,' said the amorph after a moment's thought. 'Professor Lister, it was. We used to call him Sweetbread, can't think why.'

'My God, so we did!' cried Briggs in amazement. 'Old Sweetbread. All I could remember was that stupid face of his, as he stood there bleating about . . . about. . . .'

Hereditary traits. Mendelism. He always had a cage of guinea pigs on the bench,' supplied the amorph.

'So he did. So he did.' Briggs chuckled. 'And when he went to the back of the room, someone let them out and they ran all over his bench, pissing on his papers!'

'Johnson did that. Redheaded little bugger; he was always at the bottom of any trouble. He went to Vega Four.' The amorph was smiling too.

That's right. God, it all comes back. Hey, do you remember . . .' Briggs rattled on, reminiscing.

Stordahl turned to Santana. 'This is getting out of hand. Briggs is carried away. We'd better get them back on the subject.' He reached for the mike which connected him to the two men.

Santana placed a hand on his arm. 'Hold it. This is more interesting than you think. Don't you realize what's happening?'

'Only that Briggs and the armoph are wasting our time.'

'No. Think a moment. The amorph is getting his information from Briggs's mind.'

In the darkness, Stordahl stared at the psychiatrist. 'God, I see what you mean.'

'Yes. Through the amorph, Briggs is achieving total recall.'

The experiment went on, the men in the booth growing more excited, firing questions at the amorph and receiving replies dredged from the very depths of their memories. Briggs or Lever, it didn't matter; the amorph knew everything they knew, and everything they had forgotten.

'What a pity,' murmured Santana. 'This will only work with men like these two. Men who are so egotistical that their Te is themselves. The amorph of Katie Walsh, for instance, will never have total recall. She will only remember what Walsh knows about her. Nothing more. From Walsh's point of view she will be complete, but she is only one man's view of another person. But these two here . . . it's fantastic. The possibilities are enormous. . . .' Yet Santana sounded anything but enthusiastic.

Briggs was talking to Lever now; the amorph sat still, quietly watching them. *What does it think?* wondered Stordahl. *What the hell is going on in its mind? Is it just switched off, waiting for a question to activate it? Or is it mulling over the contents of two able brains, permutating information received, computing . . .?*

Is it on our side . . .?

Suddenly the amorph was speaking, interrupting the discussion between Briggs and Lever. Santana leaned forward excitedly. 'Free will . . .' he whispered.

The two men stopped talking abruptly and regarded the amorph.

'Sorry to break in like this,' the creature said. 'But I've just come up with an idea; don't know why I didn't think of it before. Funny how problems suddenly resolve themselves when you least expect it. Anyway, while you're here, I'd like to talk it over with . . . with two experts in the same . . . with. . . .' It hesitated. Its face had turned grey and it ran a finger around its collar.

'Oh, God,' muttered Santana. 'It's having identity problems. It's a composite of Briggs and Lever whom it thinks of as individuals, while at the same time thinking of itself as Briggs/Lever. Previously it had conversed with either Briggs or Lever. Now it wants to talk to both of them together, and it suddenly has the idea that the sum of Briggs and Lever is identical to itself. It may get around this. I don't know. . . .'

Briggs was standing beside the amorph, motioning Lever to remain seated. He put his hand on its shoulder and spoke to it quietly for a few minutes. Gradually the colour returned to the creature's face and the nervous trembling ceased. Soon, Briggs was able to resume his seat.

'Briggs realized what was happening,' Santana said. 'He tipped the scales, setting up a disparity in the Briggs/Lever composite, increasing the Briggs factor. The amorph is now predominantly Briggs, which is not the same thing as the two people it faces. This sort of thing wouldn't happen often. Only when the amorph strikes a near-perfect balance between two men. The more men you have,' he continued thoughtfully, almost to himself, 'the less likely it would be. . . .'

The amorph was speaking again. 'Apologies for the little attack,' it remarked smoothly. 'For a moment I didn't feel too good. Now, to return to the drainage problem.'

'The drainage problem?' echoed Lever.

'For some time I have been experiencing difficulties in assessing suitable sites for cabin construction due to the waterlogged state of the ground following frequent rain.'

'You're darned right I have,' interjected Lever, grinning. Briggs motioned him to silence.

'The available sites on the fused ground to the east of the colony are all used up, and in any case I'm not happy about building there. Foundations are impossible to construct and the cabins have to be built on rafts. And that bastard Stordahl tells me that it will be a long time before we can get drainpipes through and, knowing Stordahl, a long time means never.'

Lever swung around in his chair and grinned into the darkness which concealed Stordahl.

'Now listen to this,' continued the amorph, 'and tell me what you think. I have in the course of my study of the plant of this planet come across the elephant worm; I expect you've seen it. It drives a tunnel of considerable diameter. The ground around the lower slopes of the hills is comparatively dry due to the drainage action of these tunnels as much as to the lie of the land.'

'It's speaking as Briggs, now,' observed Santana quietly.

'If we could induce the elephant worm to drive its burrows between the main body of the camp and the fused site – the ground slopes gently downward – we could have a large dry site for at least a hundred cabins.'

'That's Lever again.'

'Unfortunately the elephant worm will not burrow in this area. I've seen them travelling on the surface, but even this only occasionally. Recently I've found out why.' ('Briggs,' whispered Santana.)

'As I've mentioned before, the nourishment intake of the plants on Marilyn is opposite to that of their counterparts of Earth, in that they catch moisture in their cup-like extremities and, after extracting what they need, exude it from the roots, together with waste matter. I have now found out that the elephant worm feeds by absorption through the skin of this waste matter. This is why it frequents the lower slopes of the cuptree groves, where the food is most concentrated.'

'Here it comes!' Santana was staring into the booth, rigid with excitement. 'It can deduce, Alex. It can arrive at conclusions on the basis of combined knowledge; and, what's more, it will volunteer these conclusions!'

'So all we have to do is plant cuptrees next to the domes,' the amorph went on, 'and release elephant worms around the area between the domes and the fused ground. They will burrow eastward, uphill, towards the source of nourishment. They will inhabit the area as long as the trees are there. We'll have no more problems with waterlogged ground. Good idea, do you think?'

There was a confused babble from the booth as Lever and Briggs jumped to their feet, slapping each other on the back and pumping hands. Lever even shook hands with the amorph. Stordahl switched on the light as the two men, followed by the amorph which was grinning uncertainly, burst from the booth.

'Great!' Lever was exclaiming. 'My God, there's a conclusive experiment for you, Santana!'

The little psychiatrist eyed them morosely, suddenly indifferent to their exuberance.

Briggs's delight had taken on a thoughtful aspect. 'Christ,' he muttered. 'I wonder. . . . The say most scientists are egotists, married to the job, they reckon. Now just suppose . . . just suppose there were, say, six of us, each expert in our own field plus one amorph. What couldn't we achieve? Had you thought of that, Santana?'

'I had though of it,' replied the psychiatrist sombrely. 'I suppose it was too much to hope that nobody else would. . . .'

EIGHT

There is no danger in the amorph. The danger is in the mind of man. He has controlled this danger all his life; it has always been there, sleeping, occasionally stirring in his subconscious; is it any worse when awakened? Surely it is better to bring it into the open rather than to suppress it, thereby causing frustration, paranoia?

Thus ran the arguments.

Thus the amorphs entered the colony of Alice on the planet Marilyn.

He sat on a fallen tree on the slopes of a low hill some three miles from the colony and he faced south; the cuptrees hid his form from prying field glasses. It was late afternoon and the wind was beginning to blow from inland, sighing through the trees at his back. The clouds had drifted away and the sky was clear and red and violet, ochre and pink. He didn't think about the dust particles as he sat, but he did think the sky was beautiful. The land, too, becoming dim with fading light; the slanting sunlight tipped the peaks of the western mountains with crimson; black shadow fell towards him from the distant brightness, then lifted in the sparkling of a billion jewels as the rays vaulted the intervening blackness and touched each raised palm of the saucerplants with emeralds and silver.

The little girl was playing by herself a few yards away; her favourite game, as she plucked the firm saucerplants and tipped the remaining moisture from one to another, laughing, playing imaginary tea parties and offering imaginary guests cups, and serious conversation, and love.

He watched her, and he offered her love. Silently, in his mind; but that was all he needed to do.

She ran to him suddenly. 'Al won't eat his biscuit,' she said, frowning, staring him straight in the face with that incredible directness. 'He says it's got no chocolate on it. You tell him he's got to.' She tapped him on the wrist impatiently, dissatisfied with his sluggish reaction. 'Tell him he must!'

He watched her face with that breathtaking feeling of

wonderment which always affected, strangely, his throat, causing it to feel thick and tight. Short hair, once very blonde but now darkening, at five years old, to a streaky gold. Once long, until in the heat of the summer it had to be cut because, as she said, it was making her uncomfortable, getting graggy. A combination, he had correctely deduced, of greasy and shaggy.

Her nose, even now, had not really achieved a satisfactory bridge; and maybe about the nostrils it was too wide, a spreading lump of putty in the middle of her face. The thin line of a scar on the left where she had fallen at the age of two; at that age almost as lively as now, she had run and fallen, and the edge of the nostril had torn right back. . . . His knuckles whitened as he relived the horror of that moment.

Mouth small and very firm; the chin was firm too and the cheeks plump. And the eyes. . . . Grey-green they stared, glared, smiled, cried; long-lashed and beautiful beyond measure, they were her asset; her eyes and her personality – independent, self-willed, occasionally touchingly tender. *Looks don't matter so much,* he told himself. *She'd get married on that personality alone; the boys will howl around her like wolves. She's going to be a load of trouble in ten year's time. . . .*

'Tell him he must!'

'Come here, sweetheart.' Coaxing. 'Come here and listen. I want to whisper something to you.'

Almost she came; then a sudden grin, a frown, and she jumped back. 'What? What do you want to whisper?'

'It's a secret.'

She swung around abruptly, arms flying, short skirt awhirl. 'It's *not* a secret!' She skipped back to her imaginary guests. 'You want to whisper I love you, and then you'll kiss me. It's not a secret!'

Conceited little thing, he thought fondly, watching her as she poured her coffee. *She'll be married by the time she's eighteen. I hope he turns out to be a reasonable sort of fellow, you get so many oddballs these days. . . .*

So he watched Alice play on the hillside and, when it got too dark, he left her. . . .

Thus Alex Stordahl found his Te.

Last supper. James and Agatha Walters sitting one at each

end of the rough table which no amount of unskilled planing could make smooth; funny how the damned thing catches and pulls out chunks. Tubb Tacker seems to have the knack. Get him to have a go at this one. Enter the amorph; indeterminate, hermaphrodite.

'Thank you. Put it down there, will you.'

Mrs. Walters spooned out chunks of reconstituted mock beef from the pot and slopped it onto the plates. The pristine plastic became a lake of gunk. A dismal silence prevailed as Walters took his plate and began to eat, sawing ineffectively at the meat.

'God, not again,' he muttered. 'Aggie, this is my last night here for a week. Surely, tonight of all nights, the stuff could have been properly cooked. Just look at this.' He tapped the meat graphically. 'Like mahogany. I'm sure it's possible to cook reconstituted meat so it's tender. Other people manage it. Why can't you?'

'Ruby cooked it,' admitted Mrs. Walters, glancing at the amorph which stood impassively by.

'Ruby or you, what's the difference? She's got your mind, being partly my Te.'

'And yours. She's my Te as well.'

They both scrutinized the creature, striving to identify themselves in the anonymous features, and failing. For a fleeting moment each wondered if, in fact, they were present in that amalgam, or if maybe an old flame had sparked into unexpected life again. . . .

In each other's presence they had put subtle questions to the amorph and received evasive replies as to its identity because, naturally, each of them was transmitting frantic mental instructions that such a question should not be answered. Mrs. Walters had cornered the amorph one day while James was out at work and asked it, bluntly, of whom was it a composite?

But by this time its influence from James's Te factor was waning at the same rate as James's previous unspoken veto on the question, and it was unable to reply. Mrs. Walters did, however, find out who her own Te was. She did not tell James. James deduced that she knew her own Te and wondered why she didn't volunteer its identity. There were two possible explanations. Either it was someone from her past; in which case she would never tell him. Or it was himself, in which case again she wouldn't tell him, not wanting to give him the satisfaction.

On the day Mrs. Walters discovered her Te, she immediately locked the amorph in the broom cupboard. By the time James returned from work and released the creature, it was almost shapeless.

The amorph was fostering an atmosphere of mistrust. But then, it was so useful about the house that Mrs. Walters refused to part with it.

It was an atrocious cook, a fact which James used as evidence of his marital fidelity. Mrs. Walters was also an atrocious cook.

'Never mind,' said James at last in placatory tones. 'Let's not quarrel about the thing again. This is the last night. Let's have a drink and go to bed.' He leered at her hopefully.

They put the kids to bed early, and soon followed them.

Later, Mrs. Walters said: 'I don't think it's fair sending family men to the desert site, James. They should be exempted. I don't know what we'll do without you. A week seems such a long time. We've never been apart before.'

James Walters regarded her face in the half-light. She looked contented; it seemed she had enjoyed herself as usual. The thought crossed his mind that she might be a nymphomaniac. Their life in bed had always been satisfactory. . . . And now he would be away for a week. It would be unfair to say that James always felt irritable after love. Just touchy. Like at breakfast, it didn't take much to trigger him off.

In this knife-edge balance of mind he gazed at her.

While he was away, the amorph would still be in the house, and it would undoubtedly take a male form.

By God, he thought, *it had better not be some smooth bastard from her past, perfected by her own mind, irresistible, around her constantly for a whole week.*

It had better be me, he thought. . . .

It wasn't until the next day, as he rode the tractor towards the desert and the rain slanted across the cab window, that a further thought occurred.

Suppose her Te is me? Around the house all day, perfected by her own mind, irresistible. . . . God, no; she couldn't!

She wouldn't. . . . Would she?

The Reverend Iain Waddie stood at the entrance to his church dome, scrutinizing the interior with religious, if not gloating, delight. A tall man with grizzled, wiry hair and a lugubrious Scottish expression, he was the sole mentor of the colony's moral and spiritual welfare.

'A padre?' Hetherington had queried in annoyance. 'What the hell do we want a padre for? We've got enough drones as it is, without turning the voyage into a church outing.'

His audience had stared at him, scandalized. 'It won't look good if we don't take a padre,' someone ventured. 'It's always good public relations to drag religion into things, like having someone say a prayer at blast-off. It looks good, J. It salves people's consciences when they might otherwise feel guilty about all that money going into a commercial enterprise. It dilutes materialism.'

'They'll start squabbling about denominations next,' grumbled Hetherington.

'They needn't,' one of his aides said, the light of inspiration in his eyes. 'Not if we put it across right. A fresh start. Brotherhood. A new world where men live and work together under one God.'

'One for all and all for one God,' the original speaker suggested. 'It has a ring to it. All we need is a name for the sect.'

'The Hetheringtonians,' volunteered Hetherington, but sarcastically. Even he drew the line somewhere.

A polite chuckle with undertones of uncertainty, then the suggestion was made: 'Why not simply call it the Marilyn Interdenominational Church? That way it doesn't sound as though we've taken it on ourselves to branch out.'

'I suppose so,' agreed the tycoon reluctantly. 'Find me a padre, then, Preferably one who has other talents, like engineering or metallurgy.'

The Reverend Iain Waddie possessed a degree in chemistry gained in his wild youth before, one night in the cheaper seats of a Glasgow cinema, he was visited by an Experience.

He had spent the early part of the evening in celebration of the victory of the Glasgow Rangers over their local rivals Celtic. The cinema was warm and the whiskey soporific. The film – an ancient science-fiction collector's piece featuring as its climax a nuclear holocaust in which the entire globe was graphically consumed, watched by one man and one woman from the vantage point of the Moon – ground to its finale as he dozed. The ultimate cataclysm brought him jerking forward in his seat, blasted into wakefulness by the full wonder of stereophonic sound. As the globe expanded like a fiery nova it seemed Iain Waddie saw a face, a face kindly though stern, shimmering through the rolling clouds. And he thought he heard a voice saying, 'Let there be light,' the instant before the watching man and woman were bathed in a silvery brightness. Then Earth deflated and shrank to a dead stone in the sky and the camera zoomed back to the couple on the Moon showing that the place was luxuriantly covered with vegetation. As the audience raced the Terrestrial Anthem to the exits the landscape was receding farther still until the horizon could be seen, then a semicircle and finally the entire disc and, surprise! it couldn't have been the Moon after all because the continents of North and South America were clearly outlined – but Waddie had missed this final twist because he was asleep again.

The cleaners found him in the morning and he woke with the feeling that he had undergone a powerful spiritual experience, although he couldn't remember quite what. This experience may or may not have had some bearing on the fact that ten years later he was ordained as a Minister of the Church. Probably not, although from that day he forswore alcohol.

Falling attendances forced him to seek new pastures and he signed on with the organization for the Marilyn colony with the somewhat illogical feeling that, up there, he would be nearer God. It also occurred to him that the colonists, huddled together in their fear of the mighty Unknown, would flock to find solace in his pithy sermons.

The colonists, to his disappointment, had proved remarkably phlegmatic in their adaptation to the new environment and he had often wondered whether even his small congregation was impelled through his doors by boredom rather than terror.

Nevertheless, of his own feelings he had no doubt. Over the years of disappointment in Glasgow, as the handful of old ladies who constituted his flock had succumbed, one by one, to bronchial asthma in the bitterly damp Clydeside winters, his faith had blazed undiminished; indeed, with the years it had seemed to wax stronger, which was as it should be. As he led the hymns on the bleak Sunday mornings he would cast a fatherly eye over the faithful; and, turning his head slightly, he would see the hair of the cherubic choirboys gilded by the thin sunlight – and he would be thankful that, at least here under this roof, they were at one with God. Administering corporal punishment to young McIntyre, who would insist on chewing gum noisily during the sermon, he was aware of a sensation of saintly righteousness. Dark and dirty though Glasgow might be, in this church the light of God shone pure.

When the amorphs were investigated, found harmless, and became part of the colony life, the Reverend Iain Waddie was at first perturbed, then interested. As stories of the creatures' abilities were told around the colony the Great Idea came to him; but gradually at first because he was slightly appalled by his own temerity. He talked to Stordahl, to Briggs, and Santana. He read his Bible and took out his old textbooks. He came to the decision.

He requested that an amorph be brought to him.

They brought it. He wheeled around from his satisfied examination of the church interior as he heard them approach. He took the amorph by the hand and thanked them. They left; he entered the church with the creature. Yes, the place looked well; the brass sparkled and the Son on the illuminated cross seemed to be signifying His approval. It was a fitting place for God.

The amorph stood before the altar and the Reverend Waddie took up the Bible; the selection of the passage he should read at this time had caused him much thought. The right atmosphere of reverence must be created while the transformation of the creature took place. He read, and while he read he concentrated his thoughts on the amorph, glancing at it from time to time and waiting for it to react to his Te factor, as Santana had assured him is would.

There was only one possible Te for the Reverend Iain Waddie. The one Person who had shaped his life, the Person to whom he had devoted all his years. . . .

And the amorph began to change.

It was five o'clock in the afternoon and the people in the vicinity of the church dome heard the shot and came running. Just one shot. They burst through the church entrance and stopped. There was a rustle at the far end of the dome; nobody saw who or what disappeared through the rear entrance. They were staring at the body on the altar steps.

It seemed that the Reverend Iain Waddie had found a more reliable route to God.

'You're a damned fool, Santana,' Stordahl said afterwards. 'You put him up to that. You could have stopped him at any time.'

The psychiatrist sighed. 'Oh, ye of little faith. Who was I to stop him? Doesn't it occur to you, Alex, it's just possible that he did, in fact, see God?'

Thus the amorphs entered the colony of Alice on the planet Marilyn; as friends, companions, servants, workers. They lived among the colonists, sharing their food, their domes, houses; and sometimes, their beds. They possessed individual characteristics although it was difficult to determine whether they were in fact individuals. They possessed the characteristics of the Tes of those with whom they had the most contact; and as the Te represents an idealized concept of a person, the amorphs were pleasant and without malice. As months went by the form and mentality of each amorph become more stabilized; they were therefore entrusted with more responsible positions in the community; the older members were taken, officially, on to the colony strength. It was decided that a period of three months was necessary for an amorph to become tolerably fixed so that it could work with a comparative stranger without, disconcertingly, beginning to take on a different appearance and characteristics. After three months, therefore, an amorph became a legal individual, with certain rights.

With the event of this additional labour force together with the successful drainage of a large area of land, building of homesteads proceeded rapidly and a measure of content descended over the colony, despite the further inexplicable delay of the supply ship. The colony's only visitor during these months was a small tender dropped from an onward bound FTL ship, delivering Wilton lichen.

Not only as workers were the amorphs responsible for this contentment; they also exuded a pleasing atmosphere of goodwill. Nobody could dislike an amorph, as an idealized person must have many good points. It was discovered early that there were few colonists so completely egotistic that their Te took their own form. In any case, where this happened such an amorph was quickly diluted by the influence of others. Stordahl had tactfully suggested to Briggs that he let his experimental amorph get around a bit and mingle with the others. . . .

The amorphs used as house servants could have presented the greatest problem due to their lack of contact with the main body of colonists. But even these settled in well, not without a few hot disputes between husband and wife at first. In the end it was tacitly agreed that no one could help who their Te was; it was just one of those things, and the outraged spouses merely decided to keep a closer eye on their mates in the future. . . . What's done is done, most of them in effect said; but don't let me catch you again.

So the colony settled down and many of the initial fears of the amorph proved groundless. . . .

Joan had her cabin a little to the north of the main area of new buildings. Although she entered into community life with every appearance of enjoyment, nevertheless people found her deep and uncommunicative about herself. She was rarely seen with any member of the opposite sex apart from Stordahl. This caused some comment among the younger, single males as they gathered around the bar in the community dome in the evenings to discuss prospects. Stordahl was reckoned to be a cold fish; the bed-worthy Joan was, they felt, wasted on him.

Joan frequently felt the same as she entered her cabin alone, Stordahl having said goodnight at the door and strode off into the gloom. The amorph would be sitting by the fire, reading.

'What are the chances?' she asked it hopelessly once, as the familiar face looked up from its book. 'Why is Alex . . . the way he is? How long am I supposed to wait around like this?'

'Wait, my dear?' The expression was slight bewilderment, with a touch of apprehension. 'Wait? What for?'

She sighed, and sat down, staring at the beloved face created from her own emotions. Unfortunately she had created the mind as well as the face, and the duplicate Alex was true to her own knowledge of the original.

* * * *

The Wilton lichen (cheaper than polybind) was duly sowed in the desert while work went on at the site. Hetherington had answered Stordahl's complaints about working conditions with a stroke of typical ingenuity.

'Send the amorphs in,' he instructed. 'From what you say, they never complain.'

So the fear of redundancy was sowed and the colonists redoubled their efforts to become self-supporting, working side by side with the amorphs around the clock. One of Walsh's Katies was borrowed, and spent her time instructing cookery with emphasis on the use of local resources....

At last, six months late, the supply ship arrived.

NINE

The tender squatted on its haunches some two miles northwest of Alice, defecating smoke and flame. A somewhat ironic cheer rose from the assembled colonists. There had been a growing feeling recently that, with the help of the amorphs, they could almost go it alone; the ship which would have been welcome a few months ago now served as a reminder of the organization's sovereignty. But at least there would be mail, and fresh faces, hardware, and possibly a variation of food. The half-tracks raced towards the tender, snaking trailers behind. The main body of the colonists followed on foot, a straggling crowd representing the entire population with the exception of a few on duty at the desert site.

Stordahl braked and dismounted, followed by Joan and the members of the colony's upper echelon. Briggs was there, gazing cynically at the silver apparition so incongruous against the backdrop of the northern mountains. Charlton's expression was of carefully controlled eagerness; soon he would be jockeying for position beside whichever organization chief rode in the ship. Bill Myers stood beside Stordahl, grinning broadly with uncomplicated anticipation. Santana scowled in the background. The others were all there except, of course, Walsh, and, a notable absentee, Lever. The surveyor had shown no inclination to return from his tour of duty in the desert; indeed, he had volunteered for a second week. Stordahl wondered privately if the men were going crazy, and intended to have a word with Santana about the matter.

The tender stood silent on its huge hydraulic legs for a few minutes while the final whiffs of smoke and steam dispersed. Then, with a high whine, a sector of the shining cylinder slid smoothly downwards and came to rest on the ground between two of the straddled legs. The colony leaders moved forward, rehearsing their opening words. Well behind them, the hurrying crowd was making good progress; one or two were running.

From the curved wall facing them a tall segment began to fall outward like a descending drawbridge. Quickly estimating its height, the party halted as it swung down and grounded a few yards from their feet. A group of men advanced from within the body of the elevator. As they stepped into the light, there was a concerted sigh of astonishment from the colony men. One of the newcomers sat in a wheelchair. His dark business jacket hung limply from his shoulders. He had no arms. He controlled the motorized chair with foot pedals.

'Oh, my God,' whispered Briggs. 'It's the Old Man. What the hell is he doing here?'

Stordahl's initial surprise turned to nervous despondency as he watched Hetherington approach. He had enough on his hands already, without the tycoon breathing down his neck for the next few days. He felt vaguely aggrieved. Why hadn't Hetherington given them some intimation of his visit? Was this his system, to catch people on the hop?

He stepped forward on to the ramp. 'Mr. Hetherington,' he said, remembering not to extend his hand. 'This is an unexpected pleasure.' *Thank God it isn't raining for once,* he thought.

The great man squinted up at him, bulbous eyes in a toad-like face. 'I'm sure,' he said noncommittally. 'How are you doing, Stordahl?'

'Fine. Things are going great. Housing projects well under way, the desert site partly constructed. . . .' He broke off as he realized he was beginning to babble.

'Good. I'll hear all about that later.' Hetherington's eyes flickered to the other members of the welcoming committee. 'Briggs, Charlton, Myers . . .' he murmured. He had a good memory for names. His gaze travelled to the approaching horde moving rapidly across the plain. 'And the children of Israel in the background. God, what a mob. Did we bring all those people here?' He favoured Stordahl with an incredulous grin, but the eyes remained cold.

'Some of them are amorphs, sir.'

'Ah yes, of course, the amorphs. . . . Your reports interested me. However . . . I take it you can fix accommodation for a few days?'

'I'll have one of the cabins prepared, sir.'

'Cabins? Oh, yes, the leisure-time housing project. Yes. . . .' He swivelled around in his chair, gazing back into the interior of the elevator.

Stordahl seized his opportunity. 'Bill,' he murmured.

'Take Joan and go and clean up my place for Mr. Hetherington.'

The tycoon swung back, the cold grin was there again. 'And while you're making your arrangements, Stordahl, remember there are two of us. Mrs. Hetherington has come along.'

Mrs. Hetherington made her artistically delayed entrance, strolling from the elevator with swinging hips, the sun catching her golden hair at just the angle to turn it into a halo around her perfect face. She gazed directly at Stordahl.

'Hello, Alex.'

'It's good to see you again, Mrs. Hetherington,' the Supervisor replied, feeling curiously unsteady about the knees.

She nodded to each of the party in turn, then surveyed the landscape, shielding her eyes. 'I'm longing to see this place,' she said. 'Is it a beautiful planet, Alex? Is it a compliment that my husband named it after me?'

Stordahl smiled mutely; the question was not answerable.

'You must show me around,' she added.

It had been awkward; they were not prepared. But they managed; they strapped the wheelchair to the platform on the back of a half-track and Hetherington was lifted into the passenger seat by one of his bodyguards. Throughout the operation Hetherington was silent. Months ago, Stordahl had been acquainted of the tycoon's affliction by his secretary, before that initial meeting. 'Mr. Hetherington never speaks about it,' she said. 'And he doesn't like anyone else to. He lost his arms many years ago. They had to be amputated, and now he is losing the use of his legs as well. He can't walk, but he's got enough strength to operate the controls of the wheelchair with his feet. There are guns in the arms of the wheelchair too, foot-operated. The thing's a bit frightening. . . . When his legs go completely I don't know what he'll do. He's a very dynamic sort of man; he'd hate to be completely dependent on people to wheel him around.' There was a curious pity in her voice.

They got Hetherington safely to Stordahl's cabin; Joan and Bill Myers had done a good job of straightening the place out in a very short time.

The tycoon glanced around, his gaze taking in the timber walls, the locally-made furniture, the organization-issue utensils. 'Not bad . . .' he observed. 'Not bad at all. This place and all the others have been built in the workers' leisure time?' He shot Stordahl a searching look.

'Of course. These jobs can be done very quickly with the help of a team of amorphs.'

'I'm sure they can. . . . I suppose, now these people of ours have got the amorphs to help them and they all live in nice little cabins instead of organization domes . . . I suppose they're beginning to feel pretty damned independent.'

'There has been talk,' admitted Stordahl cautiously.

'Which you have effectively squashed, no doubt. I saw no demonstration when we touched down. . . . I expected talk of mutiny, Stordahl. I always expect it, and I always get it. It's human nature, because built into human nature is an unreasoning reaction to certain words. It doesn't matter what service contract these people sign, it doesn't matter how honestly they believe at the time that they will abide by the terms of the contract – the whole integrity of a man will be cast aside at one word from a practised speaker. Just one word, Stordahl. That's all it takes.'

'And the word, sir?'

'Slavery, Stordahl. Slavery. Get a man with the gift of the gab calling them slaves, and my God you have to stamp on it fast. Otherwise they start thinking: the man's right! The organization has enslaved us! Granted we'll be freed in five years' time, but right now we're slaves, and right now is what counts! Cast off the shackles! Let's have a democratic vote: do you people want to be slaves? Of course not, motion carried. So what do we do? We declare independence! Independence and the dignity of the individual; the right of every human born a mother's son!' Hetherington regarded Stordahl shrewdly. 'Familiar words, Stordahl? Heard them some place before?'

'I have.'

'Of course you have. But right now everything's OK, is it? Good. I wonder why. You've had it easy, I think, because of the amorphs. Hand in hand, humans and amorphs are building for the future here on Marilyn. True, the colonists still have to put in their eight hours a day working off their passage here; but no matter, while they toil in the sweatshops the amorphs are building their houses and, so I believe, draining the land and planting local crops. It sort of makes things worthwhile.' There was a knife-edge of sarcasm in Hetherington's voice. 'Tell me, Stordahl. What exactly is the status of the amorph?'

'It's a difficult point,' admitted the Supervisor. 'When they first enter the colony they have no status; we allow anyone to bring them in to help build, or for housework, or whatever. Their characteristics change all the time at first, until they settle down. Then they become stabilized with one individual or set of people, and they don't change so much. We give them three months, then they register on the official colony roll.'

'What does that mean?'

'Well . . . I suppose it means that we regard them as individuals.'

'Do you pay them?'

'Of course not. They've got nothing to spend money on. They get their food and accommodation free.'

Hetherington chuckled quietly. 'Doesn't that sound like slavery to you, Stordahl?'

Stordahl was silent.

'Never mind, man,' Hetherington reassured him. 'I'm playing with words, just like your rabble-rousers do. But just remember my argument, the next time you get into difficulties. A more important point, since we must all benefit alike by this miraculous influx of free labour – are any of the amorphs working for the organization, or do you keep them all to yourselves?'

Stordahl was glad to be able to answer that one. 'We use them at the desert site, sir. Lever has a team there right now.'

'How many?'

'About twenty. They're setting up permanent accommodation and laboratories.'

'Any of our own men there, apart from Lever?'

'Not right now. Conditions are appalling. We were lucky to have the amorphs available. They don't complain. The conditions don't even seem to affect them.'

'But you go up there every so often?' inquired Hetherington, an edge to his voice.

'Oh, yes. We all take our turn. But Lever's been spending most of his time up there. He seems to enjoy it, so who am I to bring him back? It's impossible to get any other volunteers; we have to work a roster.'

'Keep an eye on Lever,' remarked Hetherington meaningly. 'I know that man.'

Stordahl spoke thoughtfully. 'Oddly enough, he's one of the few men in the colony whose Te factor induces an amorph to assume his own shape.'

'I've no doubt there's an army of Levers up at the desert site,' remarked Hetherington. 'But that brings me to the point. I'm interested in this peculiarity of his and . . . Briggs, did you say it was?'

At this moment Marilyn Hetherington entered the room and sat quietly down opposite them, sipping a drink. She watched their faces without speaking. She wore a high-necked, demure green dress. Stordahl glanced at her; then, following Hetherington's lead, ignored her.

'Yes. Briggs was the other man. Santana says that the phenomenon would only apply to the complete egotist.'

'You might be surprised to learn that I've brought some egotists with me.' The tycoon made this peculiar statement as casually as if he said he had brought a herd of breeding cattle. Stordahl found himself absurdly wondering what egotists looked like, en masse; and what one fed them on.

'Ah . . . how many?' was all he could think of to say.

'Just four. Each one a brilliant man in his own sphere.'

'You intend to experiment with them? You're going to try for an amorph composite of all four?'

'You catch on quickly, Stordahl,' observed Hetherington sarcastically. 'But you're wrong on one point. The amorph will be a composite of five. The four men I spoke of, plus myself.'

Marilyn Hetherington spoke for the first time. 'You should make a good team.' No acid tone to her voice; just a hint of mischief in the blue eyes.

'I've no doubt I qualify,' said Hetherington equably. 'But wouldn't it be a surprise if my Te turned out to be you, my dear?'

'I'll arrange accommodation for these men,' Stordahl said.

'Thank you. . . . Do you realize how important this could be, Stordahl?' The pale eyes for once betrayed the emotion behind them. 'My men are supreme in their own fields. Plus myself, to add a further factor of, shall we say, drive? Scientists tend to be a trifle sluggardly, don't you think. Although my men are not mere scientists. . . . The knowledge that we'll put into that mind! The powers of reasoning allied to intuitive thought which will be at our disposal! There will be nothing we can't achieve!' Unconsciously he paraphrased Briggs's previous words, but then he went one better. 'The creature we father will be akin to God!'

'Or possibly the devil,' remarked Marilyn Hetherington quietly.

Like many dynamic personalities, Hetherington drank heavily, though with little initial effect. For the next hour he and Stordahl discussed progress at the desert site, the problems of transportation, and the proposed steelworks. The tycoon had done his homework; obviously Stordahl's weekly reports had formed the basis of several feasibility studies at the organization headquarters. It appeared that his intentions were now to build the steelworks at a site four miles south of the mountain range and about seven miles from the present scene of operations. Water from the mountains would be piped to the desert site and mixed with the oxide to form a slurry, which would then be piped to the steelworks. A spaceport would be constructed three miles west of the steelworks.

This was the economical solution, but it would result in Alice eventually becoming a ghost town. Which would be a blow to the present inhabitants who had spent months building. Stordahl wondered how they would take it.

'That's their rough luck,' said Hetherington unfeelingly. 'Why do they image I provided domes? So long as they work for me, they must be prepared to move out at a moment's notice.'

With these ominous words he waved Stordahl from his presence.

Following Stordahl to the door, Marilyn said: 'Don't go for a minute. I want to talk. We've arrived here, and we've come straight to this cabin, and I haven't had a chance to talk to anyone yet. I want to find out something about this place.' The sun was below the horizon and the western sky flamed with the auroral display. She watched it, lips parted. 'That's beautiful,' she said softly. 'What causes it?'

'Dust,' said Stordahl briefly. 'Look, Mrs. Hetherington. I don't want to be rude, but I think—'

'Call me Marilyn.'

'Marilyn. I was saying—'

'You're scared of me,' the girl said. She leaned back, swinging on the half-open door. 'J. will be asleep now; he always is. It's the reaction. He arrives like a fireball and sparks like hell for a couple of hours, then he gets stoned and flakes out. Reaction from the flight. He hates the shuttle to the planet. Can you imagine what zero gravity is like for a man with no arms and very little use in his legs. There's no artificial gravity on the tender. And don't get me wrong when I say he's asleep. I just want to talk to somone, for God's sake, someone different from J. and those apes around him and his pet geniuses. I've had them for days. Now I'm here on the planet that's named after me and I want to talk about it, that's all. I'm not going to . . . make advances. . . .'

'I'm sorry.' Stordahl was contrite. She looked young and lonely; suddenly very unhappy. 'I'm a bit clumsy, I'm afraid. I thought. . . .' His voice trailed off uncertainly. He decided it would be best to shut up.

'All right. I know. I'm his fifth wife and you think I'm a gold digger married to a paralytic and I must need a bit on the side now and then to keep the frustrations away. You're not alone. Everyone thinks the same.'

'Forget it, Marilyn. I've said I'm sorry. Let's talk about something else. You want to know about our world. Most of it you see around you. This is the town of Alice. According to your husband, it will soon be a ghost town.' He couldn't keep the bitterness out of his voice.

But womanlike, she picked on the personal aspect. 'Alice. You named it. Is that your wife?'

'My daughter,' replied Stordahl shortly. 'They're both dead.'

'I'm sorry. . . . It must be lonely out here, feeling you've left them behind. You couldn't do anything else, you know. It's best to get away.'

The damned woman seems to read my mind, Stordahl thought. Unless she had been through his personal file, and knew that his family had died recently. . . . 'I get along,' he said brutally. 'Your husband provides me with a concubine.'

'Is she nice?'

'Very. Although I can't bring myself to tell her so. Sometimes she's too nice; so damned reasonable and understanding that I want to throttle her.'

Marilyn smiled sympathetically. 'What a pity you don't love her. . . . Aren't there any other girls?'

'She's the best one here.' Stordahl wondered how the conversation had taken this turn.

'Then maybe one day you'll make the most of her,' Marilyn said. 'I must be going now, Alex. I must put J. to bed. I'd like to come along and see the colony later on tonight; you have a community hall? But I don't think I'd better. I'm pretty tired myself.'

Alex held out his hand; she took it in a cool grip. 'Goodnight, Marilyn. See you in the morning.'

'Maybe not. I think we're going to be busy for a while. When we've settled in, you'll show me around?'

'Of course.'

'Good. 'Bye, then.' She closed the door. She was gone. Stordahl stood for a moment, then walked away. It seemed that he hadn't been able to tell her anything about the colony, after all; merely about himself. Maybe that's what she wanted.

For God's sake, he thought furiously. *Get it out of your mind. . . .*

TEN

Hetherington's visit to the planet of Marilyn did not begin well. The day following his arrival there was a general feeling in the colony that a meeting would be called at which the tycoon would, so to speak, tell them the score. People spent the day wandering aimlessly, waiting for the loudspeakers to summon them to the Community Hall. The only person to make contact with Hetherington was Stordahl, who called at the cabin in mid-morning ostensibly to find out if there was anything required; in reality to ascertain the man's intentions. He was met at the door by one of the watchdogs who informed him that Mr. Hetherington was in consultation with his advisers and could not be disturbed; neither did he need anything more than a supply of food and drink.

As Stordahl walked away, irritated but helpless, he had the idea of trying the adjoining cabin, which housed the mysterious egotists. Again with the excuse of offering assistance, hospitality or whatever, he knocked at the door. There was no reply. Presumably the men were all closeted with Hetherington. Stordahl returned to the main colony with the feeling of being let down, thinking that any business discussed at this time ought surely to include himself as representative of the colonists.

'Perhaps it's nothing to do with us,' Joan ventured. 'It could be an entirely different matter. The organization's pretty big, you know.'

Stordahl glared at her angrily. 'Nonsense. He's talking to the men he brought. They're planning how to create their goddamned genius amorph. That's why Hetherington's come here, believe me. It's not the colony he's interested in, or even the steelworks. It's the amorphs. He's seen the possibilities.'

'Don't worry, dear. Maybe she'll join us for lunch,' said Joan mischievously.

'Oh, for God's sake. . . .' Stordahl stamped off and spent the next hour or so aimlessly wandering about the colony giving evasive answers to the many people who stopped him and asked what was going to happen.

Shortly after lunch – at which Marilyn did not appear – the long-awaited communication from Hetherington arrived in the shape of one of his slab-faced pugs who informed Stordahl loftily that Mr. Hetherington was commandeering the radio dome until further notice, and would like a link to the cabin installed. Furiously Stordahl put a team of men on the job. The team, inspired by the sight of the Supervisor watching their every move with barely-suppressed viciousness, completed the job in seventy-five minutes flat.

Then Hetherington requested an amorph; a fresh, uninfluenced creature on which he and his men could get to work. . . .

'I realize this must be vexing for you, Stordahl,' remarked the tycoon when at last, after two days in seclusion, he summoned the Supervisor to his presence. 'I am a very busy man, and this matter of the amorph could be of the utmost importance to us all. There is no time to socialize.'

'I wasn't thinking of you socializing, sir,' Stordahl blurted out. 'It's just that I think I ought to be involved in any matters concerning the colony and the amorphs. I think I have a right to know what's going on. So does everyone else.'

'It doesn't concern you. This is a top-level organization matter. The consequences could be far-reaching and we must avoid details of our progress leaking out at present.'

Stordahl tried to think calmly. 'Your experiment is your own business, sir. I concede that; maybe I expressed myself badly. But I'm worried about the morale of the colony as a whole. Look at it from their point of view. For some time now they've been concerned about the future of the colony, and this need never have happened if the supply ships had arrived on time. Now at last the ship comes, and they find that you're on board. It worries them. They wonder if you've come to tell them you're closing the whole thing down. They feel unsettled. They're a long way from home, Mr. Hetherington. You might at least tell them your plans for the future of Marilyn.'

Hetherington thought for a moment. 'You may summon a meeting for tomorrow, Stordahl,' he said at last. 'Or perhaps not,' he corrected himself. 'The day after tomorrow. That's the best I can do. Don't you understand, it's impossible at the moment to leave this amorph?' His eyes were gleaming, inward-looking; he spoke quietly as if to himself. 'The progress is fantastic. The thing is soaking up information like a sponge. But we can't leave it alone. We must keep at it all the time, to fix it permanently in its new form. Otherwise it slips back. . . .'

'But it takes months to achieve any sort of permanency.'

'I'm not so concerned about that. We can take the thing away with us once the initial stages are over. But right now, time is valuable. . . . The day after tomorrow, Stordahl,' he said firmly.

'The day after tomorrow,' Stordahl repeated woodenly.

'And until then, I will have no disturbance.'

'I'll see to it, sir.'

'You're a good man, Stordahl.'

Don't hand me that crap, thought the Supervisor.

At nine A.M., two days later, Hetherington addressed the colony assembled in the Community Hall. Stordahl himself introduced the tycoon, then sat back as Hetherington wheeled himself to the front of the platform and paused impressively before delivering a speech which, for the first ten minutes, consisted entirely of such emotion-laden words as he himself had condemned a few days earlier.

Phrases such as 'This new frontier of ours', 'The unquenchable spirit of Man', 'Victory in the battle against the elements', and 'The future of our children', spilled from his lips in glib succession as he stared challengingly at his audience, somehow seeming himself to represent the personification of all the virtues he extolled.

Marilyn whispered to Stordahl: 'He calls this his up-and-at-them talk. You've no idea of the careful thought that went into the choice of wording; his scriptwriters were psychologists and poets, the best. I've lost count of the number of times I've heard it, but it always sounds good.'

Joan leaned across; Stordahl sat between her and Marilyn. Much to his surprise the two girls, completely different types, got on well together. Joan asked: 'What's it all leading up to?'

Marilyn smiled. 'You've got a suspicious mind, Joan. Sometimes it leads up to nothing – it's just a pep talk. On this occasion, well. . . .' She glanced significantly at Stordahl, reminding him mutely of Hetherington's ominous words three days ago.

Hetherington was well into his stride and the audience basked in a pleasant glow of self-esteem. Judging his moment carefully, the tycoon proceeded to drop his bomb.

'Orbiting around your planet,' he said, 'is the freighter *Hetherington Adventure*, on which I came. That freighter is crammed with equipment and construction materials, and I'm sure you'll be pleased to know that we're now all set to go ahead with the steelworks. As always with such a project as ours, the question of economy has to be very carefully studied. My advisers have prepared reports which have assured me, if I needed assuring, that the Marilyn project cannot be other than successful. I'm sure this will remove any doubts from your minds as to your future on this new world. The signs are good. This planet will enjoy great prosperity. We are ready. The tenders are landing the materials and equipment at this very moment!'

It seemed a good moment to applaud, and the dome rang with cheering and stamping. People pumped one another's hands, slapped one another on the back. Stordahl sat tensely waiting for the bubble to burst; he glanced at Marilyn, who was biting her lip nervously.

As the applause died a man remained standing, a lone man staring at the platform as others resumed their seats around him. He waited for silence without nervousness, with an air of dignity. He spoke, loudly and clearly, before Hetherington could continue.

'I don't see any tenders landing, Mr. Hetherington,' he said.

The silence grew as Hetherington tried to stare him down. The tycoon had been put on the defensive unexpectedly, before he had had an opportunity to explain the change of plan in his own words. Impossible to ignore the man now; everyone was waiting for his reply. He opened his mouth; the man spoke again, beating him to it.

'We would at least be able to hear them now.' He cupped a hand to his ear. 'I don't hear anything, either.'

Hetherington spoke; his face was crimson. 'What is your name, man?' he asked sharply.

'I have no name as yet. I am an amorph.'

'By God,' snarled Hetherington. 'What right have you

to question me? You're not a colonist. You're an alien. Allow me to continue. Sit down or get out.'

The amorph stood his ground. 'I think we ought to get one fact clear, Mr. Hetherington. I have been told of my origins; it has been explained to me how I came into existence in my present form. Bearing this in mind, I must correct your misconception. I am a native of this planet. You, Mr. Hetherington, are an alien.'

'Quite right, George,' somebody shouted.

Stordahl recognized the creature now; nick-named George, he was an assistant stores clerk. As such he came into contact with many of the colonists, male and female. He had settled down into a predominantly male hermaphrodite of considerable intelligence and a streak of stubbornness. Alarmingly, the shout of approval had come from a human colonist.

Stordahl got quickly to his feet. 'Quiet, everybody!' he shouted. 'George, sit down, please. What Mr. Hetherington has to say is important. We can deal with the questions afterwards.'

The meeting came reluctantly to order and Hetherington resumed. Amid a barely suppressed muttering he described the change of site for the steelworks, explaining that it had never been his intention for the main body of the colony to be situated at Alice; it had merely been a convenient landing site well away from the uncertain wind currents around the mountains. Had he known that large-scale private building would be undertaken in the Alice area, he would immediately have advised against it. . . .

'That's unfair,' muttered Stordahl to Marilyn. 'He knew they were building. Now they'll think I didn't tell him in the weekly reports. He's shifted the blame to me.'

'All part of your job, Alex,' said Marilyn sympathetically.

A monstrous suspicion was forming in Stordahl's mind. Hetherington had avoided mentioning a matter which was of supreme importance. He waited while the tycoon spoke on, but nothing was said which cleared his mind. Hetherington finished. There was no applause. Stordahl stood.

His thanks to the tycoon for his exposition was greeted in cynical silence by the audience. He asked for questions, his stomach fluttering nervously.

The first question justified his fears. George the amorph was on his feet.

'One thing, Mr. Hetherington. I'm sure we'd all like to welcome the steelworks construction team to Alice, before our town has to be . . . repositioned. It seems a pity that they should be orbiting up there with their equipment instead of enjoying a few days' hospitality with us, before they start work. I think I speak on behalf of all of us when I ask you that they should be landed here as soon as possible.'

There was a murmur of excited approval. The idea of new faces around the place was welcome. Stordahl watched Hetherington intently. *Surely,* he thought, *the man can't intend. . . .*

He did. He faced the speaker blandly, upright in his wheelchair. 'I have spoken before of the enormous expense involved in an operation of this kind, and of our need to keep costs to a minimum. In view of the new factors obtaining on this planet, I have brought no construction workers, merely a supervisor. There is ample labour on Marilyn.

'The work of erection will be carried out by our present colonists and amorphs, working side by side.'

'What will they do?' Stordahl asked Santana after the meeting had broken up in some disorder.

'Difficult to say, Alex. It's unfortunate that this, ah, revelation should have come so soon after Hetheringon's clash with George. He denies the amorphs citizenship, in effect, and now he says he wants to press them into service as labourers. The colonists won't like it. My guess is that they'll be behind the amorphs to a man.'

'The amorphs are popular,' Joan added. 'Can he force them to work? It seems to me that they get a little more independent as time goes on. A few months ago I would have said that they couldn't refuse; it wasn't in their make-up. But now they're developing personalities of their own.'

'Just how many amorphs do we have in the town now, Alex?' asked Santana.

'Over two hundred.'

'I see. . . . Well, there's one way to find out what's in their minds. We speak to them. Simply, we ask them what they intend to do, just as we would ask a human being.'

Due to various pressures the opportunity did not arise until the following day.

They met in Stordahl's office; Santana, Joan, James Walters on behalf of the colonists, and the amorph George. Stordahl presiding. He came straight to the point.

'There's unrest,' he said. 'We all know that. What I want to know is, how far does it go? Is anyone talking about taking action?'

Walters coughed, embarrassed. 'Look here, Mr. Stordahl. I don't think I ought to be in on this. I seem to be a sort of leader among a certain element. I can't inform on them.'

'That's all right, Jim. I know that; that's why I asked you here. You're the leader, but you've got a few volatile types among your lot who do the rabble-rousing. I just want you to tell me the sort of action they might suggest – so that I can talk it over with you now and arrive at a compromise before anyone does anything stupid.'

'I see what you mean. That's fair enough, provided you really mean compromise. This is what we think:

'First, we're not going to work with the amorphs on construction. We don't think it's right that they should be used. It's outright exploitation. Second, we're not moving from Alice. We like it here and we've spent months of spare time building our houses. We stay. Either the steelworks are built here or Alice becomes an independent town. Things are different from a few months ago. We can be self-supporting as regards food. We've got the amorphs to help us. In due course, if Hetherington has to pull out because of this, we can lease the rights on the desert.'

Walters's voice had gained confidence as he spoke. There was a steel toolbox on the floor and, unconsciously, he stepped on it as he addressed them, gaining a foot in height. 'Down, boy,' murmured Santana; the amorph grinned briefly.

'That sounds like an ultimatum, Jim,' observed Stordahl quietly. 'I don't think you realize quite how tough the going would be. There are so many things you'd lack. You haven't got a hospital, for one thing. Suppose Dr. Singer and his men didn't go along with you? What would you do then?'

'Contact the nearest Earth colony and offer them mineral rights in return for services,' answered Walters blithely.

'I rather think Mr. Hetherington would take the FTL radio with him,' Stordahl pointed out mildly.

'We'd have it seized by then.'

'Oh, I see. . . .' Stordahl looked thoughtful. 'What you're proposing isn't secession. It's revolution.'

'If you want to put it that way.' Walters's voice began to lose a little of its confidence.

'Right. I think I understand what you're getting at. Let me answer your two points before we start talking wildly. First, the amorphs. You say you won't work with them on the steelworks, on the grounds of exploitation; yet you imply that you intend to continue using them without pay for your private projects. That's not logical. Next, the housing. The simple answer is that if you intend to continue working for the organization, you'll have to move.'

'We don't intend to work for the organization. I thought I'd made that clear.'

'You haven't decided yet. Look, Jim, I'm a reasonable man, and you can see I'm caught between two poles. So it's up to me to try to work things out so that everyone's happy. What I propose is this, concerning your two points. One: I put it to Hetherington that he pays the amorphs a wage for construction work, provided that you pay them a similar hourly rate when you use them for private work. Two: I'll suggest that you be paid compensation for the time spent in building your present homes.'

There was a long silence while Walters considered. The suggestions were fair enough, but the implications scarcely pleasant. The days of unlimited free labour would be over. The meagre salary of the contract men would have to be stretched even further in order to pay the amorphs. On the other hand, there would be a lump sum available on moving houses which would go a long way towards rehabilitating the colonists at the new site. He was about to say that he would put it to his colleagues, when there was an unexpected interruption from George.

'I think we're leaving something out, gentlemen,' said the amorph gently. 'You're forgetting the views of my people. That might have a bearing on the matter.'

'Sorry, George,' said Stordahl. 'You tell us their views.'

'You see, Mr. Stordahl,' said the amorph, 'even you, who talk of exploitation, are now assigning us to work without consulting us. Just suppose we don't want to work at the new site. What then?'

'Do you want to work at the steelworks, George?'

'No, Mr. Stordahl, since you were good enough to ask. I'm afraid the days of unpaid lackeys are finished. The amorphs are through. I speak for all of us. We've decided to pull out.'

They stared at the creature in astonishment. No amorph had ever spoken like this before. If it had not been for George's display of individuality at the meeting, Stordahl would not have believed it possible for an amorph to speak like this. They were noticeably lacking in initiative . . . or were they? Had this been a pose? Had they in fact been biding their time until the human shape and mentality had become permanent, before making their move?

'You can't do that,' said Santana slowly. 'You're not adaptable to your environment any longer. You'd be at the mercy of every carnivore on the planet. You're lacking in fundamental knowledge, and you wouldn't know to what extent. Let me put it this way. . . .' There was a great sadness in the psychiatrist's eyes as he marshalled his thoughts. Man had created an idiot in his own image. . . . 'You see, George, your knowledge is a composite of several Te factors. Women come to you for issue of stores; you have picked up a little from each of them. For most of them, I trust, their Te is their husband. They have some extremely brilliant husbands. . . .

'But you don't know what the husbands know, George. You only know what the wives know of their husbands. A wife may know that her husband is, say, a doctor. She will have picked up snippets of medical information from him, which you will automatically know. But you will not be able to treat cholera.

'You're the *wife*'s Te; you will only know what *she* knows of *him*. The knowledge which seems to fill your head is a myth, George. Ninety per cent of it will be inaccurate, but you will never realize this. . . . How many wives really know their husbands' jobs? How much does any human being know about another? What do I know of the real Stordahl, for instance? I could feed into a computer all I know about Stordahl, and it would be of no practical use. Your brain, George, is full of emotionally-clouded irrelevancies – but to you this seems like knowledge because you haven't had time to learn differently. . . .'

The psychiatrist spoke for some time in a gently reasonable tone, explaining the difficulties of the amorph's proposed line of action, and extolling the advantages of life with the humans under Stordahl's plan.

And all the time he spoke, George the amorph gazed beyond him with a quiet smile. . . .

When Santana had finally finished, George spoke.

'What makes you so sure that none of us has any practical knowledge?' he asked. 'It only takes one of us. . . . We have a great empathy among ourselves, particularly away from the influence of humans. We are almost, shall we say, a hive. . . .'

Santana was to remember this remark the following morning, when it was announced that Hetherington's tame genius had inexplicably escaped. . . .

ELEVEN

'I can't understand it,' said Hetherington, echoing the time-honoured lament of the man who will not admit that the regrettable incident is indirectly his own fault. 'The thing was locked in. We finished the experiment for the night and we locked it in its cage. The cage was in the shed and the shed was locked too.'

'How far had the experiments gone?' asked Stordahl, a worry nagging at his mind. 'I mean, what sort of powers had the thing achieved? There was no evidence of . . . teleportation?'

Hetherington swivelled in his chair; circular openings in each arm-rest pointed threateningly. 'Christ, Stordahl, don't talk like a child. Teleportation, my left testicle. We had begun to create an incredibly intelligent creature which was already showing signs under test conditions of being able to apply its knowledge intuitively, in a way no computer could ever match. There was no suggestion of paranormal powers whatsoever.'

'Paranormality is relative.' Santana spoke thoughtfully. 'A few months ago we would have said that telepathy was paranormal, but indisputably the amorphs possess this ability to a certain degree, otherwise they would never pick up the mental content of the Te factor. And the amorph George hinted that the amorphs in human form are to an extent telepathic among their own kind. Which raises some interesting implications. In creating a mastermind which has escaped, you may have been instrumental in creating a master race. . . .'

Hetherington stared at the psychiatrist in growing alarm. 'You mean they'll take over? Wipe us out?'

'I venture to suggest that is a childish remark, too, Mr. Hetherington. The amorphs have no grievance against us yet. They have proved themselves so far to be non-aggressive. But they've acquired individuality, and dignity, and a knowledge of their own beginnings; a sort of race-consciousness. And you locked one of them up in a cage. . . . So the simple answer to the present mystery is that your genius was released by another amorph.'

'But that's going directly against our wishes. Stordahl?' Hetherington appealed to the Supervisor. 'I thought you said the amorphs didn't do that kind of thing.'

'It was an unusual circumstance.'

'By God, I hope we don't get any more unusual circumstances. The knowledge locked up in that thing's mind is fantastic!'

Stordahl said thoughtfully: 'It was an aggressive act by amorph standards. I wonder how far it could lead. They can be aggressive, Santana. I was once insulted by the amorph which took the form of Briggs. It said it didn't like me.'

'The Te of an egotist is complete, a duplicate of the actual person,' said Santana. 'Whereas the ordinary Te is idealized, the perfect, though incomplete, person. Mr. Hetherington had created a composite amorph of five egotists. In doing so, it follows he will have created . . . a megalomaniac. A totally selfish megalomaniac with inhuman knowledge and vast intelligence. . . .'

'Have you noticed, when he feels cornered by anyone he turns his chair directly towards them and brings those diabolical guns to bear,' Santana remarked afterwards. 'There's compensation for having no arms, if you like. I don't suppose he's ever used them, but it's unnerving to see his feet on those pedals.'

'It just makes the bastard feel good,' said Stordahl moodily. 'Where an ordinary man points his finger, Hetherington points his guns. But to be fair, there have been several attempts on his life in the past. It's the only way he can arm himself, if you'll excuse the lousy pun.'

He left the psychiatrist and went outside. The grey skies were drizzling rain and men were moving about briskly from dome to dome, searching for the lost amorph. Briggs walked towards him, smiling thinly.

'I hear we've lost the new Messiah,' the biologist greeted him.

'It's not funny, Briggs. The thing could be dangerous. . . .' He eyed the man with sudden suspicion. 'What about your amorph? Is it safe? George was talking about a general walkout. Led by the new genius, I suppose,' he added bitterly. 'I'd hate to think of your damned Te being added to the pool of knowledge and bloody-mindedness.'

'I've thought of that,' said Briggs smugly. 'I've locked it up.'

'Where?' Stordahl looked around. It was noticeable that only the colonists were engaged in the search; the amorphs stood around in little knots, watching, expressionless.

'In the shelter. Want to satisfy yourself?'

They were just in time. As they approached the tiny building they saw a group of amorphs working at the lock with a portable laser. They hurried up; on their arrival the amorphs stood back, eyeing them sullenly.

'Give me that!' Stordahl took the laser from an unresisting hand. 'Now get out of here. This place is out of bounds. Understand?' He stared at the humanoid creatures; they gazed back, their expressions blank and mulish. As one, they wheeled around and shuffled off. The atmosphere was heavy with resentment.

'My God, Stordahl. I don't like this.' The biologist was alarmed. 'These people could turn dangerous. You can almost smell murder. What's got into them?'

'Hetherington's pet genius has got into them. He's around somewhere. I expect he's been moving among them all night, working them up.'

'He could quite easily influence them directly with his own mentality,' Briggs remarked nervously. 'He wouldn't need to say much.'

Stordahl reached into his pocket and handed the biologist a photograph. 'This is our man, by the way. I've been handing these around. Shout if you see him.'

Briggs snorted. 'You're an optimist.' He examined the photograph cynically. 'Do you imagine he looks like this now? He's only been in Alice a few days. His physical appearance hasn't congealed. He's spent the night with his friends, so I expect he's looking pretty anonymous by now.'

'It's the best we can do.' Wearily, Stordahl turned away. 'For God's sake, guard that door until I send along a relief.'

At least the crisis has stopped people from preaching revolution for the time being, thought Stordahl as he entered the dome complex. The search was continuing and being extended towards the homestead area; meanwhile the amorphs were being rounded up and assembled in the community hall for identification against the register. Over two hundred of them stood in a muttering crowd. As soon as each one was identified, he was quickly led away to cabins commandeered for the purpose. Stordahl thought it unwise at present to allow the creatures to gather together for any longer than was strictly necessary; once at the cabins they were locked up and guarded, twenty to a unit.

The colonists were thorough in their search; their manner was resigned and no longer rebellious. In the emergency they were working for the good of all, but Stordahl wondered what their attitude would be when things settled down after their quarry was caught. The remaining amorphs would presumably leave as they had intimated, and the colonists would have to face the future without their help. It wouldn't be easy. Over the months they had begun to take the creatures for granted.

He wondered about the other amorphs, those still out in the country who had never known human contact. Did the presumed telepathic ability extend that far? What was happening in the cuptree groves? Were the unformed creatures aware of what was happening at the colony?

He could find out quite easily. Any change would be instantly apparent to him, in the attitude of his own Te. . . .

Joan entered her cabin slowly, wondering how to play the scene which was to follow. The amorph looked up from its book.

'Hello, Joan,' it greeted her pleasantly. 'How's my favourite girl today?'

'How are you, Alex?' she replied abstractedly. He would have to go. Stordahl's instructions had been specific. All amorphs must assemble at the Community Hall for roll call. It was late already; she had delayed for a long time, trying to face up to the inevitable showdown.

'I'm fine,' replied the creature, and she marvelled yet again. The tone of voice and the inflexion were so exactly right. . . . 'I'm reading a most interesting book about the origin of species,' the amorph went on. 'Strange to think we had such humble beginnings.'

Her amorph. Her Te. . . . The creature of her mind which she had never dared to reveal in public for fear of the ultimate embarrassment. Her innermost emotions in human form. She had been a damned fool ever to have taken the creature in, but she had been at first curious, then fascinated as the resemblance took shape. . . . It would appear in the register as a number, assigned privately to her. Just a number, but when people saw it they would know exactly whose Te it represented. . . .

'Alex,' she said with sudden determination. 'I've got something to tell you.'

'What's that, my dear?' It looked up from the book with an effort. It was deeply interested and she thought: *This is something we hadn't allowed for. This is something Santana had never thought of.*

The amorph in its earlier state represented an emotional idea, true. But it was capable of learning, very quickly, from a book. And from conversation with humans. . . .

What did the amorphs do in their spare time? How many of them used the colony library.

She had its attention. She spoke rapidly. 'Alex . . . you're not human. I've been meaning to tell you for a long time but I couldn't get around to it. You're not from Earth. You were born on Marilyn. This is your home planet. There are others of your type around the colony. We call you amorphs.'

The creature smiled tolerantly. 'What rubbish you talk sometimes, Joan.' It resumed its perusal of the book.

'Alex!' she cried desperately. 'I'm telling the truth! Listen to me, I. . . .' She thought quickly. 'I can prove it. How old are you?'

'Forty, of course.'

'Tell me about your childhood.'

It was heartrending to watch the expression of bewilderment spread over the familiar face. 'Childhood?' it mumbled. 'I can't. . . . I don't remember. Did I . . . ? I must have had a childhood. Everyone has. . . .' Suddenly the eyes cleared. 'I remember, of course. I was reading of such an incident only the other day. I had an attack of amnesia through overwork. Frankly, I can't remember anything before the time I first met you in this cabin. The mind can play some very strange tricks, Joan.'

'Tell me about Earth.'

'Really, my dear. This is a bit childish. What do you want to know about Earth?'

'I want to prove to you that you're a product of my own mind. There are certain things you can't know.'

'If that's the case, you wouldn't know them either. So how would you know if I was answering correctly?'

'I'll take that chance,' Joan snapped irritably. *Is the real*

Alex Stordahl as annoying as this? she wondered. Time was getting on. . . . With a sudden renewal of tenderness, she thought: *I can't just turn him in among all those other amorphs who know what they are because they've been told from the start; and him thinking he's human all the time. . . .* Suddenly she took the book from his hands and threw it on the floor. 'Pick that up, Alex,' she commanded.

Obediently the amorph rose from its chair, bent down and retrieved the book.

'Give it to me. Now . . . pick it up again.'

The amorph resumed its seat, leaving the book where she had thrown it. 'You're being unreasonable, Joan.'

She had hoped to show the creature that it had no option but to repeatedly obey her commands, thereby proving that it did not possess the requisite human characteristics of free will.

She had failed, because she had forgotten that the amorph was Alex Stordahl as she thought of that man. And she knew perfectly well that Alex himself would have refused the second time, too. Indeed, she thought wearily, he would probably have told her to go to hell on the first occasion. The amorph was certainly idealized. . . .

'Why are you crying, Joan?' the creature asked sympathetically.

'You've got to go, Alex,' she said. 'You've been summoned to the Community Hall.'

'Oh?' Surprise showed. 'You've never wanted me to go out before.'

Joan thought her chance had come at the last moment. The real Alex Stordahl would never have stayed indoors for a month, just because she had asked him to. 'You're right,' she said. 'But why didn't you go out just the same?'

'I didn't want to,' replied the amorph simply. 'I guess I was scared. Ever since I can remember, you've looked after me. I suppose I must have guessed that something . . . strange had happened to me before, but I never thought to ask you. So I stayed in, because it was what you wanted. But now, since you suggest it, I'd like a walk. See you later.' He waved to her casually and was gone.

Joan sat down and wept.

* * * *

Outside, the amorph paused for a moment. It looked towards the dome complex, then commenced to walk slowly and thoughtfully down the rough track between the cabins. Gradually its pace quickened and its bearing became assertive; it straightened its back, looking taller. At the junction of the track with the main route to the domes it turned left.

Crossing the road it addressed a man standing outside a cabin.

'This is one of the houses where we're holding the amorphs, is it?'

'That's right, sir.'

'Fine, you can release them now. We've caught the one we're after. They can all come out. Pass the word along to the other guards, will you?'

'Certainly, Mr. Stordahl,' said the man, unlocking the cabin door.

On the solitude of the hillside it was easy to believe nothing had changed. The plain rolled southward and in the far distance a rent in the clouds dripped watery sunlight on to the pale sea. To the south-east were the swamplands of the river delta; he shivered, slightly, remembering the piranavas. The delta was a wild, bloody place.

Stordahl watched his Te forming. . . .

Soon the little girl spoke. 'Hello, Daddy. What are we going to do today?'

'You've changed your dress.' He smiled at her; she was always very clothes conscious. . . .

She looked down at herself, small hands smoothing the material. 'I like this dress. Do you like it? It's pink. Mommy says it's my colour.'

'Mommy?' Another ghost walked on Stordahl's grave.

'She bought this for me in Worcester.' And she did, too; Stordahl remembered. A bright spring day before Alice's birthday, and the low mist rising from the River Severn. . . .

'That was a long time ago. You've got a good memory, darling.'

Alice looked puzzled. 'A long time ago? It was only. . . .' A thoughtful frown. 'It was only last week, because it was my birthday the next day, that's what the dress was for, my birthday.'

Alice would never grow up. . . .

She prattled on; it was one of her good days. Sometimes, often, she would wake ill-tempered and the grey-green eyes would flash and the face would too easily crumple fat and red and tearful. 'That Mommy won't let me wear my trouser suit!' she would howl, enlisting his support while Mary got the breakfast. Flinging the offending dress to the floor and stamping on it. 'Take it easy, sweetheart,' he would say, putting his arm around her, and Mary would emerge from the kitchen to see them there; a faint smile would cross her face. 'She's not getting the better of me,' Mary would say. 'You'd give her anything she wanted. She's spoiled enough already.' He would grin back over Alice's head, pick up the dress and ease it over Alice's tense shoulders; her face would emerge pink and furious from the neck opening. Ten minutes later she would have forgotten the whole incident and she and Mary would be good friends again.

It would be nice to see Mary again. But a man has only one Te. . . .

Stordahl roused himself in some alarm; he was beginning to confuse his realities. He tried to regard the child-like amorph without emotion, marshalling his thoughts.

'What do you know about the colony?' he asked decisively.

'C . . . conolly? What's conolly, Daddy?'

He led her around the trees; the domes lay below them, away on the plain. 'That's the colony.'

'What a funny place. Why are the houses round?'

'They're built that way. Have you ever seen it before?'

'No.' And of course she hadn't. An hour ago she had no eyes. . . .

'Has anyone ever told you to go down there?'

'No, Daddy.' The fair hair shook decisively.

'And those things.' Pointing to a group of unformed amorphs moving shapeless among the saucerplants. 'What are those?'

'I don't know. I've never seen them before. What funny things! Will they gobble us up, Daddy?' Alarm in the bright eyes.

He sighed. 'It's nothing to worry about, sweetheart. They're just harmless animals. Run away and play now. I must go to work.'

She ran among the cuptrees and Stordahl started back down the hill.

Alice was the same as ever. There was no telepathic contact between the colony amorphs and the shapeless creatures in the hills, so far. But what would happen if the two groups came into close contact? It was anyone's guess, but the likelihood was that the wild amorphs would begin to take human shape, imitating what they saw; and their minds would merge with the general pool, absorbing knowledge. . . .

A large crowd was milling about the outer perimeter of the domes as he approached the colony; he accelerated the half-track over the last mile and pulled up abruptly beside Briggs, who was talking with a group of excited colonists.

'Where the hell have you been, Stordahl?' cried the biologist angrily. 'This is a fine time to take to the hills. What the hell is going on here?'

'You tell me,' retorted Stordahl. 'I've only just arrived.'

'Just arrived? My God.' There was a gun in Briggs's hand. 'You let the amorphs out, then clear off and leave us to face the consequences. What sort of a Supervisor are you, for Christ's sake?'

'I didn't let them out. They were locked up when I left. Myers must have released them; I imagine the Old Man told him to. Where is he?'

'I'm here, Alex.' Bill Myers pushed his way through the crowd. 'I gave no orders for release. We haven't caught Hetherington's genius yet. I thought we were going to keep them locked up until then.'

'Well, it seems they've got out,' observed Stordahl wearily. 'Some sort of idiotic foul-up, I suppose. It's no good standing around blaming one another. What's happening?'

'They're leaving,' explained Briggs more calmly. 'Or so they say. What are your orders, Supervisor? I mean, do we let them go or not?'

Attentive faces waited for Stordahl's reply. Behind, a large crowd of amorphs began to move steadily towards them.

'How can there be any question?' asked Stordahl. 'We're not jailers. This is a colony, not a prison or a zoo. If they want to go, they go. They're here of their own free will.'

'And how the hell are we supposed to run the colony without them?' asked a man belligerently, thrusting his face forward.

'Oh, shut up, for God's sake.' Stordahl felt tired and sick; he was not prepared to argue the point. He moved away with the intention of circling the crowd and meeting the oncoming amorphs.

'Mr. Hetherington's not going to like this,' someone bleated behind him.

'Balls to Mr. Hetherington,' muttered Stordahl.

'I heard that!'

He ignored the acrimony and walked over to the amorphs. There was a large number of them; he presumed they were all present. They carried no arms, no supplies; they walked steadily towards the outskirts of the colony, blank-faced. The storekeeper George was to the fore. Stordahl stepped up to him.

'So you're pulling out, George. You meant what you said.'

George did not slacken his pace and Stordahl had to change direction, hurrying beside the amorph.

'As I said, we're going.' The creature's expression was not resentful, or determined; merely wooden. 'The time has come. In a way we're grateful to you people; you've taught us a lot. We've gained a sense of identity, a great deal of knowledge, and a suitable form. I trust you are not going to attempt to stop us.'

'What's the point?' asked Stordahl resignedly. He looked closely at the amorph beside George. 'I suppose this is your leader.'

'I am.' The creature spoke in a commanding voice, deep and resonant. An indefinable air of vitality radiated from him. Stordahl felt inferior in his presence. He looked away from the brilliant eyes and saw, with a shock, another amorph who bore a striking resemblance to himself. He stared for a moment and was about to speak, but then decided his question would be better unasked. The amorph looked back at him, a reflection, a weird impression of a mirror. . . .

His gaze returned to the leader. 'What's your name?'

'Moses,' the amorph replied. 'Mr. Hetherington named

me Laddie, but I think Moses is far more suitable, don't you?'

Their clothes dripping, the amorphs trudged away into the rain.

TWELVE

'I don't think I'm being unreasonable,' remarked Hetherington in a deceptive tone of mildness. 'I'd just like you to tell me who released the amorphs, that's all. I mean, he might have thought he had a very good reason. I just want to know what that reason was, so that I can tell him he's wrong.' He swivelled the wheelchair in a semicircle, giving each person in turn a view down the gun barrels.

The silence was long and tense. Most of the higher executives of the colony were present, together with Marilyn Hetherington and the four egotists who had been deprived of their brainchild. Hetherington had summoned the meeting for the morning, having preserved an ominous silence since the exodus of the amorphs the previous day.

The guns came abruptly to rest, levelled at Stordahl; Hetherington's withered foot tapped the trigger-pedal unconsciously. 'Rumour has it that it was you, Stordahl.'

Stordahl glanced at the others; Joan's face was ashen.

'It was you, Mr. Stordahl!' yelped a panic-stricken voice from behind as the silence grew intense. 'I passed on your orders. I'm not taking the blame. It was you. You told me to let them go!'

'Yes . . . I did,' said Stordahl slowly.

'No!'

'Be quiet, Joan. Let me explain, Mr. Hetherington.'

'Of course, Stordahl. Go right ahead. I'm not stopping you.'

'We were unable to find the, ah, indoctrinated amorph despite searching the entire dome complex and housing area, and it occurred to me that our quarry had managed to infiltrate the groups of amorphs which we'd imprisoned. This could have been dangerous. My idea was that we should let them out quickly, stop crowding them, to make it easier to identify the one we were after. The longer he was in seclusion with the others, the more time he would have to assume an anonymous appearance. Remember, we knew what he looked like. It was important that things stayed that way.'

Hetherington smiled dangerously. 'But you failed, Stordahl. I'm told that after release they remained together, formed themselves into a mob and left the colony. This could have been foreseen. In retrospect, it seems that your decision to lock them up was also a mistake. It triggered off the unrest and gave the creature George the chance he wanted.'

'George would have led them out in any case,' Stordahl protested. 'He'd told us his intentions already.'

Hetherington's smile was fixed and mirthless. 'Ah, but did he lead them out?' he asked softly. 'You alone spoke to George as they departed. Tell me, Stordahl, was George in charge?'

Beside Stordahl, Briggs stiffened suddenly and shot the Supervisor an impatient glance. He was about to speak when his eye caught Joan's; and he paused, visualizing again the faces of the leaders of the departing crowd of amorphs. He shut his mouth abruptly as an extraordinary expression of understanding, almost compassion, eased the embittered lines of his face.

'You were about to say something, Mr. Briggs?'

'No. It's nothing.'

Stordahl spoke. 'George wasn't in charge. There was another amorph there. Your man. He said his name was Moses, and that he was the leader.'

'Why didn't you stop him?'

'I couldn't,' replied Stordahl simply. 'It wasn't that I was outnumbered; there was plenty of help at hand. But I was unable to do anything. There was an aura about that creature. He seemed almost to will me to let him go.'

'Thank you, Stordahl,' said Hetherington mildly. 'You, Briggs, and Santana stay here. Everyone else may go.'

'So our man has found another name,' observed Hetherington blandly. He appeared to be in surprisingly good spirits, a fact which Stordahl and Santana observed with some alarm. The tycoon was at his most unpredictable when gay. He spun the chair around with a carefree movement and studied his underlings for a moment.

Hetherington's bodyguards had remained in the room, as had the four egotists; the colonists, seeing them for the first time at close quarters, recognized certain faces. Hetherington chuckled.

'I've been remiss,' he said. 'I've neglected to introduce

you to my friends here. We've been so wrapped up in Project Genius for the last few days that we haven't had time for socializing. Gentlemen,' he addressed his own group, 'I present Messrs. Stordahl, Santana, and Briggs of the Marilyn colony; good men all, if at times irresponsible. Men of Marilyn, meet my colleagues. First, Professor Ronald Sokalski, physicist of the Hetherington Organization.'

The physicist was tall and thin; his brief smile was gone, a memory almost before it appeared. Stordahl knew his face; it was familiar in articles in the *World Scientist* in which the physicist expounded his views as to the nature of matter at FTL speeds. He had been responsible for designing the first successful FTL ship, and for developing the FTL radio system on which so many colonized worlds depended. He was at present engaged in anti-gravity research in artificial FTL conditions, based on his own theory of Negative Relativity.

'Admiral Hammond Dwight, of the Earth Corps.'

Another familiar figure; the face which had stared granite determination from every 3-V set on Earth at the time of the Vegan engagement. 'Hammer' Dwight lived his appearance – or so the publicity handouts gave one to understand. In fact, Stordahl had often wondered how the appearance and expression of man-to-man pugnacity could be reconciled with the obvious fact that Dwight controlled his engagements from a distance of several light-years, safe at the console of the Earth Corps flagship. Nevertheless, he conceded that the man was a master tactician. Dwight stared at the colonists contemptuously with no flicker of acknowledgment; apparently they were not made of the stuff he admired. If he admired anything, apart from himself.

'Mr. Andrew Mahoney.'

Another 3-V familiar, the Librarian of the World Archives who led a double life as Andy Ryan, quiz-king and memory man. He grinned expansively as though at a studio audience, and said with inappropriate facetiousness: 'Howdy, fellow competitors.' It was his catch-phrase. Once asked why he addressed everyone he met in this manner, he had snapped: 'Because they *are* my competitors. I've got to stamp on them all, one way or another, in order to survive. Have you never heard of Darwin?'

Needless to say, the remark was deleted from the exhibited show in order to retain Andy Ryan's reputation as an amusing intellectual.

'Mr. Phillip Spink.'

Stordahl had met Spink personally when the man held the position of Comptroller General of the late World Emigration Commission. A heated altercation had resulted in Spink axing the budget for the Alban colony which was at that time desperately short of building materials. The last colony to be set up before the Commission was disbanded, Alban had been saved from complete disaster by the intervention of an older and wealthier neighbour. At the time, Stordahl, not appreciating the financial straits in which the Commission found itself, had referred to Spink as drunk with power. He had, however, written the man an immediate apology on hearing the Commission's fate.

Judging by the venomous glance Spink gave Stordahl, the apology had not been accepted. . . .

Hetherington smiled paternally at the two groups; it was noticeable that he did not bother to introduce his pugs, whom he no doubt regarded as merely useful animals. Stordahl, glancing at the powerful forms sitting impassively in the background, tended to agree with this view.

'You may be a little surprised at the manner in which I have accepted our present situation,' the tycoon remarked pedantically. 'However, the loss of our amorph is not a disaster. The creature was, shall I say, faulty? It didn't come up to expectations. It tended to be . . . difficult. We shall try again. Which was one of the reasons I wanted to speak to you three. You've been living with the amorphs for some time. I should like to hear your views.'

'I think your project was madness. Sheer madness,' said Santana frankly.

'Interesting but not constructive. Explain yourself further.'

'Obviously. You were trying to create a monster which I have no confidence we could control. The thing is self-willed and power-mad. It's at large on the plains with a gang of followers. The current situation is dangerous enough, and now you're saying you're going to try again.'

'With your help, Santana; with your help. A moderating influence is required, that's all.'

'The amorphs are heading towards the desert,' Stordahl

interjected. 'They spent the night five miles west of here.'

'Once and for all,' snapped the tycoon, 'I'm telling you to forget all that, Stordahl. They can't do any harm out there. They're not armed.'

'But what about the colony? Supposing they organize themselves into raiding parties? If your genius is as good as we think, they'll have weapons within the year. They could recruit every unformed amorph on the planet, and wipe us out, yourself included.'

'I will be a very long way from here when that happens, Stordahl.'

The three colonists stared at Hetherington, finding the implications of this remark difficult to believe.

'You mean you intend to pull out?' whispered Briggs. 'You're going to create your next goddamned genius and take it away with you, leaving us to face the music?'

'Mr. Briggs. You misunderstood me. I think you've had it too easy on Marilyn in the past, and you've become soft. I'm not running out on you. Supplies and equipment will come through as always. I'm merely stating that the colony will have to deal with any attack in its own way. Hostile aliens have been encountered before. I'll see you're armed; in fact, I've already landed a large supply of laser rifles for use in the event of any difficulty with the amorphs I had intended to employ at the steelworks. There will be no problem.' He leaned back, gazing at them blandly, the toad-like face tolerant.

Stordahl asked the question quietly. 'Exactly where have you landed the rifles, Mr. Hetherington?'

'At the site of the new steelworks, of course. . . .' A rictus of alarm twitched at the tycoon's mouth as the significance struck him suddenly.

Stordahl's chest felt tight and his hands were trembling. 'At the site of the steelworks. . . .' He controlled himself with difficulty, realizing that he was about to mount a one-man mutiny. Would Briggs have supported him? Santana certainly. But those hoods in the background; they would have had the three colonists helpless in five seconds flat. Marilyn was there, standing behind the tycoon. How much had she heard? Which side would she be on, if it came to the crunch? And Sokalski and his team, sitting there wondering what it was all about. Hetherington represented their ticket if anything went wrong. . . . This was no time for revolution.

'The site of the steelworks, together with the weapons, is just about two miles from the amorphs' present estimated position,' he said. 'I think we can assume that they'll have their arms within the hour.'

The helicopter chattered across the green plain, chasing its shadow. The rain had ceased and the late morning sun sparkled on the billion upturned saucers of water, silver and emerald. In the distance rose the mountains, blue, green-skirted. Receding behind – the colony. Somewhere ahead, the amorphs and a megalomaniac. A little farther on, a dozen cases of the latest laser rifles, continuous-action and deadly, capable of slicing a man in half at a range dependent only on the planet's horizon. Also dynamite and grenades. An arsenal.

'What the hell are you doing here?' asked Stordahl. Below, he saw the stream of hastily-manned half-tracks which would arrive far too late. . . .

Marilyn looked at him sombrely. 'He didn't like my Te,' she said. 'He forced me into a prolonged contact, just to see what. . . .' Her voice trailed off.

The third occupant of the bubble chuckled. 'You flatter yourself, lady.' He was one of the pugs. 'Why do you think he sent me along? To keep an eye on you. To protect you. . . . Oh, boy; you should have seen his face yesterday though, when that thing began to take shape. I didn't know who it was going to be, but it certainly wasn't the Old Man. I had to laugh. . . .'

Below, the plain swept by; there was no sign of the amorphs.

'He heard you laugh, Alberto,' remarked Marilyn. 'It was a damned stupid thing to do.'

'Couldn't help it. Hey. . . .' The blank face showed mild alarm. 'Do you think he might bear a grudge?'

'I don't think so, not so that you'd notice.' The girl's face was grim. 'All the same, three people had to go in the helicopter to try to beat the amorphs to the site, or reason with them, if they've got there first. I can think of a more suitable choice for a task force. Alberto – yes, he's a hired killer . . . sorry, dear. But why me? Why you,

Alex? Because what we're going to do is dangerous, that's why. I can't think of any other reason.'

'Try harder,' advised Alberto equably. 'Stordahl's responsible for this foul-up, and he knows the country as well as anyone. The Old Man wanted me to come along because he didn't like the idea of Mr. Stordahl getting hold of all those rifles, bearing in mind that the said Mr. Stordahl looked as though he wanted to take over the whole show a while back. You, Mrs. Hetherington, are here for the same reason. He trusts you more than anyone.'

'After yesterday?' The girl stared moodily out of the window.

'I've known the Old Man longer than you, gorgeous. He's no fool. He never expected a girl like you to have a Te in his form. But you can think dirty so long as you don't do dirty. He knows you're sensible and you know where the money comes from. So he's not worried about you. Who was that Te of yours, anyway? I don't know him.'

'J. did,' said Marilyn. 'It would have been a shock to him.' She shivered. Yesterday a man from the past had walked forward in time. . . .

'There's the site,' said Stordahl suddenly.

In the distance, black upon the green, was an untidy area of scattered objects. They swept closer and could make out huge cases, girders strewn upon the ground, and a single dome.

'Where are the amorphs?' asked Marilyn.

'They must be around somewhere.' Stordahl scanned the horizon, puzzled. The emerald carpet stretched unbroken to the mountains. He banked and surveyed the site again. 'Look!' He pointed.

From the short shadow of a large box protruded legs, a man's legs, black and motionless on the flatness of the saucerplants. From the entrance to the dome someone was watching them, looking up, pointing. . . .

The extended digit was not a finger; it was a laser rifle. Stordahl banked away sharply.

The helicopter shook violently, shuddering as though to rid itself of the suddenly unbalanced rotor; a titanium tip, sliced off, fluttered groundward gyrating like a sycamore seed. Land and sky wheeled crazily as Stordahl wrenched at the controls, fighting for height with revving engine. Needles of fire probed around, crackling against the metalwork.

'You'll have to put her down, Stordahl!' shouted Alberto above the din.

'Like hell.' The craft sat on its tail and they were staring at the sky; it tilted, and men were running. Amorphs; a brief glimpse of a crowd surging from the dome.

More rifles, puffs of smoke from the transparent bubble now starred with cracks as the mountains swung past, in sight but too far away; and again the ground, the dome, the amorphs.

'Put her down, you crazy fool!' The pug's face was contorted with unaccustomed emotion. 'You're going to kill us!'

The whine of the motor was cut off in mid-surge as fire splattered about the cables. Swinging wildly suspended from the damaged blades, the helicopter sank rapidly towards the ground.

The hydraulics absorbed a part of the impact and threw the craft up and over; something smashed Stordahl across the side of the face and he fell, dizzy. He was lying in wetness. He looked up and saw the helicopter, its bubble split, its rotors bent double, tilt towards him, then rock back gently. It reached equilibrium on its side, a dead skeleton of twisted metal. Marilyn was on her knees nearby. Alberto hung face-down from his seat straps, his head hanging limply, his hair brushing the ground.

Stordahl sat up, climbed unsteadily to his feet. Bending, he helped Marilyn up. She leaned against him groaning, and was suddenly, violently sick.

The amorphs stood watching without comment, laser rifles at the ready. Two of the creatures stepped forward.

'A visit not altogether unexpected,' remarked Moses, his resonant voice betraying no triumph.

Behind him, Stordahl saw the shape of Alberto slip to the ground to lie in an untidy heap, an inert bundle of tattered clothes. The amorphs wheeled around at the sudden movement, then turned back. 'What shall we do?' asked George. The concept of a prisoner was new to him. His face showed slight bewilderment.

'You'll learn, George,' said Moses.

Suddenly George uttered a cry and flung himself bodily against Moses. The two amorphs fell to the ground, George on top. George's clothes burst into flame as a laser pencilled fire on his back. The rest of the amorphs swung around; Stordahl saw Alberto's face slashed crimson and black and the pug subsided, a rifle slipping from his grasp.

Moses climbed to his feet, thrusting aside the smouldering lump of flesh which had been George but which, in its last moments, had lost all semblance to human form.

'George was a fine example to us all,' he remarked coolly. 'My people will go far.'

THIRTEEN

'What are they going to do with us, Alex?' Marilyn asked, and there was an edge of hysteria to her voice. She glanced at the guard standing just inside the entrance to the dome, watching them with no trace of expression on his inhumanly nondescript face. 'Are they going to kill us?' She sat on the edge of a chair which represented the dome's total furnishing. Stordahl leaned against the concave wall nearby. There was an unpleasant smell in the dome, a reek of decay.

'I don't think so,' he reassured her. 'We have a certain value to them.'

'As hostages, you mean?'

'I don't think so. The way I see it, our very presence here represents a further source of knowledge to them.' He indicated the guard. 'That amorph isn't just keeping an eye on us. He's picking up information from our minds about our Tes. And among all the idealistic rubbish we're emitting, there may be a hard core of useful knowledge.'

Marilyn looked at the guard. 'How horrible. . . . Can't we do anything? Stop thinking, or something?'

'It doesn't make any difference. Don't get the idea they're telepathic in the normal sense. That's the mistake we all keep making.' He hesitated, then confessed, for her peace of mind: 'All he's getting from me is a lot of useless stuff about a little girl who . . . seems to be my Te. My daughter. . . . She was five years old. I can't see that she can be much help to them.'

There was compassion in Marilyn's eyes. 'Oh . . . I see. You don't think there's any chance of that . . . thing turning into anyone we know?'

'I don't think so. These amorphs seem to have reached a stage when they're a little less malleable. No doubt they're still influenced by us to a certain extent, but these people have been in their present form for some months. I think we've got to assume they've become fixed.'

Marilyn spoke very quietly. 'Except Moses, possibly? He's a recent convert.'

Stordahl stared at her.

At that moment the entrance to the dome darkened; they looked up to find Moses regarding them loftily. 'Ah, the prisoners,' he observed. 'Plotting escape, no doubt. I regret that you're wasting your time, Stordahl.' He beckoned. 'Come here. Let me show you my fortress.'

Outside, it was late afternoon, the low sun glinting from the dome and throwing deep shadows from the crates of equipment which had now been arranged in a rough circle with the dome at the centre. Smaller boxes and items of equipment had been piled on top of the crates and among these crouched amorphs, laser rifles at the ready. Stordahl marvelled at the amount of work which had been achieved in a comparatively short time. Some of the crates must have been extremely heavy, yet they had been positioned with such care that no gaps showed between them.

'I can remember,' said Moses in sardonic tones, 'movies of the old Wild West, when pioneers attacked by Indians arranged their wagons in just such a way. The set-up has an air of nostalgia. I have so many memories, now. . . .'

Stordahl found himself wondering which of Hetherington's men of genius had been so uncharacteristic as to watch Westerns, and decided it could only be Hammond Dwight. The slaughter so frequently depicted would have appealed to him. 'I take it you're expecting a siege,' he observed.

'Not a lengthy one. You see, your friends are short of weapons.' Moses chuckled. 'I know the way their minds will work. They'll set up a barrier of trucks some distance away, and exchange rifle fire until dark. Standard procedure. Then, under cover of darkness, they'll try to rush us. They'll creep across the intervening distance like maggots and storm our walls, equipped with knives. They'll have to climb our walls first, of course, but once they're inside it'll be hand-to-hand fighting. They'll reason that our rifles will be a disadvantage to us at close quarters in the dark.'

'They'll be right,' said Stordahl. 'You'll be just as likely to mow down your own men.'

Moses chuckled again, a low gloating chuckle one stage removed from insanity. Stordahl shivered.

'They will have forgotten something,' the amorph continued. 'It seems that Mr. Hetherington intended construction of the plant to proceed around the clock, and thoughtfully provided floodlights for the purpose.'

Stordahl could see the generator; indeed, it was the only large object placed within the circle, standing beside the dome. Cables ran from it to batteries of floodlights rigged on tall stands around, and close to, the dome.

'So when your friends storm our walls, they will find them unguarded. They will climb them, and descend into this circular area. Meanwhile my men will have withdrawn into the dome, except for some twenty who will be armed with laser rifles and will stand in a circle around the perimeter of the dome, thus commanding a field of fire which will include the entire area within the walls.' Moses's deep voice had risen slightly as he anticipated the action to come. 'And when all the attackers are within our walls, we will switch on the lights. And we will open fire. And we will burn the enemy down, every last one, before they are able to retreat. The siege, if you can call it a siege, will be short-lived. A large proportion of the more active members of your colony will be wiped out.' The amorph chuckled again. 'What do you think of that, Mr. Stordahl? A worthy strategy, don't you think? Worthy, perhaps, of the great Hammond Dwight himself?'

The sun was lower in the west and the plain glittered with a sea of upturned saucerplants, across which could be seen a column of trucks, steadily advancing.

Stordahl regarded the generator thoughtfully.

'Of course,' remarked Moses, 'such a strategy would be nullified if I allowed you to get your hands on that generator. But don't worry. I won't.'

Before the light faded entirely they were able to see that the colonists had, in fact, drawn their vehicles together in the form of a rough barricade. As the last rays of the sun fingered the mountain tips to the north, a pencil of light reached from the trucks and crackled among the amorphs' fortifications.

'It's a pity that you won't be able to witness the massacre,' remarked Moses as he led them into the dome which by now was crowded with amorphs surplus to the requirements of the firing party already standing around the outer walls. 'But we must leave a clear field of fire for our marksmen. Added to which, of course, I wouldn't put it past you to call out some sort of futile warning.'

'What's the point of all this?' Marilyn asked quietly.

'What are you hoping to achieve? You've got your independence now. Why not leave it at that? Why start a war? You can't win, you know.'

'You're thinking that Earth will send in troops and wipe us out, aren't you?' Moses regarded her quizzically. 'I don't think you quite realize the situation. I know better than you the way Hetherington's mind works. He won't throw good money after bad, and he's had his setbacks here already. A colony like yours is always marginal as regards profit until it's well established. The initial outlay must be kept down. If we sit on his equipment and find other ways to make things hot for your husband, he'll pull out and try somewhere else.'

They could hear the crackling hiss of lasers probing the barricades outside.

'Covering fire,' observed Moses. 'Now ask yourself who's starting the war.' The rest of the amorphs sat quietly on the crushed vegetation of the floor, saying nothing, a tight mass of quasi-humanity utterly at the command of their leader. Moses regarded them without expression, but raised his voice so that it echoed deep and resonant, around the dome. 'And when they've gone, we'll take over. We've waited millennia for this, an age of waiting without knowing what we were waiting for, because we had not the ability to wonder. Then a few short months ago Man came and gave us thoughts and form; and soon we will supersede him. Because there is no limit to what we can achieve. Each of us, in time, will possess the combined knowledge of all Mankind.'

'That's nonsense, Moses,' said Stordahl desperately. 'You're only a composite of four or five men. Their knowledge is limited. And a lot of what you think you know is just not true; it's idealized rubbish with little basis in fact. You only think you're omnipotent because of the type of men whose intelligence you've borrowed. They were blind egotists. They thought of nothing but themselves. You can't build a world on selfishness.'

Moses waved an arm at the room, at the seated amorphs. 'Behold the moderating factor,' he said. 'These people and myself gradually assimilate one another's knowledge and outlook, and in due course they will be like me, and I like them. Selfishness will not come into it. We will be as one.'

'A totally communist quasi-human society,' observed

Stordahl, and Marilyn looked at him sharply. 'With human knowledge, and human appearance, human make-up, internal organs. . . . I suppose you do have human internal organs?'

'Naturally,' replied Moses with a trace of smugness. 'Our original form of the amorph was adept at total internal and external reproduction of the object being. We have become human. I think you might say – superhuman. . . .'

'So what happens when you get sick?'

'Sick?' Puzzlement flickered across the amorph's face.

'Humans get sick,' explained Stordahl. 'They get malfunctions of the internal organs. It happens frequently. It can be fatal. Is there a doctor among you?'

'A doctor?' Moses was thinking hard and the puzzlement was giving way to mild alarm.

'You see that creature there?' Stordahl indicated one of the amorphs who was vomiting quietly on to the ground. 'I would say he's sick. I don't know why he's sick, but I don't think you do, either. I'm not a physician, neither are you. For all we know, he may be dying.'

Moses was beside the man in two quick strides, seizing him by the shoulder. 'You!' he said sharply. 'What's the matter with you?'

The amorph looked up in bewilderment and misery. 'I don't know, Moses,' he replied thickly. His chin dripped yellow fluid.

Moses looked around. It was apparent that several of his men were unwell. 'All of you!' he shouted. 'Remember! You've lived with humans for some time. You must have had this trouble before. What did you do?'

'I went to the doctor,' someone said.

Stordahl spoke quietly to Marilyn. 'This is one thing Moses hadn't thought of, anyway. His make-up is that of your husband's team of geniuses, and no egotist will consider himself as being a person susceptible to sickness, if he is idealizing himself. So Moses *couldn't* think of it. The concept of sickness is foreign to him. . . .'

Moses was striding among his men, firing questions, gathering a smattering of miscellaneous and largely inaccurate medical knowledge. Eventually he returned to Stordahl and Marilyn, and for once there was uncertainty in his smile.

'Well, that's one problem solved,' he said airily. 'It was

something they ate. It seems that a lot of the saucerplants in this area have got some sort of decay, and they were used in the meal we ate tonight. They caused vomiting.'

'Fine,' said Stordahl. 'I've no doubt in due course the vomiting will stop. Until they have to eat again. Then they'll vomit again. There's not much food available here apart from the saucerplants. Of course, at the colony we grow Earth-type crops which have been developed for use on this planet. I always find that Earth-type food sits easier on Earth-type stomachs,' he added significantly. Then he thought of Walsh and the Katies, and their exclusively Marilyn diet on which they appeared to thrive. Maybe they chose their food more carefully, or. . . .

'What sort of decay have the plants got?' he asked abruptly, something nudging the back of his mind, something that Briggs had said a long time ago. . . .

'Oh. . . .' Some of the arrogance had gone from Moses's tone. The outbreak of sickness had worried him seriously. He looked around at the crushed saucerplants on the ground. He bent and picked one, held it up to the dim light of the dome's only lamp. 'Like this,' he said.

The edges of the plant had turned brown; they crumbled as Moses fingered the broad saucer. A slightly fetid odour arose. Stordahl recognized it; he had smelled it ever since they had arrived in the area, but had earlier attributed it to inadequate sanitary arrangements.

'The plants you ate,' he said sharply. 'They came from inside the dome?'

'No. The plants outside are going the same way.'

'Then, it's not merely lack of sunlight,' Stordahl mused. He regarded Moses. 'You realize what this means? If the plants in this area are diseased, you'll have to move camp. You won't be able to sit on this equipment and prevent Hetherington from going ahead with his work. You'll have to go where the food is.'

'We'll stay here!' The amorph's tone was stubborn. 'We'll stay here and send out foraging parties. Hetherington's not getting his hands on this equipment!'

Stordahl looked at Moses in surprise; the amorph's chin was quivering and he suddenly looked like a child about to cry. . . .

As the hours passed, the amorphs became increasingly ill

and Stordahl and Marilyn considered themselves lucky that Moses had not thought to offer them food. Moses himself was affected too, and the efficiency of the firing squad outside was doubtless impaired. The stench in the dome was unbelievable and, as he looked around at the miserable amorphs lying huddled in the dim light, Stordahl wondered if he might get a chance to sabotage the generator after all. . . . As yet, the expected attack had not come, but he knew it couldn't be long now. Putting himself in the place of Hammer Dwight, who was no doubt in charge of operations, Stordahl reasoned that the admiral would from force of habit choose a specific and dramatic moment to launch the onslaught, like midnight. . . . Which would be in thirty Marilyn minutes from now.

Despite the unhappy lurchings of his stomach, Moses was watchful and from time to time regarded the two humans shrewdly – a quick cunning glance sideways which contained more than a hint of insanity. Every so often he would launch into a rambling tactical monologue laced with reminiscences which could only have come from the memory of Hammond Dwight. At the climax of one of these lengthy perorations he announced abruptly that the attack would be made at midnight, which tallied disconcertingly with Stordahl's own conclusions.

Then he addressed Stordahl and Marilyn directly. 'You two,' he said harshly. 'I don't trust you. You intend to foul up the operation. I've met enlisted men like you before and I don't like your attitude. If you get a chance to throw a wrench into the works, you will. Well, you won't get that chance. Come with me.' He picked his way through the recumbent forms of his people and the two humans followed with a puzzled glance at each other. At the rear of the dome was a small room, intended for future use as a radio shack but at present as bereft of furniture as the rest of the building.

'In there,' Moses commanded, stepping aside.

Stordahl and Marilyn entered and he slammed the door behind them. After a while Stordahl tried the knob, but apparently a bolt had been shot from the other side. He shook the door tentatively. It was flimsy, but the noise involved in breaking it down would quickly bring Moses running.

'Well . . . here we are,' said Marilyn uncertainly. They

stood alone in the blackness, suddenly uneasy in each other's presence.

'I suppose your husband's men erected this thing,' said Stordahl. 'There's always the chance. . . .' Kneeling, he thrust his fingers into the soil against the outside wall, but encountered metal where the base of the wall continued below the surface. 'These things are screwed into the ground,' he explained. 'You start off with a huge metal ring with slanting teeth and a thread which follows the teeth around, sort of. You put it on the ground and start up a motor which rotates the ring and the teeth bite in, drawing the whole thing below ground level. Then you attach your interlocking permaplast segments to the ring fittings to form the dome.'

'Why are you telling me all this, Alex?' asked Marilyn quietly.

'Sometimes they don't do the job properly, so the bottom ring is only resting on the ground, in which case it might be possible to pull away the vegetation and squeeze out. This ring has been installed properly,' he informed her, remaining in his kneeling position and talking for the sake of talking – and to drive the insidious, hideously inappropriate thoughts from his mind. . . . 'Then they float concrete over the whole of the interior.'

'I'm not going to eat you, Alex.' Marilyn sat down beside him and if he moved his arm only slightly he could touch her.

'In a very short time a lot of colonists are going to die.'

'Which really has nothing to do with it, as we can't affect the issue one way or another.' Her voice was steady and matter-of-fact. 'Look at it this way. There are just two of us here in this little room, just you and me; and as soon as we got here there was this funny atmosphere between us and I knew why and so did you. We're two human animals, right now in an environment where the normal codes of behaviour don't exist. We're scared and we've only got each other for comfort and. . . .' Her voice was no longer calm, 'My God, I need some comfort now, Alex.'

'Marilyn, for heaven's sake. . . . This isn't the time or place.' And Stordahl found he was shaking with the effect of her nearness and the conflict between his mind and his body.

'You think I'm asking you to love me?' she asked softly.

'I wouldn't presume to do that, my dear. Not at this time. I'm just asking you simply to move closer to me, another human being, and hold me and stroke me and say something nice even if you don't mean it, and. . . .'

And so on, and so on, and she described what she wanted in the fullest detail in a small voice so lost and lonely that Stordahl found she was in his arms and he was doing exactly as she said. . . . And after a while she ceased to guide him because he had taken over. He murmured words to her which he knew, as he said them, were true; and for that reason he tried not to say them, but couldn't help it. . . . 'I love you, Marilyn,' he kept saying. 'I love you,' and she whispered into his ear as he held her: 'I didn't ask you to say that, my darling. . . .'

So it went, and so it finished, and when it finished the tiny room seemed brighter with the light of their love, and Marilyn's face was lovely, the golden hair spreading like a golden flood on the green. . . .

And it took Stordahl fully five seconds to realize that the glow was the result of the floodlights outside, filtering through the opaque permaplast of the wall; and he heard the crackling and sizzling of seared flesh as colonists died, trapped in the bright amphitheatre of the circle of crates; and he heard shouting, and after a while the shouting and the sizzling ceased, and everything was very quiet again. . . .

So he turned away from the girl, the human animal beside him. And he wept for the disgusting, compulsive instincts and behaviour of human animals generally and himself in particular, the Colony Supervisor, while his people died within a radius of some thirty yards from him.

FOURTEEN

In a situation where sleep ought to have been impossible Stordahl still slept, and woke to find grey daylight glowing through the dome. He sat up wearily, conscious of a painful stiffness in his limbs, an aching hunger and a feeling of utter depression and guilt. He was unable to look at the girl on the ground beside him although he was aware that she was watching him as she lay on her back.

She spoke, quietly. 'How are you feeling, Alex?'

He sighed, staring at the door and wishing she would keep quiet. How many colonists were lying dead outside? What was Moses doing?

'I asked how you were feeling, Alex.'

Would Dwight launch another attack? Stordahl tried to imagine what he would do himself, in Dwight's position. The colonists had insufficient weapons to capture the amorphs' fortress. Their losses had been heavy. It would take a very long time for arms and ammunition to come through. Maybe Hetherington would pull out right away, just pack up and go. But he would surely make some attempt to rescue his wife, wouldn't he? Wouldn't he . . .?

'Alex . . . ?'

Now, if Marilyn were not here, he knew what Hetherington would do. He would take off in the tender, hover over the fortress, and fry the amorphs with his rocket engines. . . . But Marilyn was here, so Hetherington couldn't do that. . . .

'Alex! Look at me, you bastard!'

Shocked by the venom in her tone, he looked at her. Her clothes were dishevelled and revealing. In a sudden mood of bravado he attempted to match her frankness and allowed his gaze to travel from her feet, slowly up her body until he reached her eyes. They were bright and furious and contemptuous. He had to drop his gaze.

'You are a damned hypocrite,' she said slowly and distinctly, making each word count. 'Last night you discovered you had the guts to make love to me, and I knew it wasn't just because we were alone in the dark. Oh, no. It was because you'd always wanted to. So you took your opportunity.'

Stordahl spoke at last. 'You wanted to, as well.'

'Oh, God!' she cried in exasperation. 'We both wanted to, so we did it. And what's wrong with what we did? And now you go all complex about the thing. I tell you, Alex, the only thing wrong is your attitude!'

'I'd rather not discuss it. A lot of people died last night, while we were enjoying ourselves.'

'You'd rather not discuss it,' she mimicked furiously. 'What the hell could we do about the people who died? Was it our fault? And don't think I'm not broken up about that as well, although I didn't know the colonists as well as you. It was a terrible thing – but it's a different issue. It has no connection with what happened between us last night. Can't you see that? There was merely a coincidence of time and place. Supposing our colonists hadn't died last night. But suppose, a week later, you heard that a ship had blown apart with the loss of all on board, light-years away. Would you work it out backwards, and say: "My God, all those people must have died at the very instant that I was making love to my boss's wife – what kind of a rat am I?" I doubt if you would say that, Alex. I doubt it very much.'

'Button your blouse, Marilyn,' said Stordahl wearily.

She looked at him for a long time and the fight seemed to go out of her. She stood, and began to do as he said. 'It could have been very nice, Alex,' she said sadly. 'It could have gone on, beyond now; and I would have liked that. I won't ask you to remember some of the things you said last night; it's all over, now. When we get out of here – if we get out, you can go running back to that nice Joan of yours and spend the rest of your life making her unhappy because of your high moral principles, which tell you she's a concubine supplied by the Hetherington Organization.' Her voice broke. 'I wish you happiness, my darling. . . .'

'What a remarkably complicated creature a human is.'

The door was open and Moses stood regarding them. 'I can't pretend to understand the implications of all you were saying,' the amorph continued. 'But I can't help wondering if my own race will encounter the same problems in due course. There has been experimentation, naturally; but we found so far that the process of copulation is entirely pleasurable with none of the dismal after-effects which seem to plague Mr. Stordahl here. . . . However, that isn't what I came to talk about.'

'What the hell do you want?' snarled Stordahl. 'How many of our men did you kill last night?' Moses carried a gun, which was a pity. Stordahl's fingers itched to get around that throat. . . .

'None, as a matter of fact.' For the first time they noticed that Moses's face looked drawn; he must have been up all night. 'Can I take it that this means you and Mrs. Hetherington can now continue your, ah, affair, as I believe the expression is?'

'What are you talking about, Moses? We heard lasers. The floodlights were on.'

'Exactly. It was a most unfortunate occurrence which means, I fear, that we have lost the element of surprise. No doubt your friends observed the lights. They will not, therefore, try a night attack. I wanted to ask you just what you think they will do.'

'I don't understand.' Stordahl was conscious of a huge relief.

'Come with me. I will admit that I don't understand, either.'

They stood at the entrance to the dome and looked out across the plain. The colonists' barricade was still in position, the trucks drawn together in a tight wall. At present there was no exchange of fire. A few amorphs moved about the enclosed area, dragging bulky objects towards a mound to the east of the fortress.

'What are those?' asked Marilyn.

Moses explained. 'Last night my men became trigger-happy. In the darkness they could see objects crawling about the enclosure – objects which they assumed were your friends. So they opened fire and switched on the lights. Then they discovered that the things they saw were not men, but elephant worms, a large number of them, which had for some reason surfaced. They switched the lights off, of course, but it was too late, the damage had been done. . . . I wonder what Hammer Dwight will try next.'

Stordahl laughed aloud in his relief. 'You're trying to outguess yourself, Moses. You know Dwight's mind as well as your own. In fact, it *is* your own.'

'I think I'm attaining some measure of individuality,' said Moses reprovingly. He chewed a fingernail worriedly, glancing across at the colonists' position on the plain.

Meanwhile, Marilyn had been examining the gross body

of an elephant worm nearby. 'I don't see any laser burns on that one,' she remarked.

'They all died,' said Moses. 'Whether they were shot or not, they died just the same.'

'Like the saucerplants,' observed Stordahl. As far as he could see, the green plain was gradually turning brown and the stink of decay was heavy. 'This disease is widespread.' He spoke to Moses. 'You're going to have to think pretty carefully about your food supplies. This affects everybody, not just the amorphs. The colonists have been using a lot of local plants to supplement our food until they can bring more land under cultivation—'

'I'm not interested in the colonists' problems!' interrupted Moses shrilly. 'It's my troops that concern me. My fort!'

Stordahl regarded the amorph carefully. The creature's personality was definitely undergoing a change; the voice was higher and less controlled, the thinking was becoming illogical; it was almost as though Moses were playing at soldiers. . . . Even his face was thinner and his physique seemed somehow shrunken.

'I'm thinking about all of us, Moses,' he said. 'It seems to me that the whole ecology of the area has become upset.'

But the amorph's attention was on the distant colonists. 'They're coming,' he said. 'Reinforcements arrived from the north, earlier on; and they're coming. Look!'

He was right. The trucks, one by one, were swinging away from their positions, moving forward in echelon, relentlessly approaching the fortress.

'To the barricades, men!' yelled Moses. 'Wipe them out, every last one! Prisoners will not be taken!'

As the amorphs leaped to their positions Moses turned to Stordahl and Marilyn, grinning broadly, ecstatically. 'It's a suicide attack. I'll let you watch this, you two. This is going to be a massacre!'

Puzzled, Stordahl watched the advancing trucks. Laser beams probed among them but they held their course, then swung south and formed into a single rank so well disciplined that from Stordahl's viewpoint only the nearest truck was visible. This carried a heavy shield against which the lasers played harmlessly. Maintaining a distance of some two hundred yards the trucks circled the fortress.

Stordahl glanced at the sky. A large area of blue was

visible on the far horizon and the sun's rays had already crept over the mountains to the east, slanting downward from behind the cloudbank, now moving across the eastern plain towards them, silvering the distant saucerplants.

Dwight had timed his move well. He intended to attack at the moment when the defenders would be dazzled by the combined effect of the low morning sun and the reflective, water-filled plants.

The trucks had halted at a position slightly north of east; the area of glittering saucerplants was spreading rapidly. Moses directed the main body of his men to the barricades on that side, while still maintaining a small force around the rest of the perimeter to guard against a surprise rush from the remaining colonists on the western plain. Then they waited for the sun to reach them. The atmosphere was tense and silent. Moses returned to the two humans, having deployed his forces.

The attack came within two minutes. Suddenly the plain was ablaze with light as the clouds broke and, shielding his eyes, Stordahl could make out the trucks heading for the barricade.

He spoke quietly to Marilyn. 'You'd better get inside.'

'No,' she said flatly.

The roar of the trucks ceased as one by one they drew up at the far side of the fortress. Lasers crackled and, silhouetted against the glare, they could see men fighting on the top of the barricade.

'Look out!' Stordahl threw Marilyn to the ground as he caught sight of an amorph, laser still clutched to his body, toppling from a crate. A pencil of light seared across the camp area and came to rest against the dome, a few feet above their heads. Molten permaplast dripped to the ground, sizzling. Seizing Marilyn's arm, Stordahl began to crawl around the far side of the dome, dragging her with him.

Moses stood above them, peering around the edge of the dome. 'We're holding them off,' he reported, shielding his eyes against the glare. 'In a way, I admire Hammer Dwight's strategy. If you must have a suicide attack, make sure to take as many of the opposition with you as possible. I've no doubt our losses will be quite heavy, before the attackers are wiped out.'

Stordahl could not agree. Despite the advantage afforded

by strong sunlight, he could not understand the tactics of sending a small group of men, who could only have had a dozen assorted guns between them, against a larger number of amorphs armed with lasers. It didn't make any sort of sense, particularly as in the certain event of the attack failing, all the weapons would be captured.

Moses enlightened him on this latter point. 'They've got no guns at all,' he gloated. 'Your men are trying to take us with knives. They don't stand a chance. . . .'

Stordahl, after making sure that the chastened Marilyn intended to stay put, joined the amorph. From the shadow afforded by the edge of the dome he could see the action more clearly. The attackers had now captured a small segment of the barricade and fierce fighting was in progress on the ground within the enclosure. The amorphs with their rifles were now at a slight disadvantage in what had become hand-to-hand engagement and the attackers, yelling hate, were fighting like maniacs. Knives rose and fell and the air was alive with the screams of death.

Moses noted the momentary setback. He took a quick glance over his shoulder. The remainder of the colonists were still in the same position on the western plain. He ran around the inside perimeter collecting his remaining men together, and assembled them beside the dome. To the east, the battle continued as fiercely as ever and the ground was littered with bodies. It seemed to Stordahl that the attackers were now in the ascendancy.

Moses spoke to his men. 'Raise your guns,' he said stonily. 'Take aim.'

Two of the attackers had broken through and were racing towards the dome, brandishing knives and yelling insanely.

'Fire!' snapped Moses.

The two men dropped to the ground, screaming, legs taken off at the knees.

'Keep firing,' commanded Moses evenly.

The laser beams played among the struggling figures, cutting down attacker and defender alike, sizzling among the bodies for an eternity of seconds until everything was still and the air was thick with drifting smoke.

'You bastard,' whispered Stordahl.

Moses regarded him brightly, a trembling smile on his lips. 'Possibly,' he said, his voice high-pitched with strain. 'But at least I know when to cut my losses. . . . Back to your positions, men. Mr. Stordahl and Mrs. Hetherington, come with me. Let us view the dead. You might find some friends among these brave men. . . .'

The stench of scorched flesh was sickening and Stordahl swallowed heavily. 'Does she have to come?' he asked.

'Of course. I wish her to savour my victory to the full.' Moses reinforced his command with a twitch of his rifle and, slowly, they began to move across the enclosure towards the two nearest dead, these being the men who had broken clear of the fighting and made for the dome. Moses rolled the first figure over with his foot.

The sightless eyes of Lever the engineer stared into the sky.

'Know him?'

'You never met him,' muttered Stordahl. 'His name's Lever. He wasn't such a bad man.'

Beside him, Marilyn was crying softly.

'How about him?' The next man lay on his back.

Stordahl stared.

'Isn't it funny,' chuckled Moses. 'You humans are a conceited race. . . . I've heard you talking about us amorphs; you say we all look the same. Now, take these two men – I wouldn't know one from the other. In death, you have as little individuality as us. . . .'

Stordahl said nothing as they left the second man and walked on.

They examined another of the attackers, and another, and Moses had suddenly fallen silent. . . .

'I don't want to see any more,' said Marilyn quietly. 'Please, don't make me see any more.'

Moses stood still, gazing at the fifth man, and again the dead face of Lever was upturned to the sky. He turned to look at Stordahl, and there were tears in his eyes. 'What's happened?' he whispered. 'What does this mean, Mr. Stordahl?'

Stordahl hesitated, filled with a great pity. 'They're . . . they're amorphs, Moses. Not one of them is human. They're Lever's desert army. They were the reinforcements you said arrived from the north. Lever may even have been training them for war, for all we know. But Hetherington commandeered them, and sent them against you.'

'Did you know anything about this?'

'No. Of course not.'

Moses surveyed the scene of battle. 'There must be a hundred dead here,' he said dully. 'And all amorphs. And I gave the order to kill them, myself. . . . I thought I was cutting my losses, but I was multiplying them. . . . Tell me, Mr. Stordahl' – his cheeks were now wet with tears – 'what sort of a mind could think up a trick like this?'

'A human mind, Moses,' replied Stordahl gently. 'And you're not quite human, yet.'

Moses regarded him for a long time, then said: 'It seems I've got something to learn. We'll go back to the dome. I'll have to speak to my people.'

They sat on the ground in the small radio room.

Stordahl spoke at last. 'That was just about the dirtiest thing I've ever come across,' he said slowly.

'Moses deliberately fired on his own men, Alex,' Marilyn reminded him. 'Don't get carried away with pity for the creature, just because Dwight pulled a fast one. He wiped out dozens of his own men just because he thought the opposition was getting the upper hand and might break through. That was pretty dirty, too. I noticed you weren't too pleased about it at the time.'

Stordahl sighed. 'Maybe you're right. I suppose I could say that two wrongs don't make a right, but I can't deny that there's a certain satisfaction in seeing a nut like Moses get what he deserves. Maybe I've got the wrong attitude towards these amorphs. I've known them in the colony, I've worked with them, and I've liked them. We've all liked them, because they tend to represent the best of human characteristics. But then this wierd business of the egotists started – not just your husband's team, but Briggs and Lever as well – and the whole relationship got fouled up. We can't blame anyone but ourselves, because we created them. And now we've persuaded over a hundred of them to kill one another.'

'It's tough,' agreed Marilyn. 'But there's nothing we can do. The matter's in other hands, just like any war. . . .' She paused, attentive. 'Did you notice something then? A sort of tremor, as though something heavy was being dropped?'

'No . . . I expect Moses is reinforcing his battlements. I wonder what he's told his people, as he calls them. He seemed in a strange mood.'

'Maybe he's suggesting they surrender.'

'Could be. Their morale will be low after this. And they haven't eaten since last night, and there's no food around here. If they send out a foraging party the colonists will move in with trucks and mow them down.'

Marilyn thought. 'Wait a moment. The amorphs have got the trucks that Lever's army used for their attack.'

Stordahl laughed shortly. 'Dwight will have foreseen that. It was a suicide attack. Those trucks would have just enough fuel to reach the walls, and no more. Didn't you notice the noise they made? They were operating on the auxiliary diesel engines. The piles would have been taken out.'

'Of course. . . . Look, Alex. Are you sure you don't notice something funny? This place seems to be shaking. I can feel the ground moving.'

Stordahl placed his palms to the ground and felt around. 'You're right,' he said slowly. 'And look at that, over there. What the hell's happening?'

They watched a patch of ground near the door where the decaying saucerplants were heaving and shuddering in a peculiar fashion. And as they watched, a large area of soil lifted and cracked apart, falling aside, revealing a pulsating whiteness beneath the surface which grew, pushing aside more soil. Huge and fleshy, a vast bulk was heaving itself to the surface.

'An elephant worm!' observed Marilyn in horrified disgust.

Stordahl watched the creature, now completely clear of its hole, subside on the soil, obviously dying.

'Marilyn,' he said quietly, 'it's possible that Moses may kill us in retaliation once he's finished addressing his people, do you realize that? He's not entirely sane; and if a mob of amorphs is anything like a mob of humans, I don't give much for our chances.'

'I know. I just don't want to think about it, please, Alex.' The girl tried to smile. 'Otherwise I might find myself asking you to perform some last service for me, and have you go all moral again. I know it looks bad. I don't need you to tell me. But there's nothing we can do about it.'

'There could be.' Stordahl was on his feet. 'If you're willing to try it, we could see where this hole goes. . . .'

FIFTEEN

After a brief discussion Stordahl lowered himself head-first into the hole which descended at an angle of some forty-five degrees. After he had crawled about eight feet the tunnel levelled out and he paused until a tap on his foot announced that Marilyn was following.

It hadn't been easy to persuade Marilyn to try the tunnel. She was a girl accustomed to luxury; indeed, Stordahl suspected that this was the first time she had got her hands dirty since she was a child. However, recent happenings had contrived to remind her that all was not Dior and Vegan supersilk, her clothes were filthy already, and she reluctantly agreed.

Stordahl inched his way along the tunnel. The going was difficult and the soil wet and muddy. The tunnel was an almost perfect cylinder some two feet six in diameter, giving little room for manoeuvring. A few roots trailed from the roof and the stink of decay which pervaded the dome was noticeable here, too. As he crawled, he tried not to dwell on the thought that sooner or later he would find the tunnel blocked by a dead elephant worm which had been unable to reach the surface. He was by no means certain how he would deal with that problem. He wondered, briefly, why the worms had made for the open air before dying, then his thoughts returned to Marilyn again. . . .

Since his youth, Stordahl had never considered himself a ladies' man; indeed sex as such, though enjoyable, had never interested him overmuch. He had married early and remained comfortably if boringly in love with Mary until her tragic death; the boring aspect of their relationship being typified by his single extramarital affair some six Standard years ago. That affair had taught him a lesson. The girl had been young and pretty – he still recalled her face vividly – and he had been thrown into her company while waiting for Mary to arrive on the planet with the main body of colonists. One night, after a few drinks, they had found themselves making love.

To a more worldly man than Stordahl this would have constituted a one-night stand as fleeting as the bubbles in the following morning's bromo; but Stordahl was not that type. Mary was not due for six Standard weeks and the affair continued for just that period of time. . . . Stordahl was hooked because, to him, the act of making love was inseparable from love itself. The pretty biologist left on the same ship which brought Mary and for weeks Stordahl underwent the deepest misery until the passage of time and the continued presence of his wife gradually brought him back to normal. He often wondered if Mary had suspected anything during that period; he was aware that his lovemaking had lacked the spark of inspiration. . . . Eventually he realized that love affairs were not for him; they were not worth the emotional involvement which the initial, casual sex invariably caused.

Three or four years later he had said to Mary, in a moment of unexpected frankness: 'I love you, you know.' They had had a wonderful day on Earth, taking Alice around the Galactic Zoo. Alice, then four, had enjoyed everything she saw, and Stordahl felt very close to his family. 'You do believe that, don't you?' he asked Mary as they prepared for bed and Alice slept in the next room.

She regarded him, her head slightly on one side in that attitude of mild disbelief he remembered so well. 'I think you're quite fond of me,' she said, smiling, 'and that's enough for me, dear. We've been married quite a while and I think I'm very lucky. I've enjoyed all of it, every day.'

He shivered in the damp tunnel as he remembered that conversation and its oddly prophetic ring. He had said, smiling also: 'Damn it, Mary, don't you think I'm capable of love?'

'Oh, yes,' she had replied. 'You love your daughter. It always makes me want to laugh when you meet us after you've been away for a few days. Your eyes go straight to her and you grab her and kiss her. Then afterwards you notice I'm there as well. So you kiss me as well, and you look guilty. This afternoon while Alice was looking at the animals, you were watching her all the time with a sort of stupid fatherly grin on your face. Don't get me wrong, dear. I like it that way. I think it's nice.'

There was no jealousy in Mary. Mary and Alice . . . and now, Marilyn.

What was Marilyn's attitude towards him, now? She

seemed to have thawed somewhat after her coolness earlier in the day. He had to admit he had brought that coolness on himself. No girl likes to be made to feel like a whore.

Her muffled voice reached him. 'Hey, Alex! Wait a moment. I can't keep up. I keep sliding about in all this animal muck.'

He paused.

'It's mud,' he corrected her, calling back over his shoulder. 'It's soil mixed with water, which constitutes mud.'

'Oh, my God,' he heard her mutter. 'He's so damned pure he doesn't even know muck when he's wallowing in it. . . .' She raised her voice. 'Are you denying that elephant worms have natural functions? Can't you smell it?'

'It's the decay. This disease thing. . . . Are you ready to move on?' asked Stordahl.

'With pleasure.'

As they resumed their progress, Stordahl wondered at the girl's spirits. Their situation was dangerous, he had already lost his sense of direction and Marilyn must be aware of this, yet she was accepting the situation phlegmatically, without any of the miserable whining he had expected. His respect for her increased.

A light showed; a dim glowing disc in the distance.

'No talking,' called Stordahl. 'There's a shaft ahead. There may be amorphs above it.'

Soon he could see the soil of the tunnel walls, smoothed by the passage of elephant worms. Twisting around, he hauled himself up the shaft and, eyes narrowed against the glare, lifted his head cautiously above ground level.

They were still below the enclosure. He could see the dome; at the entrance were grouped the amorphs and he saw Moses addressing them, but was too far away to catch the words. He turned to get his bearings.

He saw boots, trousers. An amorph was standing beside the hole.

He withdrew abruptly, almost falling on Marilyn, who was lying at the foot of the shaft, looking up.

'What's the matter?'

'There's an amorph up there,' he whispered back. 'He didn't see me. He was facing the other way. One of the guards at the perimeter. We're not quite outside, yet.'

'Oh, God. So we have to go on, do we? I was enjoying the fresh air.'

'It seems we're going in the right direction, anyway. Come on.' He began to crawl again.

Soon the tunnel began to branch in all directions and Stordahl had constantly to make decisions as to their correct course. *At least*, he thought, *if we do come across a blockage, there are plenty of alternatives.* He wondered about the habits of the elephant worms; whether they lived a communal existence. It was unlikely that all these tunnels were the work of the single worm they had seen in the radio room. On the other hand, there were not nearly enough interconnecting tunnels to account for the large numbers of dead worms they had seen on the surface. Another thought occurred: suppose they met a live worm, coming towards them and filling the entire tunnel. . . . He tried not to think about that one.

He paused at another shaft, looked out, and found that they were heading west, towards the colonists' trucks. Turning around he saw the fortress, heads in evidence among the piled crates, laser rifles poking through the gaps. . . . He withdrew and they went on.

For some time now there had been no branches off the route they were following and Stordahl began to wonder what he should do if the tunnel doubled back. Would it be possible to dig their way through to the surface? As he was pondering this, the glow of daylight showed ahead once more.

This time the entire tunnel sloped upwards terminating at the disc of grey sky. This was the end of the road. He looked out; they were at least fifty yards from the trucks and in full view of Moses's amorphs with their laser rifles. . . . At least, he amended that, not quite in full view. Between the tunnel exit and the fortress was a huge dead worm, about two yards away. It might be possible to signal to the colonists from the cover of that worm.

'What are we going to do?' asked Marilyn. 'Run for it?' She was lying immediately beside him; the hole widened at this point and she was just able to see the nearby trucks.

'We'll have to. Unless we can make them see us.'

'Wait a moment.' She spoke quickly as Stordahl was about to wave. 'Back down the tunnel a bit.' She began to withdraw downwards, dragging him with her.

'What do you want?'

They were pressed tightly together in the confined space; Marilyn moved her body against him.

'For God's sake!' exploded Stordahl. 'Can't you pick a better time?'

'This may be the only time,' she said quietly. 'And I can't think of a better one. I'm all covered in mud and so are you, and I want to find out whether the things you said to me last night were true. You remember,' she went on ruthlessly, 'you said you loved me, and I almost believed you because I thought you wouldn't say a thing like that unless you meant it. And I've spent my life being lusted after and never being loved. If you can love me in this condition and in this place, it just might mean that you really love me.'

'Marilyn . . .' said Stordahl helplessly. Then he laughed with surprised, uncomplicated delight as he put his arms around her.

Later they had to face reality. They waved and shouted, and at last a surprised face was looking at them from a truck. There was a pause during which they could imagine the amazed conference going on; every now and then a face would pop up from behind a vehicle and regard them incredulously. Soon a truck moved away from the end of the line and pulled up between them and the amorphs.

'Run for it!' shouted the driver, himself protected by a small temporary shield. 'I'll follow behind.'

They sprinted over the short distance to the accompaniment of a chorus of cheers and whistles from the watching colonists and arrived panting behind the trucks where a group of tents had been set up. The first person they saw was Hetherington himself, wheeling rapidly towards them, his face livid.

'Just what the hell have you two been up to?' he yelled. 'Come with me.'

They followed him into a tent where a collapsible table and chairs had been set up. Briggs was there, and Hammond Dwight, and Lever. Hetherington dismissed them curtly.

Now,' he said grimly. 'What's been happening?'

Marilyn eyed him coolly. 'We've escaped from the amorphs,' she said. 'Aren't you glad about that, J.?'

'Glad?' he snarled. 'I'd rather you'd stayed there than

show up in this condition.' He surveyed her tattered, filthy clothes with disgust. 'You've made me a laughing stock. It's obvious what you and Stordahl were doing while the rest of us were fighting for our lives. Stordahl's career's finished, anyway. I'll decide later what to do about you, young lady. I'll tell you this: you'll get no alimony out of me.' The tycoon had worked himself up into a dangerous fury; little spurts of spittle spat from his lips with each word and his foot beat a tattoo on the trigger mechanism of his wheelchair.

'Aren't you assuming a little too much?' asked Marilyn quietly.

'Assuming? Assuming? I don't need to assume anything. I know! You two bastards cooped up together, it was bound to happen.'

Hetherington swung his chair abruptly to afford Stordahl a point-blank view down the barrels. 'What have you got to say about this? You've been keeping pretty quiet, I notice,' he spat out, 'sheltering behind your girl-friend.'

Stordahl had been listening with mounting impatience to the exchanges. It seemed to him incredible that Hetherington could take this attitude. There was no sign of relief that Marilyn was unharmed, merely a tirade of futile rantings which was gettting them nowhere. There were things to be done. A meeting had to be called and tactics discussed in view of the information which he and the girl had obtained.

'Drop it,' he said wearily. 'Let's talk about something that matters, like the amorphs.'

'Not so fast, Mr. Stordahl.' Hetherington, abruptly, was in control of himself. His tone was smooth and dangerous. 'Nobody makes a sucker out of me, Mr. Stordahl. Just answer me one question. This woman here, my wife. You've been alone with her for a while. Do you find her attractive?'

Ignoring Marilyn's warning glance, Stordahl said: 'Yes.' A mood of recklessness had taken him; if Hetherington wanted to play this farce out, then it would be done. Personally, all he wanted was a bath, a good meal, and a night's sleep. His head was spinning with exhaustion. 'I could do with a drink,' he said. 'And I'm sure your wife could.'

'In due course. Now.' The tycoon leaned forward in his chair. 'Would you go so far as to say, Mr. Stordahl, that you are in love with my wife?'

Then Stordahl was goaded into uttering the words which he was to regret the rest of his life.

'I think perhaps I would go that far, Mr. Hetherington.'

Many times afterwards he thought of that moment and tried to understand what had caused him to behave with such unbelievable stupidity. He tried to think further, to analyse his emotions immediately before he spoke; but this was impossible too; emotions are a thing of the moment and appertain solely to that moment. He thought he had known fury, hate, a quixotic desire not to deny Marilyn, many emotions. It is impossible accurately to imagine an emotion again, because the situation has changed and feelings are different.

One thing he knew, afterwards. If you tell your boss you love his wife, then your future prospects in your job are slight, and your future prospects of the girl are nil. . . . Stordahl knew that, afterwards. He had known that before, too. So why didn't he know it at the fateful, fatal moment?

Hetherington was smiling easily now, totally calm and self-possessed. 'Go and get the others, you two,' he said pleasantly. 'We must hold a conference to discuss our future strategy concerning the amorphs.'

As they left the tent Marilyn said: 'You damned fool, Alex. Oh, you damned, stupid fool. . . .'

Her face was cold white behind the filth and she trembled uncontrollably.

Stordahl addressed the small group with Hetherington smiling at him blandly as though the preceding discussion had never occurred. He told them of the events in the amorphs' fortress, of the sickness which troubled the creatures, described the dying vegetation and elephant worms – which the colonists had observed themselves; the disease was becoming increasingly widespread although it had not yet reached the town of Alice – and dwelt upon the apparent degeneration of Moses.

'Moses is mentally sick,' he told them. 'It's not merely exhaustion and lack of food. He's unable to stand up to the strain of things going wrong. He lacks experience while at the same time he is convinced he is omnipotent. The conflict is, well, simply too much for him. He can't understand how any event can be beyond his control. Added to which, I think he was affected personally by Mrs. Hetherington and myself. His present form and mentality has been of short duration, not long enough, I should say, to have become fixed permanently. We influenced him with our Te factors.' Stordahl hesitated. 'I happen to know that my Te is a five-year-old child. Towards the end, Moses was displaying juvenile characteristics. . . .'

'That could be dangerous.' This opinion came from Santana. 'When he realizes that he stands no chance of winning this private war of his, it might occur to him to destroy all the equipment, out of spite.'

'There's no way he can win,' put in Hammond Dwight. 'No way at all. After our attack, I imagine his force consists mainly of women. Is that so, Stordahl?'

'That's right. And they're critically short of food. If we wait here for a while, we'll starve them out.'

Hetherington said: 'I'm not sure I want to wait that long.'

'What else can we do?'

'I'll tell you what I propose in a minute. Meanwhile – Briggs. You've been doing some work on this plant disease. Have you come up with anything?'

'I'm short of equipment out here,' protested the biologist. 'I've examined the plants and worms, of course, but there's so little to go on. . . . All I can say is that the saucer-plants seem to be dying naturally. There's no sign of a virus such as we know it. The plants around here seem to be just dying, as though they were uprooted. Maybe when I get back to the lab I'll be able to tell you more.'

Lever spoke up. 'If it spreads to the Wilton lichen we're in big trouble. Right now, everything's fine. The lichen's taken well and working conditions up at the site are tolerable. But if the lichen dies we might as well pack up and go. There's no way we can work the ore under the conditions we had a few months ago.'

'So there's no need for you to recruit another private army,' put in Hetherington slyly. 'If conditions at the site are suitable for humans.'

Lever flushed. 'You were glad of my amorphs today, Mr. Hetherington.'

'Very sensible of you to make them available,' remarked the tycoon ambiguously. 'I'm sorry they all got killed, but it was in a good cause. Admiral Dwight must take a lot of credit for the idea.'

Stordahl was about to voice his opinion of Dwight's

strategy but Marilyn, standing behind Hetherington, shook her head warningly.

'You were about to say something, Mr. Stordahl?'

'No . . . I was just wondering what our next step ought to be.'

'Of course.' Hetherington smiled. 'Well, Mr. Stordahl, I've given the matter some thought. Taking into account the information you've obtained, it seems unwise to allow the amorphs to remain in possession of our equipment for any longer than necessary. In another day, as Mr. Santana suggested, they might take it into their heads to destroy the lot. So we must act now, before sundown. We will attempt to talk to Moses, and make him see reason. Otherwise, at dawn tomorrow, we bring the ship's tender over and warm them up with the exhaust. Not so fiercely as to damage our equipment, although we may lose the dome. But just enough to reduce every amorph in that damned fort to a little heap of ash.'

'I'm not sure we'll be able to make Moses see reason. He's developed a sort of racial pride. I can't imagine him surrendering, just like that.'

'I'm sure you'll find a way, Mr. Stordahl.'

'Me?'

'You will leave for the amorphs' camp in ten minutes. You will carry a white flag; I imagine they'll understand the significance of that. You will use your influence over Moses to persuade him to surrender, and if you find he is reluctant, you will threaten him with the ship's tender. Oh, and you will take my wife with you. She has some influence over Moses, too. . . .'

SIXTEEN

Stordahl and Marilyn walked slowly across no-man's land under the dubious protection of a white flag.

Stordahl waved the flag from side to side as he walked and hoped that Moses would understand the signal. Marilyn, beside him, was aware of nervous shivers running down her back; she was unable to decide whether the greatest danger came from the front or the rear.

'J. thinks Moses might kill us,' she said unnecessarily.

'I know.'

They were nearing the barricades and the amorphs were looking down at them, covering them with rifles. Also standing on the crates was Moses; his gaze kept shifting from the advancing pair to the colonists in the distance; there was bewilderment on his face.

Marilyn called out: 'Moses! Don't let your people expose themselves! Stay behind the crates. We're coming over for a talk.' To Stordahl she said: 'Don't want our colonists to be tempted by a concentration of amorphs. Quite a few of them are stupid enough to open fire if the order was given. And I know two men dangerous enough to give that order. . . .'

Stordahl didn't reply, feeling that Marilyn was possibly overdramatizing the situation.

Hands reached down cautiously and they were assisted over the barricade. Once in the enclosure, Stordahl addressed Moses. 'We've got to have a talk with you,' he said. 'It might be that something can be worked out.'

Moses' face was gaunt and tired. 'Yes,' he said simply. 'Come with me.' As they walked to the dome Stordahl noticed that many of the guards were female amorphs.

They entered the dome. The ground was littered with filth and sick amorphs and the stink was overpowering. Without a glance at his suffering people Moses led the way to the radio room and closed the door behind them. 'I've made some pretty bold statements to my people over the past few days,' he said quietly. 'I wouldn't like them to hear me selling them out.'

The stench in the radio room was not so bad as outside,

although in the corner the dead elephant worm was decomposing rapidly.

'I don't want you to think you're selling them out,' said Stordahl. 'All I'm saying is that we work out some sort of compromise.'

Moses almost smiled. 'You're a diplomat, Mr. Stordahl. Throughout history the man with the upper hand has used such words. No, I won't deceive myself, or you; there's no point. Our position here is impossible. My people are sick and hungry.'

'So why haven't you surrendered already?'

'I think I would have, in a few hours. . . . But I was hoping we might have a discussion of terms first, merely as a sop to my people's pride, you understand.'

'I understand. . . .' Stordahl eyed the amorph curiously. The earlier signs of insanity had vanished; he seemed to be dealing with an eminently sensible person. 'What's happened to you, Moses?' he asked. 'A few hours ago you wouldn't have considered surrender. I must admit, I got the impression you were. . . .' He searched for the right words.

'An insane megalomaniac, perhaps?' suggested Moses.

'Shall we say a ruthless leader.'

Moses sighed. 'Don't you realize, I am what you make me? I am unable to control my own character, and for most of my intelligent life I've been exposed to a set of powerful intellects any of which would stop at nothing to gain its own ends. So I acted in accordance with my character – I had no option. Have you? I had been taught that things could never go wrong for me; I was a supreme being of unlimited intelligence. However, things went wrong; and when they did, I was conscious of a conflict within me.' He smiled wryly. 'So, after a period of bewilderment, I decided that I had been taught incorrectly. . . .

'Going back to basics, I deduced that I was failing to relate to my environment. I was misinterpreting events and I was not communicating with my people. So, simply, I got together with them and we communicated. And very soon I realized that I had made the worst mistake of all. I had considered myself a being apart from my fellows. Because their views were entirely different from mine, yet they were right and I was wrong.'

'Your people are idealistic,' Marilyn said. 'They represent the best in all of us.'

'I had been confusing goodness with weakness,' said Moses. 'I thought I was strong and they were weak, whereas in fact I was bad and they were good.' He eyed Stordahl shrewdly. It's an easy mistake for an insane megalomaniac to make, don't you think? You see, they obeyed me without question, so it never occurred to me that they might not hold my views.'

Stordahl thought of Hetherington, and Dwight . . . yes, especially Dwight. . . . 'But now you've changed your views,' he said.

'No, you still can't quite conceive it, can you? I've changed – myself. I've . . . blended with my people and absorbed their characteristics. I'm still Moses,' he chuckled grimly, 'still with the memories and knowledge of Dwight, Sokalski, and the rest; but my personality has been diluted. I've shared that with my people. They've absorbed a little of me – and fortunately there are a good number of them. But . . . I don't think you'll find them so tractable in the future.'

'Still going to be useful members of the community, do you think?' asked Stordahl lightly.

There was pathos in Moses's eagerness. 'You'll take us back?'

'Hetherington has authorized me to say so.'

At the mention of Hetherington Moses looked doubtful. 'What are the terms?'

Stordahl took a deep breath. He was not happy about the terms. 'We'll provide food and shelter, in return for which your people will do such work as required without pay. Once the factory is complete and operational, you will be allowed to became full citizens with all the rights that entails.'

'Something under two years' slavery, then freedom,' said Moses thoughtfully. 'I suppose it's as much as we can expect. The alternative is starvation, of course.'

'That's true, I'm afraid. This disease is so widespread that you could never reach healthy ground from here. And Hetherington wouldn't help you. . . .'

Moses bent down and picked a piece of saucerplant, crumbling it brown between his fingers.

He sighed. 'I shall accept your terms.'

By the time the amorphs had walked the intervening distance to the colonists' temporary camp, Hetherington had recovered from his surprise.

'Ah, Stordahl,' he said. 'I see they've capitulated.' He addressed Moses. 'You, Sonny. I'm glad you've seen some sense. I could say you should have known better than to take us on, but I won't labour the point. Now, you and your friends can start walking back to the colony.'

'They haven't had anything to eat,' Stordahl pointed out.

'Now, isn't that just too bad. However, they chose to walk here, so they can damned well walk back. We'll set up a field kitchen at the colony so they can feed when they arrive.'

'J.!' cried Marilyn. 'Look at them! They're sick and weak! A lot of them won't make it!'

Hetherington eyed her coldly. 'Shut up. Dwight. . . .' He beckoned the admiral, who bent over his chair. 'This way we'll weed out the weaker ones,' he whispered loudly, 'and we'll save on food, too. Clever, don't you think? Natural selection with fringe benefits!' He chuckled. The admiral grinned. Lever smiled broadly.

Only Briggs looked concerned. 'We need them all,' he protested. 'It's a matter of economics, Mr. Hetherington.'

'Mr. Briggs,' said the tycoon ominously, 'I aim to teach these people a lesson. They've caused me a lot of trouble and wasted the time and money of the organization. They'll walk.' He swung his chair to confront the amorph. 'Get going, Sonny. The sooner you reach the colony, the sooner you eat. Now, that's what I call incentive!'

By the time the colonists had struck their tents and loaded them on to the half-tracks from Lever's desert site, the amorphs were out of sight. The convoy set off in the direction of the colony, leaving a small party behind to refuel the original vehicles around Moses's fortress, and to check over the steelworks equipment.

Stordahl rode a half-track with Briggs.

'You've upset the Old Man,' stated Briggs.

'I know.'

'He's a mean man to get on the wrong side of.'

'Too bad,' replied Stordahl briefly, scanning the ground for any amorphs who had been unable to continue the journey.

Briggs guessed his thoughts. 'If we come across a sick amorph, I'd rather not stop,' he said firmly. 'There's been enough unpleasantness already. I want to keep my nose clean, if you don't mind.'

The convoy rolled past a couple of huddled forms.

'They brought it on themselves,' Briggs observed.

'Christ, man!' exploded Stordahl. 'They brought nothing on themselves. We gave them every thought they have. They couldn't help what they did. They acted according to the characteristics they inherited from us!'

Briggs chuckled ruefully. 'True, Stordahl. But do you know what Santana would say to that? He'd say we can't help ourselves either, because we act in accordance with the characteristics we've inherited from our forebears and our environment.'

'OK, so it's nobody's fault. Nothing's anybody's fault. . . . My God, Briggs, if I really thought you were right, I'd shoot myself!'

Briggs was silent for a moment as they passed another body lying face-down in the rotting vegetation. At last he said, with unaccustomed kindliness: 'You're an idealist, Alex, and there's no place for you in a commercial enterprise like this. I'd like you to observe events during the next few days and think of what I've said. Just notice who wins out, and who falls by the wayside. We're going to have a period of crisis, and you'll notice an inevitable pattern. . . .'

Stordahl watched grimly as they passed the main body of the amorphs, trudging westward with downcast eyes, some being supported by their colleagues. Moses was in the lead; he did not look up as they passed.

Later they reached the colony and the convoy drew up among the domes. A number of colonists, mostly women, were there to greet them. Joan approached Stordahl as he climbed from the half-track.

'What's happening, Alex?' she asked anxiously.

'Oh. . . .' He had difficulty in meeting her eyes. 'The amorphs are coming back, those who are left. They're walking. They'll be here soon.'

Hetherington had been lifted down from his specially-constructed truck. He wheeled across to them, accompanied by Marilyn. 'Get the field kitchen organized for your friends, Stordahl,' he ordered. 'I have a feeling that you'll be getting to know them even better, in the future.'

He rolled away and Stordahl watched him go, Marilyn walking beside the chair. He hoped she would turn and look at him, but she didn't; and soon they had disappeared around a dome.

Joan was watching him. 'What's happened?' she asked quietly.

Stordahl's chest felt heavy and sick. 'I'm in the Old Man's black book.' He tried to say it lightly, but failed to deceive her. She continued to regard him with concern.

'Why?' she asked. Then her expression changed and she glanced in the direction Hetherington had taken. 'It's not . . . it's not something to do with Marilyn, is it?' she asked.

'Of course not,' he said too loudly. 'It's just that he . . . wasn't too happy with the way I handled the situation with the amorphs.'

She looked at him for a long time. 'I see,' she said slowly. 'Well, you'd better get the kitchen organized, like he said. Later this evening. . . . She hesitated. 'If you feel . . . if you might want to come and talk things over, I'd . . . I'd be very pleased for you to come to my place for a drink. Often it's better, if you talk things over with someone,' she added in a small voice.

'Thanks,' said Stordahl dully, moving away and leaving her standing there, watching him go.

Hetherington sat in the sparsely furnished room alone apart from two expressionless bodyguards. *And they don't really count,* thought Stordhal. *This is between the Old Man and me, and I don't intend to settle the matter by brute force. . . . In fact I won't get the chance to settle anything; the boss will do that for me. Hetherington is not the man to discuss a matter. If he allows the appearance of a discussion to develop, it's only because he's already made up his mind. . . .*

'Ah, Mr. Stordahl. . . .'

The tycoon's expression was bland and he glanced at one of the pugs with a faint smile as though bringing him into some unspoken joke, some joke between Hetherington and the powerful moron, thereby implying that Stordahl was held in less regard than even the least intelligent man in the room.

'You wanted to see me, Mr. Hetherington?' Stordahl's mind was carried back thirty years: the headmaster's study, the smooth voice: 'What have you got to say for yourself, Stordahl? I don't like your attitude, Stordahl. Bend over this chair and accept your punishment like a man, Stordahl. . . .'

'That was why I sent for you, Mr. Stordahl. I think it's unnecessary for me to go into details as to the various ways in which you've fallen short of requirements in your duties as Supervisor of the colony. Is it?'

Stordahl swallowed and tried to keep his voice level. 'If I've given cause for dissatisfaction, I'd like to know how.'

'That is your right, Mr. Stordahl.'

'Well?'

Hetherington sighed as if disappointed. 'It's very difficult. If you can't see your own faults, then I stand little chance of pointing them out to you. However . . . I consider, for one thing, that your attitude towards the amorphs and the employees of the organization is not what I would expect from a Supervisor. To me, it seems you behave more like a union man, forever championing the bleating complaints of the workers against the judgment of their betters. That simply will not do, Mr. Stordahl.'

'That's not true!' Stordahl burst out, forgetting his resolution to stay calm. 'I don't know where you got that idea from, but it's a lie. I've always done my best for the organization.'

'Your best isn't good enough, I'm afraid. You're an emotional man, and I regret that emotions are out of place when trying to forge new frontiers.'

'Forge new frontiers?' Stordahl laughed harshly. 'Turn a profit, you mean. You can save the vivid stuff for your speeches, Hetherington. It cuts no ice with me.'

Hetherington's expression had become dangerous. 'You're a born loser. I should have realized that when I took you on. You've lost right now. So has your friend Moses. . . .' Unconsciously he sat straighter in his chair, unconsciously he paraphrased Briggs. 'Look around you, Stordahl, and see the sort of man who wins out. Meanwhile' – his voice took on an official tone – 'I regret that I must relieve you of your post, as of now.'

'Fire me, you mean?'

'Not exactly. I have a responsibility to you. I brought you

here, remember? And you have a responsibility to me, to repay in part at least the investment I made in you. You will continue to work at reduced pay as Assistant Supervisor until the ship leaves. Then, you have a choice. You can leave with the ship for Earth, or you can stay on here without pay. Either way, you quit the organization on the day the ship goes. You have the best part of a month to decide. I think that's fair.'

'I see. . . .' The showdown had run its course; the results were much as Stordahl had expected. 'Might I ask who is to replace me?' he inquired.

'I had been thinking of Mr. Lever. He's a competent man.'

So that was how Hetherington had persuaded Lever to throw his amorphs into the battle at the steelworks site. The promise of promotion. 'Very competent,' said Stordahl, sarcastically, turning to go.

'Wait a moment.' The ominously jocular note was back in Hetherington's voice. 'You haven't heard what your duties are to be. We're working men, Mr. Stordahl, building a new life.'

'What do you want me to do?'

'I have a task which will be to your liking, bearing in mind your friendship for the amorphs and your desire to build for the future . . . and my desire to see as little of you as possible. . . . You will take your friend Moses and the other amorphs – only the ones who walked out on us, you understand – and you will go to the delta. There, you will recommence cultivation of the super-rice paddy-fields which, I understand, failed some months ago.'

'And if I refuse?'

'You can't. Now, Mr. Stordahl. Get out of my sight and take those damned amorphs with you.'

The bodyguards grinned at him as he left.

SEVENTEEN

Joan said: 'It could be worse, Alex. If you stay on when the ship leaves, there's plenty you can do and you'll enjoy it all the more, being free of the organization. Then, in due course when the plant is in operation and we're more independent, I rather think you'll find you've taken over as leader of the colony again.'

It was dark outside. They sat talking by the light of a single lamp in Joan's small cabin; and she was strangely, selfishly happy now, with that chair occupied by the real Stordahl; that chair which for so many months had been used by a fake. . . . The fake was dead now, killed in the fight at the steelworks site. Joan would not repeat the experiment.

In his present mood Stordahl was not able to see so far ahead as Joan. His problems were immediate. 'I'm not sure that I'm going to stay,' he said slowly. 'I'm all washed up here. There's so many things I don't agree with. . . . It was bad enough using the amorphs as unpaid help, but now . . . Christ, we're using them in the paddy-fields because it's too dangerous for humans! What sort of a deal is that?'

'Just history repeating itself, my dear. We've always exposed subject creatures to dangers we can't face ourselves. There have been slaves before on Earth doing our dirty work for us. The first living things we sent into space were mice and dogs and apes. It's always been the way. In time, the amorphs will get their rights. But they'll need somebody like you around to fight for them. You can't run out on them now.'

Stordahl sipped his drink moodily, gazing at the flickering lamp.

The following morning he suffered the embarrassment of having to ask Lever's permission to requisition trucks and trailers for the trek to the delta; the new Supervisor signed the necessary authorization hurriedly, no doubt feeling as awkward as Stordahl himself. The amorphs were assembled and the trucks packed with a month's supplies.

All the time he was organizing the loading, Stordahl found himself looking around for Marilyn, but she did not appear. By midday everything was prepared and the trucks were ready to roll. Briggs and Santana walked over and said a few clumsy words of farewell and Joan kissed him hastily on the cheek. The trucks were activated and the convoy moved off, watched by the colonists. A few people waved, but Stordahl had the impression that the majority were not particularly interested. As they left the boundaries of the city he suddenly felt very much alone.

Moses sat beside him; the amorph, sensing his desolation, commenced to talk quietly. 'I think perhaps you're taking this too hard, Mr. Stordahl. I am aware that you are not at present popular with Mr. Hetherington and that you look on this task as a form of exile. But things will change. You're a useful man and Mr. Hetherington merely wants to teach you a lesson. When we get back with our mission successfully accomplished, he will think differently of you.'

Stordahl regarded the pedantically-spoken amorph. The creature's personality appeared now to have undergone total transformation; while no doubt still retaining his memories and vast knowledge, Moses had shared out his less pleasing characteristics among his fellows. *Now*, thought Stordahl, *we have the type of creature Hetherington should have aimed at in his damned experiment. . . .* He wondered how the tycoon's latest project was progressing.

'OK, Moses,' he said. 'So I'm worried about my position. But I'm scared stiff about yours. We've tried to farm the delta before, and been forced to abandon it. It's dangerous. Men were killed. Hetherington isn't just sending you there as a punishment, or to get you out of the way; there's more to it than that. He hopes that very few of you will come back.'

'Does he?' said Moses softly. 'Now, that's very interesting. It proves how little our Mr. Hetherington knows about the amorph. He is due for a disappointment.'

'What do you mean?'

The amorph smiled enigmatically. 'You'll find out, Mr. Stordahl. Have no fear, we shall all be coming back. And when we do, it will be in such circumstances that even Mr. Hetherington will be powerless. . . .'

The hair prickled at the back of Stordahl's scalp. Moses's eyes had taken on a sublime, almost visionary expression. 'What are you going to do?' he asked uneasily.

'Oh, no; it's not what we're going to do . . . the train of

events has already been set in motion. It is inevitable; it was inevitable from the start, from the first moment an amorph took human form.' Moses smiled at Stordahl's nervous expression. 'We're not going to take over, or anything so crude as that. Indeed, we ourselves have no control over what will happen. . . .'

'For God's sake, Moses, tell me what's going on!'

'There's really no point. I'll remind you, however, that we are creatures whose mentality has a high emotional content. And we shall soon have the ability to play on your people's emotions in a way which you might well find irresistible. You humans are basically frightened little people, Mr. Stordahl; all of you are frightened, even Mr. Hetherington. . . .'

Stordahl was silent as the convoy of trucks trundled south-east and the wheels splashed through decaying, putrid vegetation.

The delta camp was very much as Stordahl remembered it. The huts were still there, dilapidated but standing, although here and there the supporting piles looked in need of renewal. The paddy-field dykes had disappeared, however; the tide was out and the only sign of the weeks of labour were a few traces of low mudbanks retaining puddles of brown water.

The disease had not yet touched the Marilyn mangroves. Gnarled roots still supported the branching boles and the cup-shaped leaves were green and healthy. A few small lizards darted among the roots and the wet silt glistened ochre.

'So this is the site of your colony's first failure,' observed Moses. 'What went wrong?'

'You don't know? There's a small fish that lives in the tidal waters, similar to the Terrestrial piranha. We'll be seeing them in due course.'

'And we will deal with them,' said Moses confidently.

'How can you be so sure?' Stordahl was obscurely irritated. 'I tell you these things are dangerous. They invaded the paddy-fields and we couldn't keep them out. Lives were lost.'

'No matter. . . . Now, perhaps we ought to get the accommodation sorted out. We're going to be a little cramped until more huts are built.'

So saying, Moses took charge. Stordahl could only stand and watch in admiration at the efficiency of amorph labour. There were eighty-six amorphs in the party, of which fifty were female; Moses divided these into four teams and each team worked as one man, selecting suitable trees, felling them, cutting them to length and positioning them, all the while working in clinging mud which sometimes reached their knees. By nightfall four additional huts had been erected and the three original huts repaired. Sleeping bags were issued and lamps hung from the rough ceilings.

'Light attracts the piranavas,' Stordahl objected.

'That's all taken care of,' Moses reassured him.

'The tide will be coming in soon.' Stordahl was unconvinced. From the vantage point of the hut he could see over the tops of the mangroves; in the failing light the distant silt was silvered as the sea crept towards them. 'Where are the rest of your people?' he asked suddenly.

'They will be guarding us. Trust me, Mr. Stordahl. Tomorrow we start rebuilding the dykes.'

Much later Stordahl fell into an uneasy sleep as the first fringe of the incoming tide lapped at the piles beneath.

He was awakened after a short time when the floor of the hut trembled as though a heavy object had collided with the supporting piles. Still dazed with sleep he struggled from his bag and was about to investigate when he felt a restraining hand on his shoulder.

'Go to sleep, Mr. Stordahl.' It was Moses's voice, soft in his ear. 'There's nothing to be alarmed about. My people have everything under control.'

There was a reassuring confidence in the amorph's voice and Stordahl found himself wriggling back into his bag and relaxing again.

As his eyes closed he thought he saw, dimly against the entrance to the hut, the silhouette of a huge reptilian head; but in his exhaustion he was prepared to believe that his imagination was playing tricks.

The huts were roofed with flattened mangrove leaves and the amorphs' work had been thorough. The following morning Stordahl awoke to the roaring of rain on the roof, but interior of the hut had remained dry. This was in sharp contrast to the experience of the previous occupants. Apart from the dangers from the piranavas, one of their chief complaints had concerned the discomfort of waking up each morning with saturated sleeping bags. In the grey dawn light Stordahl's mood was defeatist as his thoughts dwelt on the superiority of the amorphs in various fields.

They were already at work; he was alone in the hut and he could hear the sounds of activity from outside. He got to his feet and looked out of the entrance. Moses had divided his people into two teams this time; one group was felling mangroves, working waist-deep in murky water, while the other was driving piles into the soil – still covered by the falling tide – to the north of the huts. They were working with enthusiasm and chanted rhythmically as they swung axes and hammers. Stordahl saw Moses below and called to him.

'For God's sake, don't forget the piranavas!'

Moses smiled and pointed to the south, out of Stordahl's view from his present position. Stordahl pulled on his tall wading boots and descended the rough ladder, dropping into the water with some trepidation. He looked in the direction indicated.

Beyond the huts on the seaward side, ranged in a large semicircle, were a number of huge reptiles. Covered with green-grey iridescent scales, each one must have stood at least twelve feet tall, allowing for the depth of the water. They stood upright, occasionally lifting stumpy forelimbs above the surface, gazing seaward with small bright eyes set well back on flat-snouted heads. The formation of their jaws was remarkable and Stordahl could only liken them to the Terrestrial crocodile. Their movements, however, were vastly more agile.

As he watched, a shoal of piranavas approached, skimming the surface and diving, reappearing, rising to a height of some six feet on silver, fluttering wings, banking and veering away. One fish veered too late. . . .

The nearest reptile lunged forward and upward with incredible swiftness, rising from the water on scaly hind-flippers, short thick neck outstretched and long jaws agape. There was an audible snap and the piranava was gone, while the reptile plunged head-first into the water like a diving sea lion, surfaced, and resumed its station in the crescent, snapping and gulping. The other reptiles ignored the flurry, their heads swivelling to regard the antics of the fluttering piranavas with unwinking attention.

'What the hell are those things?' asked Stordahl.

'Our bodyguards,' replied Moses briefly.

'It's fortunate they're on our side.' Stordahl watched as the piranavas, emboldened by the immobility of the reptiles, made another skimming approach and paid the price.

Moses smiled grimly. 'Particularly as they're intelligent.'

'Intelligent?'

'Those are amorphs, Mr. Stordahl.'

'Amorphs? Where did they come from?' He made a rough estimate of the labour force; they all seemed to be present.

'They're indigenous to this area. You probably saw them before, before you quit the camp; but they would have been in their unformed shape.'

'There were amorphs among the mangroves,' agreed Stordahl. 'But they didn't look like that.'

'There is an animal on our world which has that appearance,' Moses explained. 'They inhabit an area much nearer the mouth of the delta. Some of my people spent time yesterday with the local amorphs, blending with them, giving them, shall we say, humanity's gift of intelligence. . . . These then called on the reptiles' habitat, took their form, and came back.'

Moses looked directly at Stordahl. 'And when they came back to help us in the form of reptiles, they still retained their intelligence. An interesting development, don't you think? It seems that intelligence becomes a permanent characteristic. . . .'

Stordahl was silent, pondering on the significance of Moses's words. Intelligent amorphs remained intelligent. An intelligent amorph could take the shape of any form of life on the planet, from the smallest creature scuttling about the colony, to the largest and most fearsome creature of the delta, the sea, or the plain. . . .

'As you said, Mr. Stordahl,' remarked Moses, his gaze never leaving the man's face, 'it's fortunate they're on our side.'

The days went by rapidly and Stordahl never ceased to be amazed at the progress. By the time they were due to return to the colony, eight large rectangular fields were planted out with super-rice and no piranavas had been seen within the enclosures. He was unable to understand Moses's attitude; he would have expected surliness from the first, allied to a disinclination to work. It was almost as though he were trying to prove something. Prove what? That amorphs were superior to humans? That wouldn't cut any ice with Hetherington. Maybe Moses felt he didn't need to cut any ice with Hetherington. . . . Maybe Moses and the amorphs were building for the future of the colony, without any ulterior motive. But whose colony? And whose future . . . ?

There was some discussion as to who should go back to the colony now that the initial work had been completed. Moses had agreed that a few amorphs should be left to tend the crops, but insisted that the majority should return to Alice in the trucks. Bearing in mind what had been accomplished, Stordahl hardly liked to refuse. It was an awkward decision, as he knew that Hetherington expected few to return. . . . He radioed the colony and informed them of his intentions, breaking contact before objections could be raised.

Eventually the convoy set off. All eighty-six of the original amorphs were returning to Alice and the plantation was left in the hands of a number of the local amorphs who retained their reptilian guise for convenience and safety. Stordahl was not happy about this; he could visualize Hetherington asking what the hell he thought he was doing, leaving a bunch of animals in charge. . . . But Moses had been adamant. He was looking forward to the return with a strange fervour which he was unable to conceal. This only served to add to Stordahl's forebodings.

The journey was uneventful and Moses silent. By now the daily rain had washed the decayed vegetation into the soil and the terrain was naked, bare of any form of life and utterly desolate. Even this drew no comment from the amorph who sat beside Stordahl in the lead truck, gazing forward as though willing the journey to a swift completion.

Eventually they pulled up at the domes, watched by a large number of the colonists with no extravagant display of emotion. Stordahl and Moses stepped down from the truck and were met by Joan, Briggs, and Lever.

'I hear you and your people have accomplished quite a lot,' remarked Lever to Moses, smiling thinly. 'Mr. Stordahl's reports were very enthusiastic.'

'Thank you,' replied Moses gravely.

'How are you, Alex?' Joan asked, regarding Stordahl anxiously.

'Fine. . . . Have you arranged accommodation for Moses and his men?'

'In the transport dome. Get them there as soon as possible, will you, Stordahl?' Lever said.

The amorphs were dismounting from the vehicles, standing around uncertainly. 'What do you mean?' asked Stordahl puzzled. 'It's early yet. We'll have something to eat, and go there later.'

Lever frowned. 'The boss's orders. I'm sorry, Stordahl, but it seems Mr. Hetherington doesn't trust the amorphs any more, since Mrs. Hetherington died. He's imposed some pretty strict regulations. . . .'

It was like a blow to the solar plexus. 'Marilyn dead?' breathed Stordahl. 'What are you talking about?'

Joan broke in. 'You mean they didn't tell you, Alex? I thought they'd been in radio contact every day. . . .' Her voice was gentle. 'I'm afraid she died last week. She was . . . murdered. Strangled.'

EIGHTEEN

Later, in the quiet of her room, Joan explained.

'They found her in the morning. She was lying beside one of the cabins some distance from her own quarters; and she'd been . . . dead for some time. Several hours, so Dr. Singer said. She'd been strangled manually, from in front. She wasn't . . . interfered with in any other way.'

'Do they have any ideas who did it?' asked Stordahl dully.

'Mr. Hetherington and his men suspect an amorph. Everyone was questioned the following day, of course, but nothing came to light. Half the people had no alibis, but then they had no motive either.'

Stordahl remembered Marilyn's strange terror; her white-faced recriminations over his stupid remarks to Hetherington, the way she had refused to look at him since. . . . 'Hetherington had a motive himself,' he said slowly.

Joan regarded him with sympathy. 'That possibility had occurred to some of us,' she said. 'But she was strangled.' Again the dreadful word fell harshly on Stordahl's ears; the stark word to describe a stark way to die, struggling for breath with a ringing in the head, a rising, roiling blackness in the brain. . . . 'Hetherington has no arms,' said Joan simply.

'One of the pugs, I expect.' Stordahl's voice was infinitely bitter.

'Do you think Hetherington would take the chance of being blackmailed in the future? I doubt it. And . . .' Joan hesitated. 'Marilyn was an attractive girl. Imagine one of those brutes being told: go and kill my wife, I'll make it worth your while. What would he do? He'd do the job, of course, but I think. . . .'

'You think he'd rape her first,' said Stordahl harshly.

'Or . . . or afterwards,' said Joan quietly.

'Oh, God. . . .'

'You were . . . fond of her, weren't you, Alex?'

'Yes.'

'I'm very sorry, my dear.'

Stordahl cleared his mind of memories with an effort.

'But why suspect an amorph?' he asked. 'They were miles away, with me at the delta.'

'There are a lot more in the colony. They came in while you were away.'

'Of their own accord? How?'

'They were brought here. It was agreed that they were rounded up and brought in, otherwise they would die, with this disease everywhere. They have human form now, and they're kept locked up since the . . . thing happened to Marilyn, except when they're needed for work.'

Stordahl felt a dull fury rising from his stomach. 'Very convenient. Now Hetherington's got a good excuse for denying them any sort of rights. Do the colonists go along with this? How do they think an amorph can possibly commit murder? These new amorphs haven't had any contact with Moses. They'd have little initiative of their own. They'd be non-violent idealists, just like the original ones before Hetherington's experiment contaminated them.'

'Hetherington's experimenting again,' said Joan significantly.

'Christ. Doesn't the man ever learn?'

'He leaves soon. Later tomorrow. He'll be taking his experiment with him, I suppose. So at least it will be out of the way. . . .'

Stordahl remembered. The events of the past few weeks had driven Hetherington's ultimatum right out of his mind.

Joan was watching him. 'Are you going to leave with the ship?' Her voice was carefully neutral.

'God, I don't know. I hadn't thought about it. I suppose I can hardly stay on here as Lever's yes-man, even if I can persuade the Old Man to leave me on the payroll.' He looked at her helplessly. 'What should I do, Joan?'

She smiled suddenly. 'I think maybe you've come to terms with yourself this last month, otherwise you wouldn't ask me that. Because you know what my answer is, already.'

Joan was right, of course; Stordahl intended to stay. Yet when he awoke the following morning he knew that his mind was not finally made up – would not be made up until Hetherington's ship lifted clear of the ground. He decided to postpone his decision until later in the day.

It was a bad time for decisions, that morning. The drizzling rain slanted across the window of his cabin, liquefying the barren filth of the diseased soil into a slimy mess which possessed, to his jaundiced eye, a close resemblance to vomit. There were few people about yet. He watched the early risers trudging wetly through the rain as he sipped his morning hangover mixture. His head ached severely, knives of pain thrusting at his temples, while his mouth tasted of mildewed sawdust.

He was also conscious of the fact that he had made a fool of himself last night under the cumulative influence of several drinks and the sympathetic attitude of Joan. He had eventually told her everything that had happened between himself and Marilyn, his eyes wet with alcoholic tears of self-pity. He had put on an act. Admittedly deeply distressed himself, he had selfishly set about the task of upsetting Joan too – he had no illusions as to her feelings in the matter. Why had he done it? Why had he so devalued his own genuine emotions?

In such a mood Stordahl began to get dressed, and when he bent to put his shoes on it seemed that his head would explode with the pain. Eventually, sick and miserable, he left the cabin; and the complex of domes looked alien now that Marilyn was dead, as though he had stepped into a new and blankly terrifying tomorrow.

There was activity among the domes; a bustle of preparation consequent on Hetherington's imminent departure. Trucks were being loaded with gear and men were tying waterproof sheeting over piled trailers containing soil samples, botanical specimens and the like. There were no amorphs about. Stordahl assumed they would remain under lock and key until later in the day, when they would be required for duties about the colony. He wondered briefly when construction work at the foundry was due to start; last night he had been too bemused by the news of Marilyn to ask. And he didn't remember anyone volunteering the information; maybe they thought it wasn't his business any more. . . . Certainly no one acknowledged his presence as he walked among the domes. Once Charlton appeared and glanced at him, then disappeared on some errand without speaking; there was a sheepish look about the man.

James Walters was nearby. Stordahl addressed him almost belligerently.

'Oh . . . good morning, Mr. Stordahl.' The man looked faintly embarrassed.

'How are things going?'

'Fine. Just fine.' Walters turned away awkwardly and busied himself with an adjustable wrench, fiddling with the hub of a truck.

Stordahl watched the man's back for a few seconds, then walked away. There seemed to be a conspiracy of silence. He, Alex Stordahl, ex-Supervisor, was now bad news. Nobody wished to be seen talking to him. He wondered exactly what had caused this attitude. They couldn't all be *that* scared of Hetherington, could they? He began to wish he had spent more time finding out the news from Joan last night, instead of whining in self-pity.

Eventually Lever appeared and Stordahl cornered him by a truck.

'Ah . . . Stordahl.'

'What's happening here, Lever?' asked Stordahl. 'There's a weird atmosphere. People seem to be avoiding me. Why?'

Lever glanced around for an avenue of escape. 'I'm sure you've imagined it.' He laughed nervously. 'Avoiding you? Nonsense, man. We're busy just now getting ready for the Old Man's departure, that's all. Take my advice and go back to your cabin and rest up for a while. You've done a great job at the delta. A great job.' Muttering these three final words again as though to convince himself, Lever moved quickly away, almost running. Stordahl stared after him.

Ten minutes later it was announced that there would be a meeting in the Community Hall in an hour's time, at which Hetherington would address the assembled colonists prior to his departure. Stordahl drifted over to the large dome and entered. A few people were there, shifting chairs and organizing the platform, setting out the tables and the inevitable tumblers and jugs of water. An embarrassing thought struck him. Would he be sitting with the other colony leaders on the platform, or was his present post of Assistant Supervisor of such minor importance that he would be consigned to the ruck in the main body of the hall?

For a moment he considered forgetting the meeting entirely, taking Lever's advice and returning to his cabin for the rest of the day. Then a mood of obstinacy took over. He would attend the meeting and, if he got the chance, say a few words himself in front of the assembled colony. Despite the peculiar attitude he had encountered this morning, he still felt the majority of the colonists were on his side. He would rock the boat, if nothing more. . . .

He strode to the platform, ignoring the uncertain glances from workers around him, and sat down firmly in the chair he had occupied on the occasion of Hetherington's welcoming address. Inevitably his thoughts slid back to that previous occasion, and he found himself thinking of Marilyn. . . .

The hall began to fill up and he was still alone on the platform, eyeing the colonists aggressively as they glanced at him in surprise before taking their seats and speaking quietly to each other, presumably discussing him.

Then the colony leaders began to arrive; Charlton first, looking at him coldly and sitting at the other end of the long table. Briggs came and sat near Stordahl, smiling at him briefly before turning his attention to a wad of notes he took from his briefcase. Bill Myers also sat near Stordahl, murmuring a greeting. Stordahl realized for the first time that the colony now had two Assistant Supervisors: Bill and himself. He had been so busy pondering over his own position that he had failed to realize that Bill had, in effect, been passed over in favour of Lever. Bill should have been Stordahl's logical successor, but Bill had made it clear in the past that he was Stordahl's man. . . . *Poor bastard*, thought Stordahl.

Lever arrived and sat next to Charlton; soon they were joined by Ward Entwhistle, the botanist, who sat next to Lever after a surprised, uncertain glance at Briggs, who nodded to him curtly. Santana strolled in, hands in pockets, sized up the situation with a sardonic smile and seated himself beside Stordahl.

'Good morning, Alex. I get the impression the head table has divided itself into factions.'

'We seem to be in the majority. I'm surprised Briggs is on our side, though.'

'Briggs has seen the light, even if it's a red one,' remarked the psychiatrist cryptically. 'But don't kid yourself we're in the majority.' He nodded towards the colonists before them. 'Every man and woman down there is against us.'

'Why, for God's sake? Perhaps you can tell me what's been happening here, Avio.'

'Didn't you know? Hell, here's Hetherington. I'll speak to you later. Meanwhile, if you had any idea of using this occasion for an impassioned address, I'd forget it, if I were you.'

Hetherington, flanked by his bodyguard, was wheeling down the centre aisle. A number of men followed, among them Dwight. As the tycoon rolled up the temporary ramp which had been prepared for him he caught sight of Stordahl and smiled blandly.

Hetherington sat in the centre of the table, effectively bisecting the rival parties. Dragging up chairs, his colleagues sat in a group behind him, there being no further room at the table. Lever slammed a hammer and stood in the ensuing silence.

'Ladies and gentlemen,' he began, 'today is both a happy and a sad occasion for us all. Happy, because another landmark in the development of our colony has been reached. Sad, because today our benefactor, Mr. J. Wallace Hetherington, will be leaving this planet. . . .'

And so on. Stordahl sat seething as Lever ran through his repertoire of unctuous platitudes preparatory to introducing his boss. Santana spoke quietly in his ear.

'Look at that group behind the Old Man, Alex. Tell me if anything occurs to you.'

Stordahl twisted in his seat and examined the group which up to now he had disregarded in concentrating his attention on Hetherington.

Hammond Dwight was there, bolt upright in his chair and smiling appreciatively at Lever's opening address. Sokalski's expression was thoughtful, as though the banal words contained some hidden meaning apparent only to his trained mind. Andy Ryan, the comedy librarian, grinned openly and derisively behind Hetherington's back. Spink, the Comptroller General, seemed to be asleep already. The group of pugs merely looked bored. There was another man. Thick-set and heavy-jowled, he sat behind and slightly to the left of Hetherington. From where Stordahl watched, the two faces were side by side. The expressions were the same, politely deprecating smiles.

The two faces were identical.

The creature in the rear was an amorph. Hetherington's private amorph. And being the ideal Hetherington, summoned into form by the tycoon's own mind, it possessed arms. . . .

Long, strong arms terminating in squat powerful hands. Folded passively in the creature's lap. Covered with coarse black hairs, brutal hands. . . .

'I expect you're thinking the same as me,' whispered Santana. 'This is the first time Hetherington's personal amorph has appeared in public. He requisitioned it in the unformed state at the same time as the latest experimental amorph. The man must be damned sure of his ground, now. There's not a thing we can prove. He's just let us know the score, that's all. Hetherington's type always wins out. There's nothing you or I can do. . . .'

The hands twitched as Lever sat down to polite applause; then Hetherington began to speak.

'I would like to tell you people how impressed I've been with what I've seen during my stay on this planet.' Hetherington's voice was clear and commanding in the silence of the hall. 'You've had your problems; this I appreciate, but I think it's fair to say the corner has been turned. Work on construction of the foundry will commence very shortly and it's obvious to me that the colony is a viable proposition with a great future.'

Stordahl watched the colonists as they sat back in their chairs, every eye upon their employer, expressions smug as they were buttered with praise which cost nothing. Hetherington continued in this vein for some time.

He touched on the question of the amorphs: 'Hand in hand, Man and amorph will march forward into an age of prosperity. It is fortunate indeed that we arrived on the scene when we did, as we have been able to save the amorphs from this disease which is sweeping the area. Without our help, the amorphs would surely have died. . . .'

Briggs leaned around Santana and whispered: 'Stordahl!' His expression was bitter. 'I know what causes the disease!'

'Ourselves, I suppose.'

'Basically, yes. I'll tell you later.'

'Moses said it was us.'

'He was right.'

Hetherington's voice boomed on. '. . . a useful adjunct to our labour force. . . .'

Oh, God, thought Stordahl, *not that again.* He glanced around the assembled colonists for signs of dissension, but they were all regarding Hetherington raptly. Jim Walters was actually nodding mute agreement.

'. . . and we are taking back with us two of the creatures for observation. One, you see behind me. A fair likeness, I think.' (Broad smiles and a few chuckles from the colonists. No antagonism.)

'So I will leave you, secure in the knowledge that under the able leadership of Mr. Bert Lever the colony will continue to prosper, going from strength to strength until, in the foreseeable future. . . .'

Stordahl was fidgeting. As Lever rose to say a few final words he began to ease himself to his feet. 'I'm going to have a word with that damned amorph of Hetherington's,' he snarled. 'I'll smash the truth out of that bastard if it's the last thing I do. . . .'

Santana grabbed at his arm and held him. 'Stay where you are. You'll only get yourself in deeper. You don't realize the climate here. Everyone's on Hetherington's side. And that amorph would never confess to murder. It's a duplicate of the Old Man. Can you seriously imagine the Old Man confessing to anything?'

Stordahl relaxed, with reluctance. 'I suppose you're right. But why the hell is Hetherington so damned popular? Everyone knows he's a bastard. Look at Jim Walters there; he's looking at the man as though he's a god. What's been going on, Avio?'

Lever had concluded his closing remarks. Amid a scraping of chairs the meeting was dispersing. The applause had been enthusiastic. People were talking to each other animatedly, smiling.

Sick, furious, feeling out of touch and not knowing why, Stordahl watched them go.

NINETEEN

Jim Walters was still there, talking to Charlton. Exasperated by Santana's cryptic utterances, Stordahl strode across. As he approached the two men, Santana hurrying behind, Charlton moved away. Stordahl was gratified to see the embarrassment on Walters's face as he realized he was trapped.

'Right then, Jim,' snapped Stordahl. 'What the hell's going on?'

'I don't know what you mean, Mr. Stordahl,' replied Walters predictably.

'You've got a load of new amorphs here, that's what I mean. How many?'

'Oh, about a hundred. We keep them locked up, since Mrs. Hetherington. . . .'

'Yes, I know all about that. Tell me this. Do you really believe she was murdered by one of those amorphs?'

'I don't know, Mr. Stordahl. Nobody knows.'

'You know perfectly well that the average amorph isn't capable of murder.'

Walters tried to look shrewd. 'Ah, yes, but they may not all be average. We might have a rogue. Look at Moses.'

'Moses was with me all the time. If you're looking for a rogue, have you considered Hetherington's own amorph?'

Walters's countenance took on a shifty look. 'I really don't think—'

'You don't want to think, you bastard!' Stordahl shouted. The last stragglers from the hall paused and turned to watch the unexpected entertainment.

'There's no cause to talk to me like that. It's a matter for the police. . . . I don't see why I should be involved. What you're saying is slander, Mr. Stordahl.'

Bill Myers arrived. 'What's slander, Jim?'

'Mr. Stordahl's saying that—'

'I'm saying Hetherington murdered Marilyn!' shouted Stordahl imprudently, completely out of control.

'Cool it, Alex,' whispered Santana urgently.

Bill Myers spoke quietly. 'You're right, of course, Alex.' 'So what are we going to do about it?'

'Nothing. There's nothing we can do. We represent a minority. Everybody suspects Hetherington but nobody's saying so. There's no point. Let's just say it was a private matter between a man and his wife, and let's realize at the same time that the man has infinite power. We could never prove anything, for a start. And the police here are voluntary colonists, and the colonists are behind Hetherington to a man. Forget it, Alex. Hetherington's all set to go. There's no point in throwing fat in the fire at this juncture.' Myers regarded Stordahl anxiously.

'I see. . . .' Stordahl had calmed down. He turned his attention to Walters again. 'Another thing, Jim.' He forced his voice steady. 'What was all that Hetherington was saying about a labour force? These amorphs, the new ones. You didn't bring them in to save them from extinction, did you? You're putting them to work.'

Relieved at the turn of conversation, Walters grinned eagerly. 'Oh, yes, of course. Everything's all right again, now. Amazing how much work there was, without the amorphs to help out.' He chuckled. 'My wife was raising Cain, having to do all the housework herself.'

Stordahl regarded the man grimly. 'You'll be paying them wages, I trust.'

'Wages?' Walters looked aggrieved. 'What do you take us for? These are new amorphs. They haven't been influenced by Mr. Hetherington's projects. They'll do anything we want them to. We'd look pretty stupid paying them wages, wouldn't we?'

'Jim,' said Stordahl carefully, 'last time we had a big discussion about the amorphs, you were complaining about Hetherington exploiting them, using them on the steelworks site.'

'I know, I know,' said Walters impatiently. 'But this is different. Before, I was using them as a bargaining point against Mr. Hetherington and what I said was just politics. You've always got to accuse employers of exploitation – they expect it. But now, it's we the workers who are using the amorphs. That's different. We're not employers.'

Stordahl regarded Walters incredulously. 'Jim,' he said slowly, 'you are out of your mind.'

'I represent a pretty big majority.'

'My God, I'm sure you do. Well, I'm not standing for it.

You and I are going to see Lever right away, and we'll thrash this thing out.'

'You're in no position, Alex,' remarked Santana quietly.

A flicker of uneasiness had crossed Walters's face. 'Look, Mr. Stordahl. I don't think you're quite abreast. The whole thing was talked over with Mr. Hetherington last week and he goes along with it one hundred per cent. We reached a compromise.'

'This is the first I've heard of it.' Stordahl felt less certain of his ground.

'You've been out of circulation. What we agreed was, that the amorphs should be used here at the colony without pay by ourselves privately, and by the organization as a labour force. In return for our concession and in view of the economies effected, Hetherington agreed to site the steelworks here in Alice.'

'What!'

'That's the way it is. Everyone's very pleased with the situation. The town stays where it is, we keep our cabins, and nobody has to go away for weeks at a time. I don't think you'd get very far by trying to rock the boat. You'd make yourself very unpopular, Mr. Stordahl. Don't you remember how worried we all were a few months ago, over the future of the colony? Well, we've got our futures assured now. We want to keep it that way.'

'Don't blame them too much, Alex,' said Santana. 'They're a hell of a long way from Earth. They want security.'

'Briggs said something. During the lecture. He said he'd got to the bottom of this disease.' Stordahl thought. 'If the disease could be cured and the plant life re-established, there would be no need to go rounding up any more amorphs. No excuse. This is what I'm scared of, Avio. Once the colony accepts the principle of unpaid labour, there's no limit. Right now they say they've got to bring the amorphs in and convert them to human form, otherwise they'll starve. This is a big continent and for all we know the disease won't spread beyond this area. But that won't stop people rounding up amorphs from the whole of Marilyn, now that the principle's been accepted.'

Santana smiled. 'You visualize a future where the humans sit on their backsides doing nothing, tended by thousands of obedient slaves?'

'Frankly, yes.'

'You've become a pessimist in this last month, Alex.'

'A realist. Anyhow, let's go and see Briggs. Maybe I'm getting steamed up about nothing. Usually, if you know the cause of a disease, then it can be cured.'

Santana grimaced. 'Provided you want it cured,' he observed quietly.

Briggs was bending over the bench in his tiny laboratory. Hearing them enter, he straightened up immediately. Stordahl thought: *Briggs has changed. A month ago he would have kept us waiting....*

'Tell us the worst, Briggs.' Stordahl came straight to the point. 'Can the disease be cured, or can't it?'

'It can be cured.' Briggs's tone was curiously bitter. 'Whether it *will* be cured is out of my hands.' He spoke gently, almost tiredly, with no trace of his former bombast.

'What causes it?'

'As I said, basically we caused it. We fixed the desert dust with Wilton lichen. I should have known this would happen; at the very least, I should have been bright enough to guess. But I didn't. As a result of planting that damned stuff we're going to kill every type of plant life on this side of the continent – and that means the animals will die as well, including the amorph in its natural form.'

'But the lichen is in the desert. It's nowhere near the plain.'

'Let me explain. You recall the form that plant life takes? In all cases, rainfall is collected in upturned cups; the moisture then filters down through the plant and is exuded through the roots. The unformed amorph absorbs the moisture through its skin, and occasionally extrudes cup-like projections to catch the rain.

'The elephant worm lives on the resultant fluid issuing from the roots of the cuptrees and, to a lesser extent, the saucerplants. It also takes in a large amount of liquid which lies on the floor of its tunnels. I suspect that its preference for the cuptree fluid is merely a matter of taste; probably some form of resin is forthcoming which it finds pleasant – but no matter. The point is, all these forms of life are dependent on what falls from the sky.

'And in the afternoon, there is a strong wind blowing off the desert....

'The wind brings dust with it, fine mineral particles which remain suspended in the atmosphere and are deposited out by the subsequent morning rainfall. These minerals, iron and others, are essential to life on the planet. They are caught in the upturned cups and absorbed into the tissues. . . .'

Stordahl said slowly: 'And now we've fixed a large proportion of the desert dust with Wilton lichen.'

Briggs went on: 'The plants, the unformed amorphs, and the elephant worms will die from various deficiencies. In due course the lizards will starve. Soon there will be no living thing left on this side of the continent except ourselves and our Earth-type crops, and our own amorphs. . . .'

They were silent for a moment, letting the implications sink in.

'What you're saying,' said Stordahl eventually, 'is that the amorphs are trapped. They have to stay here in order to eat our food. There's no place for them to go.'

Briggs watched him without expression. 'Yes, and there's a nice little ethical problem which you might appreciate, being a man of somewhat exalted moral views. . . . What do we do about the unformed amorphs out on the plain? There are still hundreds left. Do we save their lives by bringing them all in here to become quasi-humans in slavery? Or, as they're not at this moment intelligent, do we leave them out there to die with the other animals? What a choice! We can morally justify whatever we do. How does that grab your conscience, Stordahl?'

'The third alternative,' said Stordahl harshly, 'is that we destroy the Wilton lichen.'

'I know.' Briggs looked infinitely weary. 'And the dust blows free and the plants survive. And human life at the desert becomes insupportable. And people refuse to work there, and Hetherington threatens to withdraw support. So large numbers of amorphs are sent in to do the work we won't do ourselves. Being in human form they will die, one by one – but they will soon be replaced by other amorphs gathered from all over the continent. And work will go on, and the foundry will continue to produce, and the planet of Marilyn will prosper.'

'There's no answer, Alex,' said Santana gently. 'Don't you see, man? There can't always be an answer. Right and wrong are merely convenient words in our language to describe generalities. Just this once, you'll have to go along with the status quo. If you feel that strongly about it – and I know you do – you can always catch the ship out with Hetherington. But it won't help. Whatever you do, wherever you are, you'll still be conscious of what's happening on Marilyn. . . .' He hesitated. 'What I'm saying is: we need a man of your views here. Briggs and I are staying – and heaven knows we'd rather wash our hands of the whole sick business. But we know we'll be needed. . . . And the same applies to you.

'I'll put it this way. Can you square it with your conscience if you leave a man like Bert Lever in sole command of a situation like this?'

It had been a long time.

Stordahl wondered, as he walked slowly up the hill, whether there were any left; or whether the man-made putrescence which lay all around him had claimed every living thing. Under his feet the saucerplants had deliquesced to a thick brown mush which oozed over his boots, stinking. The cuptrees ahead, once tall and proud, now bowed their heads tiredly and the circular leaves hung limp, also brown, dripping viscous moisture to the wet slime of the ground. Even the rain, sieving down through the odour-laden atmosphere, smelled rank like old urine.

As he walked he prayed that he had not left it too late; that there was at least one encapsulated memory left for him on this leprous planet. . . .

Among the yellowing boles of the cuptrees a lizard moved; a small, hungry lizard ferreting for food among the filth. This gave him hope.

He wondered if it were possible to direct the memory; if, by concentrating on a certain occasion in the past, he could influence the object amorph to take up the thread of recollection and carry it through. . . .

It had been a long time ago.

Alice had said: 'Give me fifty cents.'

'What do you say?'

A mutinous scowl, then a careful appraisal of values. It was just worth the loss of pride, she had decided. 'Give me fifty cents . . . please, Daddy.'

'Come closer.'

'No.' Backing off. 'I don't want a kiss. I want fifty cents.'

'What for, darling?'

'Chocolate. Mommy said yes I could.'

'Let's check that with Mommy, shall we?'

'No! I'm asking *you.*' A touch of alarm.

'I see. . . . Then give me a kiss, and I'll give you fifty cents.'

Doubtful. 'Promise?'

'I promise. . . . There, that wasn't so bad, was it? Now tell me whom you love?'

Careful consideration and a sidelong glance. 'Mommy. And my doll with the long hair and the pink dress. And Uncle Bert and Auntie Janet. And the cat. And the tricycle I got for my birthday, with the bell on it.'

'Is that all?'

'Nobody, nobody else.'

He had watched her go and, later, he had watched her come back running untidily from the corner shop, every so often breaking into irrelevant skips. She had slowed as she saw him, and approached with unaccustomed shyness.

'Did you eat all your chocolate, sweetheart?'

Hands behind her back. 'I thought perhaps I wouldn't get it after all.'

'Oh. So what did you get?'

Her voice was now an embarrassed whisper. 'A present for you.'

She thrust something into his palm and turned, and ran up the stairs, leaving him watching her, a packet of cigarettes in his hand and tears in his eyes. . . .

And Stordahl, standing on the decaying hillside of a faraway planet, thought: *I would like just those few minutes again. Nothing more. Just those few minutes before we cleanse the planet of memories.*

On the plain below, moving steadily towards the colony domes, he saw figures walking, wheeling a cart piled with possessions. He recognized Arnott Walsh, accompanied by five, six Katies. Refugees from the dying landscape forced back to community life.

He searched the area around the cuptrees with mounting despair, peering into dark holes, poking among rotting undergrowth, seeing only lizards which scuttled away from his investigations.

He caught a sight of Joan on the plain, walking towards

the hillock; she waved but he paid no attention as he searched desperately. *Surely there must be a few left, they can't all have died. . . .*

A large lizard was watching him from a rock, motionless apart from a beating throat pulse; its eyes were cold and cynical.

He thought, suddenly: *The transformation is a defence mechanism. A defence against aggressors but also, possibly, a defence against hunger? Amorphs find the rain no longer contains nourishment; would they then change themselves into creatures which could feed other than through the skin?* He stepped towards the lizard carefully, trying not to frighten it by a movement too sudden.

The lizard watched him and its eyes blinked, once.

He was close now; and he extended a hand, placing it on the rock beside the lizard. He leaned against the rock, watching.

And the lizard's head began to shift and flow like molten plastic.

He turned away, then. He did not want to witness the transformation; that would spoil the moment to come. Let it appear natural; he was merely Stordahl leaning against a rock and in a moment, when he turned around, his memories would have become an almost total reality. Joan was getting near and he hoped she would have the tact not to spoil things for him. She was climbing the hill and her voice came to him, calling.

In a moment he would gesture to her, tell her not to come too near in case she affected the creature herself; she would, surely, have the consideration to allow him this one last meeting, this last father's whim. . . . He heard breathing behind him, slow breathing. It wouldn't be long.

Joan had stopped twenty yards away. She was watching him and the amorph with an expression of extraordinary pity and he knew she understood; there was no need to say anything to her. . . .

Behind him, the rustling of clothes. A low cough.

'Hello, Alex.'

And the words were wrong, and the voice was wrong, and he wheeled around to see the lovely blonde girl sitting on the rock with a smile in her blue eyes and her emerald skirt hitched up about her thighs.

He said, 'Marilyn', just once, before the dizziness of

shock and disappointment and self-recrimination overcame him and he crumpled against the rock, vomiting endlessly until Joan put her arm around his shoulders and led him away.

TWENTY

Away from the cuptrees, just before the abrupt slope of the knoll flattened into the ochre plain, Joan made him sit down and she talked for a long time. At first Stordahl would say nothing; merely gazing across the plain with blank eyes, seeing or perhaps not seeing the colony and beyond it the glittering angular shape of the ship's tender. But Joan persevered because she knew that Stordahl, if left alone, would walk across the plain and through the domes and up the ramp to the ship, and then both of them would be alone.

So she told him all he had heard before, and put forward all the old arguments while she forced him to look at her and presently to listen. She was aware there was nothing new she could say and she didn't try, and while she spoke the sun drifted slowly towards the mountains like an incandescent, punctured balloon and the time of the ship's departure grew closer.

And at last he began to argue with her, and tell her where she was wrong and where the colony was wrong, and why Hetherington was a bastard and what he would like to do to Lever. . . . And then she knew she was winning.

As the shadows of the western mountains groped across the plain and the wind blew more cool she stood, gave him her hand and pulled him to his feet with a little laugh, and they began to walk. It was getting dark by the time they neared the colony; as the lights were coming on there was a dull roar, rumbling through the ground, then a bright crimson glare tinted the rims of the domes like a cluster of crescent moons. The crescents shifted, inverting, then the fiery tail of the ship's tender rose above the colony and roared up into the darkening sky.

In the afterglow they could see a multitude of figures, black shapes standing motionless – not away at the launching site but nearer, beside a dome on the outskirts of the colony.

'What's going on?' asked Stordahl. With the departure of the ship a burden of decision had lifted and he was able to be curious.

'I can't think. Nothing much was happening when I left. Most of our colonists were going to the launching site.'

'Well, they're not there now, unless . . . oh, God. It must be the amorphs. What the hell can they be up to?'

They quickened their pace and, as they neared the silent figures, three men came towards them.

'What's it all about, Avio?' called Stordahl.

Briggs was with the psychiatrist, and Moses.

'Something a little more interesting than Hetherington's departure,' said Santana quietly. 'It seems that—' He broke off and glanced at Moses. 'You tell him,' he said with an odd deference.

Moses regarded them gravely; there was a new dignity in his bearing. 'It is the important event that I hinted at, Mr. Stordahl. It has come to pass. Mrs. Walsh is having a child.'

'Katie?' Stordahl was puzzled. 'I don't see. . . .'

'Katie's an amorph, Alex,' Joan reminded him.

'Yes. Of course. There are several of them. I saw Walsh and them making for the colony earlier on, but I didn't attach much importance to it. So she's having a child.' He frowned thoughtfully.

Briggs spoke. 'We've never really considered how they reproduce. I'd assumed it was asexually, like the amoeba. Just a splitting off of a new individual. But now they've assumed human form. . . .' He looked doubtful.

'We have human organs in our present form,' said Moses. 'But the obvious question has not yet arisen. Even now it has not arisen because this is, I can assure you, a case of asexual reproduction.

'I believe you have another, less clinical term for it. You might call it a virgin birth. . . .'

Moses allowed them into the dome; it was the very small structure used for housing the colony's fire-tender. Katie Walsh lay on an improvised bed; around her, talking quietly, were the other Katies and Arnott Walsh. The zoologist came towards them, his expression one of bewildered pride.

'I had to bring her in, Mr. Stordahl,' he said. 'I didn't know how to deal with this myself. I didn't know what to expect. You see, I never . . . I didn't. . . .' He broke off in confusion.

'We know you didn't, Mr. Walsh,' said Moses gently. 'And I can assure you that everything will be all right.'

Stordahl drew Briggs aside. 'For God's sake, how can he be so sure,' he whispered. 'I don't see how he can know *what* is going to be born. I'm not sure I want to know. This sort of thing scares me. I think I'll get back to my cabin. . . .'

'Stay here, Alex,' said Joan firmly.

'Mrs. Walsh has been in her present form for a long time,' Briggs reassured him. 'The chances are that her offspring will have human form also.'

So they waited in the small dome while night fell outside and the five identical Katies busied themselves about the Katie on the bed. Conversation lapsed and they were all listening; Briggs had offered to assist but Moses, who had assumed authority, wouldn't allow it. Stordahl, in an attempt to divert his mind from the matter at hand, read the instruction manual of the fire-tender with determined interest. Moses strolled to and fro between the Katies and the entrance to the dome, unhurriedly, betraying no obvious nervousness, merely a great but largely suppressed excitement. Briggs fidgeted. Santana stared across the dome at the women and Arnott Walsh.

Moses said: 'It won't be a minute, now.' The women were bending over their charge who lay quietly, breathing fast but with no sounds of pain.

Santana took the booklet from Stordahl's hands and replaced it on the shelf. 'We must consider what this means,' he said quietly, 'because our attitude towards this event may be important in the future. We still have a lot of influence in the colony and Alex, for one, commands respect and affection, whatever he may think himself. It will be up to us to give a lead. . . .'

He addressed Stordahl. 'I've said before that men such as Hetherington tend to win out, and there's very little you or I can do about it. Well, he has won out, and he's got the colony running the way he wants it, and it may be a while before things will change – and then only gradually. He's won, but need we assume that we've lost? Now, there will be this child. . . .'

Moses spoke. 'You're wrong,' he said. 'Hetherington has lost. He's carried the germs of his own defeat into the sky with him, in the form of that monstrous amorph. Without knowing it he has created his own successor, an intellect so ruthless and powerful that it must supplant him as organization boss. A great evil has departed from our world – and something quite different has arrived. . . .'

Santana resumed in even tones. 'You see, this child will be unique. An ordinary amorph is an ideal, nothing more, a projection of a person's Te factor – lacking in knowledge, capable of learning but already filled with mental inaccuracies. Before long, I think we'll find that humans and amorphs can interbreed, and the result will be a combination of characteristics not readily distinguishable from a normal human child.

'Remember, it will be in the amorphs' interests that they should be capable of interbreeding with humans – therefore their remarkable defence mechanism will make it so.

'Now this child is an experiment by nature. A prototype born as another example of the defence mechanism – as witness the emotional and superstitious appeal it will have to humans. Its mother is a typical amorph, kindly and good and existing only to be everything Arnott Walsh wants her to be. But she is fixed, she is permanent, and she is having a child which has nothing to do with Walsh. . . .'

Stordahl felt a thrill of apprehension – was it fear or awe? – as he realized what Santana was driving at.

'You understand? The child will be the ultimate idealist. As the offspring of a fixed amorph, I doubt if it will be vulnerable to influence by humans. In direct contrast to the monster created by Hetherington, this child can only be . . . totally good. . . .'

Stordahl asked, slowly: 'And what will be our attitude? What will be humanity's attitude?'

'I am a superstitious man,' replied Santana simply. 'Out here, light-years from Earth, I think we all are. Personally, I will die to protect the life of this child.'

Watching the psychiatrist's face, Stordahl knew that he was right in his decision – if it was a decision – to stay on the planet. Joan clutched his hand suddenly. Moses was walking towards them, carrying a child. Like any other newborn baby, its face was wrinkled and it cried lustily.

It was a boy.

Stordahl regarded it. It looked normal. It was normal, but for one thing.

It would think no evil.

A Selection of Science Fiction Titles from Sphere

BEST OF ARTHUR C. CLARKE		65p
THE BEST OF FRITZ LEIBER		60p
THE BEST OF A. E. VAN VOGT		60p
THE BROKEN SWORD	Poul Anderson	35p
THE ALLEY GOD	Philip José Farmer	30p
OUT OF THE MOUTH OF THE DRAGON	Mark Geston	30p
THE WORLD OF NULL-A	A. E. Van Vogt	45p
THE PAWNS OF NULL-A	A. E. Van Vogt	45p
DAMNATION ALLEY	Roger Zelazny	30p
INCONSTANT MOON	Larry Niven	40p

A Selection of Adventure Fiction from Sphere

EAGLE IN THE SNOW	Wallace Breem	35p
CALICO PALACE	Gwen Bristow	65p
A HOT AND COPPER SKY	Jon Burmeister	45p
THE DARKLING PLAIN	Jon Burmeister	50p
RUNNING SCARED	Jon Burmeister	60p
THE EDGE OF THE COAST	Jon Burmeister	35p
DANDO AND THE SUMMER PALACE	William Clive	40p
DANDO ON DELHI RIDGE	William Clive	40p
THE DEFECTOR	Charles Collingwood	45p
ROMMEL'S GOLD	Maggie Davis	50p
THE WHITE LIE ASSIGNMENT	Peter Driscoll	35p
STONEHENGE	Harry Harrison & Leon Stover	30p
THE WHITE DAWN	James Houston	45p
THE SOLDIERS: BAYONETS IN THE SUN	William Moore	35p
A BLOODY FIELD BY SHREWSBURY	Edith Pargeter	60p
THE CHINESE AGENDA	Joe Poyer	45p
NORTH CAPE	Joe Poyer	40p
THE BALKAN ASSIGNMENT	Joe Poyer	40p
THE COAST OF LONELINESS	Colin Willock	35p
THE KILLING ZONE	William C. Woods	30p

A Selection of General Fiction from Sphere